# A Nanny for Harry

Sylvia Mulholland

A Nanny for Harry

SYLVIA MULHOLLAND

Copyright © 2018 Sylvia Mulholland

# Chapter 1

Off the coast of Long Beach, the oil drilling islands shimmered in the heat: silent, remote and mysterious. Palm trees tucked among the multi-colored buildings heightened the illusion that they were high-priced condos for the rich and famous, or fabulous resort islands. Kali Miller stood on top of the retaining wall at the end of the Millers' backyard and gazed at those islands, longing to float out over to them—weightless and carefree and unbound by space, time or the constraints of a third trimester pregnancy.

Since the start of her mat leave, Kali was realizing how small and confining her world had become. It was her size that was now making her crave unlimited space, and their 1920's house seem pokey and cramped. She and Matt could sit against opposite walls of the living room and share the same footstool in the middle. If Kali reached out a kitchen window, she could almost touch their garage on one side of their house, their neighbors' house from the other window.

As soon as Kali had found out she was pregnant, the Millers started house hunting, whipped into a frenzy by predictions of infinitely rising prices, into buying any home they could possibly afford, just to break into the market. You couldn't even get a parking space in trendy Belmont Shore—at the south end of Long Beach—for less than a hundred-grand, so the detached, single family house (with added-on guest-bedroom and bath!) that was right on Alamitos Bay—practically on the beach itself—seemed too good to be true. Which, of course, it was. The dark secrets of 67 Pine Beach Road emerged soon after closing, as the rosy pink glow of being *actual home owners* faded for Kali and Matt.

Like most other homes on or near the beach, the Millers' sat at a slight tilt: no part of it was completely square, flat or level, and the front porch was likely home to a million termites, though the Millers' agent had jabbed a pocket-knife into the top step to prove it wasn't.

The previous owner—a man by the name of Eric Proctor—had done did a quick and dirty reno on number 67, prior to listing it for sale. Though they'd never met him, Kali and Matt nicknamed him 'Hookman-Nailman-Screwman' for the number of hooks, nails and screws he'd left behind, peppering the walls with so many holes it looked as though the mob had fought a gun battle in there, once the designer furniture, paintings and photos, copper pots, wall hangings and other artful and homey touches were whisked away by the staging company.

The Millers were forever discovering bits of Eric Proctor's slipshod, penny-pinching handiwork: the wrong type of solder in the bathroom plumbing that allowed the tub water to seep into the front hall; the missing subfloor in the kitchen that led to the buckling and cracking of the cheap press-on tiles. In the halcyon days of post-home-purchase bliss, Matt and Kali had just laughed about these things, chanting, in unison, as if doing a mid-century radio ad: '*It's a Proctor! It's got to be bad*!' But they didn't laugh much anymore; Mr. Proctor's legacy was getting expensive.

Less than six months after they bought in, the market had bottomed out: house prices slumped, then plummeted. Since they would not soon recover close to what they'd paid for the house, Kali and Matt were having to accept the reality that they might well grow old and die in 67 Pine Beach Road.

~~~

A few stones from the retaining wall tumbled onto the sand as Kali stepped down off it, and she noticed, with alarm, that it was falling apart in places. One more thing their home inspector had not bothered to mention! Not for the first time—and not for the last, she was sure—the thought of suing their home inspector crossed Kali's mind.

Turning her back on the beach and the new worry of the retaining wall, she lumbered through her shabby garden, towards the Millers' house. Now that she was on mat leave, it was only her shadow she had to avoid, since there were no shop windows or mirrored walls on Pine Beach Road to confront her with her enormity. She didn't even want to know her weight when Dr. Gerber clucked about it at the start of each monthly visit, just grateful his scale only measured kilograms and she was too metrically-challenged to convert the number to pounds. But though pregnant, she wasn't yet barefoot as well: there was still one pair of Matt's old Converse sneakers that fit her swollen feet. The last pair of shoes she'd bought herself looked Cinderella-small. Now, like an ugly step-sister, she could wedge only a couple of immense toes into them.

Baby Harry (already named thanks to a clear ultrasound image) rolled over inside Kali and gave her a poke. The Millers had decided on the name Harry for its directness and simple honesty. It was a 'good guy' name; everybody liked Harrys. And the hint of royalty didn't hurt, either. Kali took a cookie from her overall pocket and quickly stuffed it into her mouth, hoping Matt hadn't come home suddenly and chosen that moment to gaze out a back window. She knew what he was thinking as he looked at her lately: that wasn't all baby, layered over her hips and bulging around her bra straps!

How huge she had become. It gave her pause, as they say, and probably gave a few others pause as well: Matt, for sure, and everyone at the law firm where Kali was a senior associate. The women were outwardly sympathetic, though morbidly fascinated, by her appearance; the men appalled or incredulous. Her arms and legs were now smooth, plump and firm, like the kielbasa sausages she'd been raised on; the rest of her pale and spongy as over-cooked perogies. Such similes popped had easily into Kali's head, offered up by her father's, Ukrainian, side of the family. It was the Old Country reclaiming her, recognizing a woman now capable of pulling a plough and swinging a sickle. Gone (but please God, not forever!) was the scrawny, smartly-dressed business lawyer of only a few months earlier.

Kali tried to view her changing dimensions with an abstract scientific curiosity, being an intelligent, highly-trained professional. It was either that or panic and throw herself into the ocean to be eaten by sharks, who would certainly relish the Big Whopper presented to them in the form of Kali Miller, attorney-at-large.

As soon as she downed the last bit of the cookie, heartburn radiated spiny fingers of fire up through her diaphragm. As her pregnancy progressed, she'd discovered that as one uncomfortable symptom subsided, it was only to be replaced by another that was worse. First had been suddenly enlarged boobs—a achy and hard as unripe melons—followed by nausea that sent her scurrying past the hotdog vendors, with their putrid-smelling goods, who were on every street corner that summer. Escalating blood pressure came next, followed by swollen legs, backaches, hemorrhoids and insomnia. Then there was the emotional messiness of pregnancy. She'd sewn a Noah's Ark wall-hanging for Harry's room, blubbering over the lousy cruel world she was about to drop him into, wondering what it would be like for the sixty, eighty, maybe a hundred (or even two hundred!) years that Harry would walk the planet, feeling wretchedly guilty that no one had bothered to ask him if he wanted to be born in the first place.

At night, she lay in bed, watching the stars glimmer between the slats of the Venetian blinds as Harry rolled and drifted inside her. What a tragically short time she and this little being would have together, she thought. In her mind, he was already eighteen, independent or off at school. And she was the mother whose phone calls he barely tolerated—rolling his eyes at her concerns about his socks and eating habits—or else avoiding altogether.

By Kali's last trimester, fears about Matt and their marriage had wrapped around her brain, digging in and hanging on for the ride. Had she made the right decision to marry a younger man, specifically, general surgery resident, Dr. Matt Miller? There were omens that their marriage would not work out, right from the start. The charming restaurant where they had lunch before the ceremony was destroyed by fire soon after; the cafe they'd gone to for cake and champagne went bankrupt the next year. Their only witnesses and guests—a couple chosen for the apparent solidity of their marriage—split up a month after the Millers' wedding, the husband running off with a much younger woman he'd met at a poetry-writing retreat. Their wedding had been tiny because Matt was still in med school at the time and Kali's dad, Boris, not a fan of the old tradition of the bride's father footing the bill for the wedding. If Kali and Matt ever hoped to buy a house they needed to save every penny, and a big fancy wedding was nothing but a massive waste of money.

'It's just your hormones talking,' Matt had reassured Kali when she hinted, darkly, about her fears concerning their marriage. 'You're not yourself. You've been taken over by an alien being named Harry. But don't worry, you'll lose all that extra weight in no time.'

And what if I don't? Kali had wondered. Matt was certainly leaving no doubt about his expectations. Was he giving her an ultimatum, a time limit? Was it a threat of some kind? Shape up or ship out? She began to worry about the nurses who flocked around him every day: scrub, circulating, O.R., recovery—all slender young women in crisp white or pink uniforms who understood the stresses of a surgeon's life the way a mere (middle-aged) wife never could—and were on the hunt for husbands themselves.

'Well look at you, in your profession,' Matt had argued, 'you've got sharp dudes in Hugo Boss suits in practically every office, and I bet they're all having impure thoughts about you.'

'So why aren't you jealous?'

'Well, Kali, I happen to *trust* you.'

'What's not to trust? Who's going to chase after a beluga whale, unless it's someone with a harpoon?' The argument had ended there, when Matt had been unable to respond to Kali's question.

And as if all of that anxiety wasn't enough, the post-natal hormonal rollercoaster was still to come. It was quite common for women to have first babies in their late thirties or early forties, but no one talked about the toll it took on them. Kali was thirty-five: five years older than Matt. She was already an '*elderly primigravida*' according to the medical profession. Matt thought she was joking when she suggested they hire a surrogate to bear their child, and of course she had been. But only to a point.

She struggled for breath as she bent over to pick some buggy lettuce to use in a salad for dinner. She'd been thrilled at the idea of an actual garden after years of apartment life and window boxes, but weeds seemed to be all that she could successfully grow. She was an arbitrary and distracted gardener—accidentally crushing delicate shoots and sprigs as she clomped around the dirt in Matt's Converses, unable to distinguish an evil weed from a nutritious vegetable.

Who would have thought that gardening could be such hellishly hard work, so unrewarding, and that things that grew out of the ground could be so *filthy*? But she couldn't expect much gardening help from Matt. He was too busy with his residency and getting his massive research paper finished. Until he did, grotesque slides of surgeries-gone-bad would litter the house: ghastly photos of body parts stapled, clipped, clamped and splayed out on laboratory tables, the morgue lighting tinting them with the lurid hues of cheap pornography. Kali refused to touch them, afraid it would hex the baby; that Harry would be born with a huge port-wine stain, a cleft palate, or something much worse.

Just then, her cellphone twittered from inside the pocket of her overalls. It was Alicia, her assistant at the firm, likely with more paranoid evidence that she was about to be assigned to another lawyer while Kali was away or—her worst nightmare—shunted into the administrative support pool, shared by a number of attorneys, thanked by none. Alicia was in her 'fifties, had never married, was highly-organized and took no shit from nobody, as she put it. She carried an elegant leather briefcase, wore perfectly polished shoes and perky scarves, and usually looked more professional than Kali. Alicia's work was her life, as she often reminded her boss, and being a *floater*, at this stage of her career, was *not* where she saw herself.

But Kali had enough of her own anxieties to deal with for the moment. She clicked off her cell and shoved it into her pocket. Then, twirling the lettuce leaves in her hand, Kali Miller, out-to-pasture-lawyer, trudged back towards the house to take a well-deserved nap before tackling the challenge of throwing something together for dinner.

# Chapter 2

Alicia gave the phone a pissed off look. If Kali didn't pick up by the fifth ring, it was unlikely she was going to at all. Even more concerning was the fact that Kali hadn't dialed in to get her voicemail messages that day. From Alicia's desk, surrounded on three sides by an upholstered divider, she could see Kali's desk, her wilting office plant (*not Alicia's job to water it!*) and the red message light winking anxiously on the side of Kali's phone. What if Kali were having the baby already? Alicia thought. That might excuse her thoughtless behavior. She checked her calendar but concluded that it was still too soon. Much as she disliked the idea of Kali being totally consumed by the processes of birthing, breast-feeding and diaper-changing, the idea that Kali would finally be getting it over with had a decided appeal.

Having nothing else to do and annoyed afresh by the fact that Kali was not answering her cell or landline, Alicia began stuffing the large envelope she meant to send over to her boss later that day. A similar package had gone out earlier, but Alicia had heard nothing back in terms of instructions or follow-up. And it wasn't as though Kali was flat on her back and incapacitated: she was just supposed to take things easy for the last few weeks before the baby arrived. Kali had pre-eclampsia – pregnancy-induced hypertension. Though Alicia had never been pregnant, she'd become an expert on pre-eclampsia through private study on Google and WebMD. As she was wrestling with a tape-gun, Rick Durham thumped on the side of her divider.

"Keeping busy, Alicia?" All breath spray and hair gel, Rick had that established-partner gloss that Alicia hoped one day to see on Kali. Partners' assistants got an immediate raise, a larger cube and increased status at the firm.

Rick was being groomed to take over as Managing Partner whenever old Mr. Biltmore (son of one of the firm's founders) decided to step down. Though he was still very much the beaky, eagle-eyed attorney, there were moments when a certain vagueness overtook his eyes and his mouth slackened as though he were wondering where he was and what he was supposed to be doing. It was times like this that gave the junior lawyers great hope and optimism about the future.

"I was about to send a FedEx over to Kali," Alicia told Rick. "She's working from home, busier than ever."

"Doing well?"

"Great! We have a ton of new work." Get your fat hammy hands off my divider, Alicia thought. I'm not impressed by your flashy college ring; I don't want to count the hairs on your knuckles. She cleared her throat and scowled at her envelope, as though offended by something on the front of it.

"No baby yet?" Rick cocked his head, smiling and trying to look interested. If he was truly interested, Alicia thought, it could be for no good reason.

"Kali thought her water broke this morning." Alicia expected the comment to motivate Rick to go away since he couldn't deal with references to bodily functions, especially female ones. But, annoyingly, he didn't move. What was he waiting for, pressed up against her cube like that? She was going to have to wipe it down with a disinfectant wipe. "It wasn't her water though," Alicia continued, as she typed Kali's address on the envelope. "It was only her mucus plug. That's what came out, in the end."

"No kidding." Rick's smile was fading nicely. "Sounds nasty."

"It's a long story," Alicia said, still typing, "if you have time to hear it." Rick scratched the top of his head, nervously, like a monkey, and Alicia was gratified that she had him off balance. "Yes, it was just that old mucus plug." She watched with satisfaction as Rick's pinstriped backside hustled off down the corridor, but she was unnerved by the encounter. What business was it of his, how busy she was? Or how busy Kali was?

It used to be that no one at Biltmore, Durham & Spears bothered too much about what the assistant was supposed to do for the three or four months that their boss took off to have a baby. But things were changing. In the worst cases (two assistants whom Alicia cringed to remember) the lawyers never came back *at all*. One of those girls was still pounding the payment and sending her resume around the internet, the other had given up trying to find work and was sitting at home, hoping to become pregnant herself.

Even when the lawyer's return from mat leave seemed certain, it was dangerous for an assistant to get too confident. The trick was to make sure you looked busy at all times, so no light bulbs went off in any HR heads indicating you had time to spare. If that happened, a girl could find herself pressed into serving another lawyer, like Mr. Biltmore, who still expected his 'secretary' to 'take dictation' and bring him coffee on a silver tray. Or worse, becoming a floater, drifting from cube to cube, filling in for any assistant who was sick or on vacation, trying your best to do unfamiliar work and getting nothing but complaints for your efforts. Floaters were disconnected, unprotected, and at the mercy of Helen Sharpe, the HR manager, who would put them at the top of her list for firing whenever the firm decided to downsize. This was never going to be the fate of Alicia Martinez. She had held together the career of Kali Miller for too many years to be tossed out onto the pavement of Santa Monica now, *muchas gracias*.

Just then, Jada Tyler, the only African-American attorney in the firm—a Yalie who was rumored to be on the partnership fast-track—stuck her head over Alicia's cube. "Any baby yet?" Her eyebrows were raised practically into her blue-black twisted pompadour.

"You'll be the first to know." Alicia finished taping the envelope, not looking up.

"Well, I somehow doubt *that*."

"It's a good thing she's away for a while." Alicia pulled over a stack of files that Kali had given her to be closed and sent to offsite storage. "Gives me a chance to get caught up. I'm swamped."

"Doesn't look like it. Seems pretty dead around here to me." French-manicured nails, like white-tipped daggers, tapped on Alicia's divider.

"That's only because we're so organized."

"Well, let me know when you get through closing out those dead files. I could use some extra hands."

"If I ever get caught up with everything, I would be glad to help you out." Alicia was stacking one file on top of another and scribbling meaningless notes, in an effort to look busy. "But I don't know what makes you think these files are dead."

"Woman lawyer intuition." Jada smiled a cat-like smile, her eyes narrowed. Alicia continued what she was doing, holding her breath, her heart thumping in her chest, until she felt Jada drift away, like a dark storm cloud moving back out to sea.

# Chapter 3

Jolly Giraffe's Daycare was on 2nd Street, the main thoroughfare of Belmont Shore, in a small storefront.

"We make sure the kids get a hot lunch every day," Mrs. Dalton said as Kali followed her broad, swaying backside into her office: a cramped messy space, where she printed 'Miller-Boy' on a whiteboard under the column entitled 'September Enrollment.' "I'll need your deposit today," she added, "to hold your baby's place."

"I have a few more questions, Mrs. Dalton." Kali was annoyed that the woman only seemed interested in getting the Millers' money. "For example, that outdoor playground. It's right out there on the busy street. Is that safe?"

"It's very well-fenced, Mrs. Miller. Go take a look, see for yourself. And the children stay inside most of the time anyway. It's so bloody hot in Long Beach, isn't it? Better for them inside. They get to watch a video every day, so when your little one gets old enough to have a favorite, you should bring it in."

"I don't think I want Harry inside watching videos all day. Babies need fresh air."

"I said one a day, not *all day*. And infants don't go out much. Two walks – at ten-thirty and two. We have strollers that take five at a time. It's a lot of you-know-what that babies need all that fresh air. You've been reading too many books."

Kali looked down at the fee schedule Mrs. Dalton pushed into her hand. "Eleven hundred a month? That's more than we expected..."

"The going rate for full-time daycare." Mrs. Dalton's eyes flickered over Kali's clothes, as if assessing how much she could afford. "The fees go down as the child gets older, but infants need the most care, of course."

"So... how many babies are there to each staff person?"

"Five to one, until they're a year old. Then it's six to one."

"But what if they're all crying at once?" Kali asked, appalled. "Or if they all needed feeding? Or changing? Or comforting?"

"Some of them would have to wait their turn, wouldn't they? Take a number."

*Take a number*? Kali's jaw dropped. "Excuse me?"

"And most important, you'll need to drop him off with at least five disposable diapers, every morning. And not the cheap ones, either. Pampers or Huggies. The store brands don't hold up."

"But we're going to use cloth diapers, Mrs. Dalton." Had the woman never heard of global warming? "For the environment," Kali added, though she'd thought that would have been obvious.

"You'll get over that notion soon enough, I promise you." Mrs. Dalton had heard this nonsense a thousand times and seen all the self-righteous mothers come to their senses in a month, tops. "So, Mrs. Miller," she was impatient to seal the deal, "do you want to keep your baby on the list? You'll never get him in if you don't confirm today, with a deposit."

"Do I need to put down five Huggies as well?"

"Mrs. Miller, please. I don't have all day."

"Why not?" Kali asked. "You don't have any actual babies to look after, do you? They're all out there, taking a number, waiting in line in their soggy Pampers since no one's going to rush to change them."

"Do you want him on the board or not?" Mrs. Dalton locked eyes with Kali.

"We're going to pass on Jolly Giraffe. No further questions. You can take his name off your board. And by the way, it's Harry."

"What?"

"Harry. Not 'Miller-Boy'."

Mrs. Dalton shrugged, grabbed a marker and aggressively drew a thick black line through 'Miller-Boy' on the whiteboard. The spot would be snapped up soon enough, she knew, with all the millennials in Belmont Shore coupling like rabbits lately.

~~~

Sunshine Children's Village was very aptly named, Kali thought, a little while later as she made a sun-visor with her hand to squint across the sun-bleached patchy grass: a scrap of a yard with no toys except a small slide, a single swing and a faded rubber ball, all of which were being ignored by the children who cried and clung to the six-foot chain-link fence. Those who were old enough to talk screamed for their mothers.

"They're new here," the supervisor told Kali, looking annoyed, "the ones making the giant fuss. It takes a while for them to settle in. They make it hard on everyone else, though."

The playground staff, two sullen young women with shaved heads, very tight T-shirts and very short shorts, sat under the single tree, half-watching the kids in a bored, desultory way. Kali had just come from the Sweet Cloud Extended Childcare Facility, which sounded like a prison to her, and was located in an office building near her law firm. There, the children played outside in a walled-in patch of baking hot asphalt, twelve floors above ground. 'You can drop your wee one off as early as six-thirty,' the owner, a fat, forty-something man named Mr. Sweet had informed Kali, 'and leave him as late as seven at night. There's an additional charge, of course, for the late pick-up. No charge for the early drop.'

What a great idea, Kali had thought, wrapping her arms protectively around her belly. And if I pay you a little more, I might never need to come and pick him up at all!

# Chapter 4

Maybe we could find a girl from the Philippines," Kali said to Matt the next evening. "Everyone says they're very hard-working, kind, patient, all that good stuff." She was painting over Matt's old waterbed for Harry's nanny, since they'd agreed that a nanny was the only realistic solution to the child-care conundrum. The daycares were not only depressing and expensive, they were brimming with bacteria, as Matt pointed out, and crawling with viruses. Did they want Harry picking up every little bug that went around? Or getting head lice, which was a near-certainty?

"Why are you painting?" Matt had taken a break from his research and was leaning against the door jamb of the back bedroom that would become the nanny's room. "Paint fumes aren't good for Harry, or for you. And I hope that's not oil-based paint you're using."

"Of course not. And the windows are all open anyway. If I don't paint it, who's going to? Don't we want Harry's nanny to have a nice room?"

"Painting that bed isn't going to make it any nicer in here. Besides, it doesn't need painting. I like the natural pine. And I don't have time to paint."

"And I do? Maybe you haven't noticed that mountain of envelopes on the kitchen table. I get two or three a day from Alicia. I see more of the FedEx guy than I see of you."

"Tell her to stop sending you stuff. You're on mat leave. Alicia needs to butt out. Your secretary works for you, not the other way around."

"Assistant, not secretary," Kali corrected him. "And she's only doing her job. She's very territorial." And more to the point, Kali was scared to death of her.

"You've got to start letting go," Matt lectured. "You can't keep up the level of productivity you're used to. You've got other, way more important, things to focus on now." Part of the problem with being married to a younger man was that he imagined himself to be older, in terms of common sense and emotional maturity. To prove this point, Matt often adopted a pedagogical role with Kali which was especially irksome when he was right. "One of the agencies has a Swedish girl we can see," he said, casually, gazing out the window with a blank look, as if the thought had slipped his mind and just re-occurred to him.

"Yeah, right," Kali snorted as she slapped more paint on the headboard.

"The least we could do is interview her. We don't have to hire her."

"The least we could do is nothing." Kali could feel her blood pressure rising. "This conversation could be hazardous to my health, Doctor. Besides, with your busy schedule, I'm surprised you've had time to sit around calling employment agencies."

"We've got to find the best person for Harry. Is there anything more important?" Kali said nothing, resenting his rightness. Or was it righteousness? "And what have you got against a Swedish girl, anyway?" he continued. "Swedes are simple and good-natured. They like to stay home and raise children."

"And I don't?"

"You think you would?"

"Did you ever bother to ask?"

Matt stared at her. "Well, look, if you really want to stay home with Harry, quit your job, I'm behind you, a hundred and ten percent."

Kali dipped the paint brush into the can again. "I'm still thinking about it. It's my career, isn't it?"

Matt ran his hands through his hair, as he always did when annoyed, frustrated or cornered. He had a ton of it—black and wavy. Kali's was mouse brown, and though it had thickened nicely since she became pregnant, the reality was that most of it would fall out after Harry was born, according to the books Kali wished she hadn't bothered to read.

"O-kay," Matt said, slowly, "but is quitting such a good idea, when you've almost got the partnership?

"No one's said that, exactly."

"It's in the bag though, right?"

"I thought so, but that was before we got pregnant."

Matt was silent for a few moments. "We'd have to sell the house. But Harry would be fine in an apartment, I guess, for a couple of years. Until I get my practice rolling. Maybe then we could get into the market again, recover from the beating we'll take if we sell this place now."

Give up their house? Kali thought. No backyard for little Harry to play in? No front walk to push him along in his stroller? No beach? They'd bought the house *for* Harry, *because* of Harry. But they'd lose a fortune if they sold now; Matt was right. Especially with all the Proctors they'd have to fix or conceal. She thought, uneasily, about the retaining wall she had yet to tell him about."

"And we might want to get Harry a dog," Matt said. "We couldn't have a dog in an apartment, except maybe an annoying, little yappy Chihuahua. Swedes love animals, by the way."

"You can't generalize about an entire race like that. All I've ever heard about Swedish girls is that they're blonde and very liberal, sexually-speaking."

"Now who's generalizing? For your information, lots of Swedes are brunettes, and it's the Netherlands that has no censorship laws. Sweden is actually a fairly uptight country. Look at Volvos – the most boring car on the market, but also the safest. Where is it made? Sweden."

"If Swedes are so boring and simple, why do we want one of them looking after Harry? Don't we want him to be intellectually stimulated?"

"I meant simple as in having simple, honest values, not simple-minded. And besides, we're not going to get a Harvard *cum laude* to look after our kid, let's face it." Matt hesitated. "Anyway, I told the agency we'd see this girl, along with a few others. They're going to set up the interviews."

"Hold on." Kali put down her paintbrush, wiping the sweat from her brow with the back of her hand. "What's the big rush?"

"Kali, it could take months. We're not going to find the right person just like that. Be realistic. We've got no time to waste."

"But we just started talking about this the other day. I'm trying to get used to the idea of sharing our house with some stranger, not to mention sharing Harry."

"You're already decorating the nanny's room, Kali. Isn't that what you're doing?"

"I thought this bed needed painting," Kali said lamely, "in case your mother comes to visit."

"The good people get snapped up fast." Matt ignored the jibe at his mom, Beth, who had yet to come and see their house. "At least agree to interview this Swedish girl, okay?"

Only if she's fatter than me, with less hair, and a huge overbite, Kali thought. But how likely was any of that? "Fine," she grumbled, anxious to end the conversation, "but we're going to interview other girls too. As many as we need to find the right one."

"Of course." Matt hustled off, whistling *(whistling?* Matt never whistled!) to get back to his research paper.

As Kali watched him go, she tried to analyze why she was so bothered by their nanny discussion. She was reconciled to the fact that they would have to give up their privacy and hire a 'live-in' nanny. A 'live-out' would charge three hundred dollars a month more than a live-in: three hundred more than they could afford. The going rate for a live-in nanny was surprisingly less than any of those heart-breaking daycares. Their house would be clean, their meals healthy and well-prepared; how nice would all that be? There was no alternative, really, for a professional working couple. And Matt was right, Kali couldn't consider giving up her law practice – not for years – for Harry's sake. Even if she wanted to – which she didn't.

She hadn't given much thought to the ethnic background or nationality of their nanny-to-be, but she had been picturing a diligent, hard-working and (though she was ashamed to admit it, even to herself) *homely* young woman, who would be grateful to have a cheery, clean room to retire to each evening. Maybe she would even wash Kali's and Matt's clothes (which they would never ask, nor expect, her to do, of course) while she was watching *Naked and Afraid* or chatting on the phone with her (equally homely) nanny friends. But a Swedish girl? Was Kali secure enough to handle seeing, first thing in the morning, a lanky blonde, with pouting bee-stung lips and tousled hair, coming out of the nursery, cradling Harry – Kali's baby – in her slender, sun-browned arms?

Why would the Millers want someone around all day saying *ja* this and *ja* that, writing little circles over the vowels of words when making out the grocery list? And they left the tops off sandwiches, didn't they, Swedes? Harry would grow up thinking that was normal. He'd be ostracized by all the other kids when he showed up with open-faced sandwiches in his lunch bag.

All things considered, having a Swedish nanny could be profoundly annoying. And if Swedes were so attracted to babies, wasn't there a risk this one might try to appropriate the Millers' baby for her own? After Kali returned to work, Harry might forget about her, or worse, reject her whenever she tried to take him into her arms. She'd heard about cases where that exact thing happened. A nanny was basically a babysitter, not a surrogate mother. Kali would be cordial and fair, but not overly-friendly; she wouldn't be the nanny's advisor or confidante. She would be her employer. Period. After all, she wasn't interested in adopting a daughter, especially a grown one, who looked like Britt Ekland, circa 1971.

~~~

There was no sound coming from their bedroom. Matt must be engrossed in his research again, Kali thought. Or was he shopping for nannies on the Internet? Maybe going through Craigslist ads – the ones with photos? She took a Snickers bar out of her overall pocket and stuffed it into her mouth, hoping Matt wouldn't hear, or pop up again unexpectedly. As she munched, dribbling chocolate bits down her chest, she checked her workmanship on the waterbed. It didn't look great, but it would do. This was a nanny's room she was furnishing, not the Ritz-Carlton. Cheap and cheerful was the goal.

Back in the kitchen, she eyed the pile of thick brown envelopes Alicia had sent over, feeling a familiar twitch of excitement. There was billable work in there, letters of instruction, maybe some work from a new client. Feeling guilty, like someone cheating on a diet, she opened the top one and pulled out a handful of telephone message slips.

Trying not to make too much noise and attract Matt's attention, she shuffled and cut the stack. Most, she noted with disappointment, were from Mike Potochnik, the client from hell, and the only referral she'd ever had from any of her relatives. He was the grandson of Kali's grandfather's best friend from the Old Country—a Ukrainian, like Kali's father, Boris. But referrals from family were destined to result in disaster: a complaint to the State Bar, ruined friendships, feuds that spanned generations.

Kali had instructed Alicia to send Potochnik's file to Accounting, to be billed out and closed. New work from that direction wasn't something Kali was eager, or likely, to get. Still, she should probably return his calls. Some of the message slips had the 'urgent' box ticked. It was too late to call him, so she would have to toss and turn and worry all night—as if she weren't doing enough of that already. She was flipping through the message slips one more time, in case she had missed something interesting, when Matt suddenly reappeared.

"As your house doc, I'm ordering you flat on your back." He grabbed the message slips from her hand.

"That kind of talk used to be a terrible turn-on."

"And I'm confiscating your precious envelopes, too."

Kali watched, licking her lips, too hot, tired and uncomfortable to fight him for them, as he stuffed the envelopes into a kitchen drawer. "I ought to at least see what's in there," she protested, "what if it's something important?"

"You'll find out in three months. Whatever it is, it isn't worth risking your health. Or Harry's."

As he hustled back into their bedroom, obviously pleased by the way he'd taken charge, Kali leaned against the kitchen counter, arms crossed over her belly, feeling light-headed and faint. Inside, Harry started to hiccup, a rhythmic beating that could go on for hours. Matt was right again. There was no 'billable time' when you were on maternity leave, and Harry deserved the best of Kali, not left-over unbilled or written-off time.

She resolved to start taking better care of herself, forget about the office and concentrate on finding Harry the perfect nanny: a capable and caring employee. Keeping an emotional distance from the nanny would be easy for her. But would it be so easy for Harry? And worse—Kali couldn't discount the awful suspicion—would it be so easy for Matt? Maybe, if she weren't old enough to have once been mistaken for Matt's mother (even if it was only by the guy who watered the office plants) the idea might never have entered Kali's head.

# Chapter 5

The next day, Kali decided to make good on her word to that awful Mrs. Dalton that she would be using only cloth diapers for Harry and do their bit to save the planet from drowning in garbage. After spending an hour in Baby Boo-Boo—a trendy Belmont Shore baby store—overwhelmed by the options for covering a baby's backside, Kali settled on five dozen pure cotton diapers and ten snazzy, Hawaiian-print, Velcro-fastened covers. The covers were part of a set that included a matching diaper bag, change pad and mosquito net. She bought those too, plus a couple of tiny shorts and Hawaiian shirts, and best of all, totally adorable baby sunglasses. Matt would be annoyed that she hadn't shopped on Amazon and saved money, but all the things in Baby Boo-Boo were so cute, creative and cool—mostly hand-made by Long Beach locals, and eco-friendly as well.

Besides, Amazon had already sucked up enough of their money for bottles, soothers, teething toys, a vaporizer, booties, hats and hooded bath-towels as well as a high chair, crib, changing table, a chest of drawers, a top-of-the-line Perego stroller, a wind-up swing and a bouncy exercise jumper that could be hung from any standard-size doorframe. As it turned out, the house had only one standard door frame, thanks to Mr. Proctor's *ad hoc* renovations.

And anyway, it was too close to Kali's due date to order more stuff online and take the chance it might not arrive before Harry, and wind up left on the front step, to be pilfered by neighbors, passers-by or vagrants while Kali was in the hospital having Harry. They wanted everything all set and ready for him, didn't they? Well, she could justify and rationalize all she liked, she realized, but she was a victim of 'the Pinterest nursery.' Kali handed her well-worn credit card to the owner of Baby Boo-Boo, and signed the credit card slip, afraid to even look at the total.

She pulled up to 67 Pine Beach Road, just before 5:00 p.m., her Honda bursting with shopping bags and boxes. There was a car parked in front of the house—an old red Mustang with a man sitting inside. What was he doing in front of their house? There was something creepily familiar about him. Kali tried to get a look at his face, but he was bending down over the seat, as if searching for something on the floor. She parked in the garage at the side of the house, then peeked around to see, with relief, that the Mustang was pulling away. There were always people sitting around in cars, doing nothing; they were a fact of life in Long Beach, as in any other city, she reminded herself. She wouldn't give it another paranoid thought.

Matt's jeep was nowhere in sight, which was good news since Kali was hoping to sneak all her Baby Boo-Boo buys into the house before he got home and avoid more complaints about her spending. The air conditioner clicked on and began humming from behind the bushes, but otherwise, all was quiet. Kali was therefore extremely surprised to enter the house and see Matt, drinking beer in the living room with a blonde, very young and extremely attractive woman.

"Honey!" He bounded out of his chair as if jabbed by the devil's pitchfork. "This is Britta Edvardsson. She had a mix-up with another interview and had to come today, on short notice. I didn't know how to reach you. I called all your usual watering-holes..."

"Watering-holes?" Kali wiped the sweat from her upper lip as she waddled into the living room. "What do I look like, a buffalo?"

There was a moment of embarrassed silence as Matt grabbed her arm, apparently not noticing the shopping bags and boxes, and pulled her towards Britta, who was unfolding her long legs to stand up. Huge blue eyes met Kali's hazel ones. A fine gold bracelet—a chain of tiny dangling stars—tinkled on her wrist as she held out her hand. She was wearing a loose cotton sweater and boyfriend jeans. It was impossible to see what her figure was like exactly, but Kali could make a fairly intelligent guess.

"*Jag heter Britta*," she said, in a soft, breathy voice. "I am Britta."

Kali took her hand, smiling vaguely. "And I'm *Mrs.* Kali Miller. I've been out shopping for diapers—cloth ones, the kind you have to wash."

"*Ja,*" Britta nodded vigorously, "The baby must have some diapers."

"Some? Try five dozen."

Britta nodded again with a giant smile. There was a space between her front teeth, but instead of making her look goofy, the flaw made her more attractive, more charming and delightful.

"You're not going to believe this," Matt chuckled, "but Britta's almost an old friend. Well, not her—I mean, her family. She was just a kid when I was over in Sweden."

"A gangly kid with freckles and braces?" Kali said.

"Gangly?" Brita's blue eyes blinked in confusion.

"Skinny," Matt said, throwing Kali a look.

"Oh, *ja,*" Britta rolled her eyes dramatically, "I was so skinny. Too much skinny!"

"Her mother's a great cook," Matt enthused. "I did some wicked freeloading off her family. They were big hockey fans. I couldn't believe it when she started telling me about her family. I didn't even recognize her, but then it suddenly hit me!"

"No kidding," Kali said, thinking that suddenly hitting him was quite an appealing idea.

"I told her she could start September first, if that's okay with you. Assuming she doesn't find another job before then."

"Matt, could you help me bring in the rest of the stuff from the car?" Kali no longer cared if he wailed on at her about her spending. "We need to talk."

"Please, I will help!" Britta said, enthusiastically.

"See? Britta wants to help already," Matt beamed.

As Britta followed Kali back through the kitchen, Kali looked back at her husband, to see him grinning into his beer. 'Did I just do something totally awesome, or what?' his expression said.

# Chapter 6

Kali arranged to meet her sister, Sofia, for lunch the next day. During a brief panicky phone call, she had explained what Matt had done: hiring Britta before Kali had a chance to think about it, get to know Britta, see other applicants, or discuss any of it with Matt. She needed to know if she was merely threatened—jealous of Britta's sex appeal and Matt's obvious admiration for it—or if there was a good reason to be genuinely concerned, for Harry's sake.

Sofia was three years older than Kali and lived in Rancho Pales Verdes, on a verdant hill overlooking the Pacific, with her Italian-import husband, Bernardo, and their daughter, Ariana. She was a real estate agent; Bernardo a successful broker. They'd set up shop and worked together as Bernardo & Wife.

The lunch was set for Panera Bread in the Lakewood Center mall. Kali got there early, squeezed herself into a booth, and settled in to wait since Sofia was sure to be late. True to form, Sofia finally appeared after half an hour, giving Kali a little wave as she entered. In her black linen dress, with a pale silk camisole peeking out from the neckline, Kali's sister looked polished to perfection, as usual: nails done, hair styled, makeup flawless. Panera Bread was not Sofia's choice for a sisterly lunch. She had suggested the Pelican Hill Golf Club, which was much too far for Kali to drive in her condition, and way too pricey. Despite being comfortably well off (even wealthy) Sofia never offered to pick up the tab.

"So, how's the little house?" was the first thing she said, before sitting down. It was a sore spot with Sofia that Kali and Matt had not bought their house through her and Bernardo. It wasn't that Kali didn't trust them, but she and Matt had agreed that they didn't want Bernardo & Wife poking through their finances, for the entire family to know about, as in what a struggle it had been to get Matt

27

and Kali approved for a first mortgage at prime. Still, from Sofia's point of view, they had snuck around behind the backs of Bernardo & Wife in an unforgivable act of family betrayal.

"I'm a bit worried about the retaining wall," Kali confessed, reluctantly throwing her sister a bone.

"I warned you about that, didn't I?" Sofia was clearly delighted. "Now, if you had bought through *us*, used *our* fabulous home inspector, you wouldn't be in this mess. Or in that silly house."

"We love the house. Cute, beachy, cozy. All that. We're really happy we bought it." She winced, wishing she hadn't used the word 'bought' as it would remind her sister of half of a six percent commission, just gone with the wind.

"Going to be a bit tight though, isn't it? You and Matty, little Harry, and your *new nanny* all crammed into that teensy 1920's beachy house?" Then, without waiting for Kali's reply, she zeroed in on the subject of the lunch. "I can't believe you let him hire a Swedish nanny. And while you were out diaper shopping!"

"A horrid but irrelevant detail."

"Not irrelevant at all. It heightens your humiliation, and the treachery of your husband. So, what are you going to do about this hideous development?"

"Nothing," Kali shrugged, trying not to sound defensive and wondering if calling Sofia had been such a good idea. "She'll be great for Harry. She seems really nice, and she's taken some child care courses, knows CPR."

"So, *he* tells you. You weren't there for the interview, were you?"

"Well, I met her, of course." Kali shifted uncomfortably in the booth and fanned her face with a paper napkin. "And Matt, being a doctor, would have grilled her on all that."

"Oh, I bet he grilled her—or certainly intends to."

"So, what do you want to eat?" Kali sighed. "I could use a glass of water right now. I feel pretty dehydrated."

"You know, Kali," Sofia moved in for the kill, "I have a friend who's five years older than her husband, like you are with Matt. She thinks it's just a matter of time before he leaves her for a younger woman. She used to be terrified, but now she's resigned to it. Can you believe it? You don't have that feeling about Matt, I hope." Her look said she hoped otherwise.

"Oh, God no," Kali faked a laugh. "He's much too busy to go out looking for another woman."

"He doesn't have to go out *looking*, Kali. She's right there, right under his nose, and Swedish!"

"I'm not all that hungry." Kali squinted up at the menu above the order counter. "Maybe just some soup..."

"Forget food. Let's get back to this Helga, or whatever her name is."

"Britta."

"Like the water filter?"

"Two t's... whatever. Anyway, I refuse to get paranoid about her."

"Paranoid? Let me spell it out for you. Matt lived in Sweden for three years, basically getting laid a lot and being very well paid. He's never gotten over those glory days as a mini sports hero. And now he's brought a little piece of Sweden right into your home—a souvenir, a memento, someone he actually knew when he lived there."

"She was just a kid back then."

"Worse! She's what? Half your age?"

"In her twenties.... not exactly half my age."

"And you're thinking of allowing this? Are you insane? Just when you're at your worst? I wasn't going to mention it—I mean, I know how crappy you must feel—but you don't look too good. Soon, you won't be able to fit into that tiny house you've got. What does Dr. Gerber say?"

"He only likes rare and interesting problems. Getting grotesquely fat is too ordinary."

"Well, maybe you should change doctors." Sofia said, as if that would be the easiest thing in the world for Kali to do at this late stage.

"No, he's fine. Hs name is synonymous with baby food, so I figured that was a good sign. And Matt vetted him, of course."

Sofia's green eyes were fixed on her sister. She was the only blonde in a family of brunettes, and with eyes so green people assumed she wore tinted contacts. She was cool and pale and in control: an enigma in a family where red-faced fussing and fulminating was the basic level of self-expression. "You don't have any ankles left at all, Kali," she added, peeking under the table, then straightening up again as she flipped back her hair. "I didn't swell up like that with Ariana."

"That was twelve years ago – you just don't remember the details." Kali was feeling short of breath.

"Oh, yes I do. One never forgets. You can forgive—I mean, you don't hold it against the baby forever—but the husband? Him you never forgive." She laughed, then got straight back to business. "You've got to be realistic about this nanny. Do you really want Gisele Bündchen lounging around in her bathrobe, getting Matty to come into her room to change a light bulb in the middle of the night?"

"Gisele Bündchen is Brazilian, not Swedish."

"You get my point."

"You should see her," Kali sighed.

"I don't have to. Matt hired her while you were out. That says it all. And sure, you trust him, but why tempt him? You'll have enough to worry about with the baby. Why ask for trouble? Invite it into your own home? *Pay* for it?"

"So, I'm supposed to fire Britta because I'm afraid Matt has a thing for Swedish girls?"

"You're not afraid he has, you know he does. Like every other man with a pulse. You need to interview more nannies, a lot of them. You're on mat leave, you've got nothing else to do. Take your time to find someone else. It's your home and your baby. Get the right person for you."

"But what'll Matt say? Britta hasn't even started. I don't have just cause."

"Stop talking like a lawyer and start thinking like a woman. And forget about what Matt has to say. You're the one who has to be comfortable with the person you hire. Matt's hardly home anyway."

"He thinks Britta should start now, before Harry's even born."

"Of course, he does!" Sofia hissed. "Kali, Kali...How much does it take to make you see what's going on? Are you blind, or suffering from hormone-induced stupidity? The only Swede I'd allow in my house is one over six feet tall, named Sven or Lars, who can give a great deep-tissue massage. You know," she leaned closer in over the table, dropping her voice, "I heard a story the other day about a woman who strangled her nanny with her bare hands. Killed her. The nanny went to answer the phone and left the baby alone in the tub. He drowned! And the horrible irony of it is, it was the *mother* who was calling, just to see how things were. Feeling guilty, probably, about being back at work. With her bare hands, can you believe it? How many of these nannies realize that their lives are at stake? There aren't many jobs where a mistake gets you strangled with someone's bare hands, not in this country anyway. But how's a mother supposed to react? Say – oh, my baby drowned? No problem, we'll just make another?"

Kali was suddenly claustrophobic, her blood pressure soaring. There were shooting pains up and down both arms. "I really feel sick. I can't eat anything. I need some air." Under the table, her swollen feet groped for her shoes.

"You're not in labor, are you?"

"I've never been in labor, so how should I know?" Struggling to bend down around her girth, Kali tried, without success, to force her swollen feet into Matt's Converses.

"I'm so glad I only need a housekeeper now that Ariana's in middle school," Sofia prattled on. "Do you ever think about how easily we working mothers turn over the keys to our homes, and hand over our precious children to the care of strangers? What do we really know about these people? Are they thieves? Psychos? It's insane when you think about it."

"I can't get these shoes on!" Kali was desperate to get outside, and away from her sister. Her face was flaming, her breath short and wheezy. "What am I going to do?"

"Oh, I'm so sorry if I upset you!" Sofia got out of the booth, bent down and picked up the shoes. She did a double take. "You're wearing Matt's sneakers?"

"Sofia, for fuck's sake!"

"Okay, calm down. I'm just trying to be a good older sister and give you my advice." She gave Kali a hug, but not big enough to crease her linen dress. "It's an imperfect system but we all have to take our chances and do the best we can. I could never give up working to stay home with a kid. I'd go bonkers within a week, and so would you. A nanny is the only option for women like us."

"I don't want to talk about nannies anymore!" Kali's lower lip was quivering. Blinking back tears, she fumbled in her bag for a tissue, as Sofia steered her outside and handed her Matt's shoes.

"Take deep breaths or something. We don't need you going into labor right here in the mall parking lot. And I have a showing in an hour, so I can't stay. It's a multimillion-dollar home, Kali. Ocean view—three sides."

All Sofia cared about was her 'showing', and not having a 'scene' to deal with, Kali thought, bitterly, blowing her nose. And it was her fault that Kali was upset enough to go into premature labor, not to mention that she was now starving. "I'm just at a really low point right now," she sniffed. "If Harry doesn't come soon, I'm going to lose my mind."

"Look at me." Sofia gripped her firmly by the shoulders. "You sure you're okay?"

Kali nodded, pressing the tissue to her eyes. There was only one correct answer where Sofia was concerned: the one that would take up the least amount of her valuable time—time that could be better spent making money.

"You go straight home now, promise?"

"Where else am I going to go? Clothes shopping? Out drinking? To a spin class?"

"Listen to your big sister. Ditch this Britta water filter person, before she has a chance to settle in, get Harry attached to her and destroy your marriage. And if you don't have the balls, I'll do it for you. It would be my pleasure."

"Thanks," Kali said, not knowing what else to say.

After Sofia had zoomed away in her Prius Hybrid Plug-in, Kali stood in the meager shade of a palm tree, practicing what she thought might be Lamaze breathing techniques, until she felt less likely to have a stroke, and marginally able to drive. She wasn't in labor, of that she was pretty sure; and if something else was about to happen to her, it would make itself known, eventually.

But she was reeling from the conversation with her sister that was supposed to have reassured her that her fears about Britta were ridiculous. She fanned her reddened face with one of Matt's Converses, not caring who saw her doing it. The love-hate relationship between sisters was indeed confusing, strange, and often very challenging. That was the only take-away she had gotten from the lunch.

# Chapter 7

Kali never had a chance to interview any prospective nannies. She awoke suddenly at four the next morning to find herself in soaking wet sheets. Trying not to panic, she nudged Matt awake. He stumbled around finding his medical bag, then returned with a strip of chemically-treated paper which he used to confirm that it was indeed amniotic fluid all over the sheets. "But it can't be!" Kali protested. She wasn't ready for Harry. He wasn't due for a few more days, and first babies were supposed to be late!

"Better bring forward that date in your iCal," Matt said.

Shivering with excitement, Kali went into Harry's room to smooth his bassinet sheets, realign the pile of folded cloth diapers and pick up bits of lint from the carpet, as if expecting a very particular house guest.

Matt went to take a shower and came out of the bathroom a few minutes later, with a towel around his waist. He grabbed his cellphone and steered Kali into Harry's room, to photograph her from several angles, standing beside the crib and doing her best to smile and try to look attractive and in control.

Kali's contractions, if that's what they were, were just vague cramping and pulling sensations, and too diffuse to even time. They felt strange but were not actually painful. According to Matt, they hadn't really started at all, but Kali didn't see what he could know, really know, about it, being a mere man.

~~~

VOLUNTEER AT LARGE it said on his badge, and he was eyeing Kali's suitcase with suspicion. "I hope that thing's not as heavy as it looks."

"No worries," Kali said, "I can manage."

"You're a lot younger than me. I didn't volunteer to be no red cap. I volunteered to be a Volunteer." Feeling vaguely guilty, though she was the one in labor and carrying not only a heavy suitcase, but sixty extra pounds of baby, amniotic fluid and fat, Kali trudged after him down the hospital corridor. As they waited for the elevator, the Volunteer scowled again at her bag. "So, what you got in there? Books?"

"I have a few. Baby books, mostly. Some files too."

"Files? You mean, like work-type stuff?"

"They said it could take a while, having the baby. I like to keep busy."

The Volunteer shook his head and irritably jabbed the elevator button. "When my wife went in for her kids, the only kind of file she would had with her was a nail file. Some people bring a whole library with them when they come in here. I can't deal with that. I'm an old man."

It was his job to show Kali to her room on the labor floor, but it was hard to imagine a less appealing tour guide, or labor floor. The corridors were a dingy grey-blue color, with wan pink borders—someone's idea of making the place look cheerful and baby-like, Kali supposed, and maybe it did have that effect, back in the 'eighties when it was last painted. Her room had the same grimy paint, but two of the walls were papered with a cheerful floral pattern, and a cute butterfly mobile floated over the birthing bed: a padded, sectional table with stirrups out the end, over which someone had popped a pair of striped oven mitts

Above the bed was a large convex mirror: the kind convenience store owners use to watch for shoplifters. Kali wondered why anyone would want a mirror over that particular bed. She should have known, but she had avoided all the pre-natal classes and hospital tours, not wanting to hear other women's horror stories. She was a worrier, and the less she knew about what was going to happen, the better. She would deal with whatever happened when it happened, as she dealt with most things in her life: *somehow.*

Next to the birthing bed was a square machine that was humming in a businesslike way, with a strip of paper threaded across the front of it and a twinkling panel of lights; behind that an oxygen mask and IV pole, neither of which Kali would have any need for, she decided. The Volunteer-at-Large was still there in the room with her, as if waiting for a tip.

"Could you open a window for me?" she asked, thinking she was expected to give him something to do.

"Nope. They're painted shut," he replied, peevishly.

"It's so stuffy in here, I thought—"

"Air conditioner don't work neither," the Volunteer grinned, looking satisfied. "Well, I'll be getting along now. They keep us volunteers busy around here. Too busy, if you want my opinion."

Kali thanked him as graciously as she could for his help, though he hadn't been of any and she was offended by his attitude. She was, after all, the patient – a woman in labor. She didn't see why anyone who *volunteered* to help in a hospital needed to be so cranky about doing it. She went over to the window to twiddle ineffectively with the air-conditioning knob.

It was a clear sunny California day, she noted: perfect for introducing Harry to the world. She felt a surge of happiness, the crabby Volunteer forgiven. The hospital parking lot was directly below her window and she could see Matt's Jeep, but not Matt. She wondered what was taking him so long. Schmoozing with the hospital staff was her guess. Dr. Miller was very popular with the staff at every hospital he'd rotated through during his residency, which was practically every hospital in Los Angeles County.

Feeling calm and in control, she undressed and put on two hospital gowns: one open at the back, the other at the front, so that her girth was completely covered. There was nothing to this birthing business, she thought, as she folded her clothes and put them into the dented locker. Alongside the locker was another padded table, with an incubator-type lamp hanging over it. On top of the table was a clear plastic tub, scale, measuring tape, tiny white knitted cap and flannel gown, a stack of blue flannel blankets and a paper diaper. No point making a fuss over the diaper, she decided: one or two couldn't do much harm to the environment.

She approved of the determined optimism conveyed by the arrangement of things on that table. Of course, Harry was on his way. Of course, he would be healthy baby boy and need a flannel gown and diaper. Of course, he would have only one head, need only one knitted cap.

There were also two blue wristbands on the table, one large, one small. She picked them up. 'Miller, boy' it said on each one, and 'Miller, Mother – Kali'. The bands were joined together, the symbolism choked her up, so she quickly put them down and climbed up onto the bed, drawing the curtains around it. Then she lay back, her head and shoulders propped up on a lumpy foam pillow.

She had to wonder at all the fuss about childbirth – all that screaming, panting and eye-rolling, the clutching of bed-posts and sheets she'd seen in movies and heard about from friends and relatives. There was nothing to it; nothing to it at all. Some women must have very low pain thresholds was the only explanation she could come up with. Suddenly, Harry started jabbing and poking at her, apparently impatient to get out. As Kali watched her stomach roll and twitch and rumble, the curtains were jerked apart by a frowning, frazzled-looking nurse. "I see you're all settled in," she said. "Has the doctor had a look at you?"

"I haven't seen him. But do you know where my husband is? Dr. Matt Miller?"

"Oh, you're Dr. Miller's wife. He's at the nurses' station, entertaining some of the staff with his stories."

"What kind of stories?" Kali asked, and why was Matt out there *entertaining* anyone instead of in the birthing room with her?

"He'll be along eventually, but there's no rush. You're not in active labor."

"How can you be sure?"

"You're not in enough pain." The nurse went about being brisk and nurse-like, officiously ripping apart the wristbands and snapping the larger one onto Kali's wrist, taking her pulse, blood pressure and temperature, buckling the fetal monitor belt around Kali's belly, then attaching it to the humming machine. She switched on the monitor, and the paper tape started to move across it, a needle-like pen graphically recording Harry's tiny heartbeat.

"Excuse me, but how do you know I'm not in enough pain?" Kali asked. "Maybe I have a high pain threshold. You can't feel what I'm feeling right now. It's quite uncomfortable."

The nurse ignored her. From her pocket, she took a scrap of paper on which were some scribbled notes. The grubby pink stethoscope slung around her neck had a baby's ID bracelet twined around it: a strand of pink, blue and white ceramic beads.

"Can I get a bracelet like that for my baby?" Kali asked, feeling a sudden urge to shop.

"They don't make these any more. Too dangerous. The baby could choke on a bead if the string broke."

"So why are you wearing one, being around babies all day?"

"Have you talked to the anesthetist about your epidural?"

Kali had been anticipating the question. "I'm not having one," she said, firmly. "My doctor and my husband have been given strict instructions. I don't care if I beg and plead, I don't want one. Billions of women have given birth without an anesthetic. I don't see why everyone just assumes a woman wants an epidural. A lot of women expect to have C-sections too—as if that's the new normal way to give birth. Booked in advance, a life well planned." Kali smoothed her hospital gown again, feeling very much on the moral high ground.

"We'll see what you have to say later." With a smug smile the nurse left, her crepe-soled shoes making sucking sounds on the tiled floor.

Kali knew her game: she only wanted her anaesthetized, so Kali would be less trouble, to make her own life easier. Hospitals had the wrong attitude. The health of the baby and mother should be most important, not the convenience of the staff. And the nurse was obviously mistaken about her labor not being active. She'd probably never had a baby herself, so how would she know? As Kali was about settle back against the pillows, her cellphone twittered.

"Thank God I found you!" It was Alicia. "I hope you're not in the middle of something."

"I'm actually in the hospital, Alicia. In labor. What's the problem?"

"I was just wondering if Mike Potochnik ever got out to visit you. He keeps calling. He's a loco guy, Kali, and he's making me crazy, too. I knew you didn't want me giving out your cell, so I gave him your address."

"You gave my home address to a stranger?"

"I thought he was an old friend, no?"

"Distant family connection. We're hardly friends."

"Well, sorry. My bad. I thought maybe he was going to bring you a baby gift or something. He came in demanding to see you—and he was really mad when I told him you were already on mat leave."

"I gave you his file to close out, Alicia. And I also gave him the name of another lawyer, if he needed more legal work done. He's a very difficult person." Kali' heart was thumping unpleasantly, the needle on the graph paper zig-zagging wildly, like a lie detector gone berserk. Harry was feeling the same stress that she was, Kali realized, with dismay.

"He wouldn't talk to anyone but you. Hold on!" Silence. "Sorry, there was someone hovering around my desk. And that's another thing. Am I supposed to just hand over your files to anyone who wants them? This is not a one-time thing, Kali. It's happening almost every day."

"Well, someone has to look after my practice. No one can do my work without seeing my files. Besides, I've got nothing to hide—they're all in good shape." Kali thought uneasily about the odd grocery list that had slipped in between pieces of file correspondence now and then; the tampon that had rolled out of a file while she was standing in the middle of the office.

'You dropped this,' one of the (young) (male) (single) lawyers said, scooping it up and handing it to her. 'What is it? Some kind of marker?'

Kali shifted the phone from one hand to the other, wiping her free hand on her hospital gown. "I can't get involved in this sort of intrigue right now. I'm supposed to stay calm." She unbuckled the monitor, climbed down from the bed and started to pace, entirely forgetting she was in the hospital. "Who's asking for my files, anyway? Rick Durham?"

# Chapter 8

Before Alicia could get into the details about Kali's files, Matt arrived, with a pile of fashion magazines, a grease-spotted deli bag and a large white envelope. "What do you think you're doing, woman?" He grabbed the phone from Kali's hand. "Your boss is in labor, Alicia," he barked into it. "Call back in six weeks." He shut down Kali's cell and put it in his pocket, over Kali's protests. Then he prodded Kali back into the bed then re-attached the fetal monitor, all the while grumbling about her health and Harry's. "What would you do without guys like me, you type-A women lawyers?"

"Actually, Matt, I really wish you wouldn't interfere with my practice."

"The one you want to give up? That one?"

"I never said I was giving it up, or even that I wanted to." Kali's thoughts flittered anxiously from client to client, lawyer to lawyer. Who was it who was always wanting her files? Her belly was twitching and cramping: Harry seemed to be performing a dance of rage in there, pummeling his mother, demanding her attention, and pissed off that she was fixating on work instead of him.

Then the nurse materialized again, to confiscate the deli bag. "She isn't allowed to eat anything, in case of complications." She gave Matt an amused look that Kali imagined was supposed to pass for a stern frown.

"Hey, isn't starvation a complication?" Kali asked.

Matt and the nurse looked at her as if to say they didn't think she was in much danger of that, but a few minutes later a woman wearing a blue smock and a hairnet brought in some Jell-O and a cup of weak tea. Kali sipped the tea, tasted a spoonful of the Jell-O and pushed the tray away.

"I've gained sixty pounds in the last nine months, and now they want to put me on a diet?" The nurse had left the room and was speaking to someone out in the corridor. "They've already started pushing for the epidural," she told Matt, in a low voice.

"I warned you."

"I'm not having one. Right? Isn't that what we agreed?"

"It's up to you. You're the one who has to go through labor."

"I'm doing it without an epidural. Let's not discuss it again. Now, pass me a magazine, please."

Together, they flipped through the magazines and then filled out the hospital's menu card, though Matt said Kali would be discharged long before that particular meal showed up. Then they tried to time Kali's contractions, without much success. They felt like strong menstrual cramps, about twenty minutes apart, ebbing and flowing—nothing that a couple of extra-strength Tylenols couldn't relieve. Kali's excitement began to wane, especially since things could continue in the same manner for hours, apparently, unless she wanted to be put on a Pitocin drip to speed things up, which she didn't. Maybe, she thought, Harry was a phlegmatic baby who would reward her for her patience by popping out easily with a minimum of fuss and bother, sleeping through the night from day one. But they didn't want him too calm, did they? She felt a small tingle of fear. What if there was something wrong with him? Kali was, after all, a high-risk, *elderly primigravida.*

Matt leaned across her bed and studied the long strip of paper, like a ticker-tape, that was looping out of the monitor and piling up on the floor. Looks like he's slowing down a bit. No—there, he's up again! Poor little fellow. What a trauma." He sat down again. "How do you feel?"

"A bit bored."

"Things will pick up. Especially if you go for the drip."

"I won't."

"Harry could be out in a couple of hours if you did."

"No."

"We could order a pizza after."

"Haven't you ever heard of letting nature take its course? What's wrong with you medical people?"

Matt just yawned and opened his envelope to shake a few slides onto the bed. "I picked these up yesterday from the lab. Some of them are really beautiful. Want to see?"

"I wish you'd put them away. Can't we share this time together, without your grotesque slides?"

Matte scooped them up, pausing to admire a couple before dropping them back into the envelope. "You're going to be too busy to care about what I'm doing. Screaming, swearing...."

"Hardly. I'm a professional woman."

"Uh huh, okay. So, if you don't want me to make good use of my time, I'll just sit here like a dummy. Maybe look through this *Vogue* again." He settled back on his chair to give Kali a mournful look. He was wearing his hospital greens: baggy drawstring pants, a loose-fitting V-neck shirt—all of it approximately the same color as the chair. Even in that, he looks devastatingly handsome. No wonder the nurses adored him. "One of the staff guys is going to take my call for a couple days after Harry arrives. He doesn't have to do that, so it's very cool of him."

"Why not let your wife relax for a while?" The nurse, who'd never really gone anywhere, was checking the monitor again. "Go downstairs, buy a box of chocolate cigars. The OB will be over in a few minutes."

"Do you want me to stay?" Matt asked Kali.

"I guess not. If it's going to be a while... you don't have to." Kali's attention was suddenly focused again on the daunting reason she was there in that birthing room. "If nothing's happening, you might as well go work on your slides and get some food. But don't go too far, okay?" After he left, Kali turned to the nurse. "Doctors are never any good when it comes to their families, are they?" she said. "Especially surgeons. And with me being a lawyer, I guess he figures I can handle almost anything."

The nurse whisked the curtains closed around the bed, clearly unimpressed to hear that Kali was a lawyer. A surgical resident with a lawyer-wife in labor was probably her worst nightmare. She would be pitying the obstetrician, the nurse practitioners, other residents, and herself. Maybe she would be lucky and go off shift before the delivery. "Now, you give a yell if the contractions start coming faster. They're going to talk to you about the drip and the epidural again. Dr. Gerber's not on tonight, and the OB covering for him has a dinner party to go to, so they'd like to get things over with. Dr. Butt would, I mean."

Kali scowled. Dr. Butt? A dinner party? Get things over with? Induced labors were rougher, she knew that much, the contractions uneven and often too close together—a wild ride. And she was expected to endure that because of some doctor's *dinner party*? "Tell him I won't be needing him," she sniffed.

"She," the nurse said, "Doris Butt."

Kali chewed her lower lip from one side to the other, trying to digest the distasteful idea of an induced labor with the sadistic Doris Butt manning the Pitocin drip, and all the while, anxious not to miss a single chilled shrimp or glass of Chardonnay at her dinner party. "Forget it," she said. "I'm not having one."

The nurse wheeled the IV pole closer to Kali's bed and checked her watch. "I'll go see if Dr. Butt's on the floor yet."

"Well, if she is on the floor, tell her to get up. She's got a baby to deliver," Kali joked. The nurse ignored her and left the room, her shoes making those sucking noises on the floor again. Kali fumed as she wondered why Dr. Gerber wasn't a no-show, and dreading the arrival of Doris Butt, who had to be in a bad mood all the time, having Butt for a surname. She settled back on her lumpy pillow, yawned and checked the time on a large wall clock. This birthing business was all really very boring, she thought.

~~~

An hour later, Kali was spread-eagled, her feet pushing against the striped oven mitts, purple-faced and pushing hard enough to blow an artery while a gaggle of nurses, interns, residents and Dr. Butt stared at her crotch and engaged in a sometimes-acrimonious debate over whether *The Phantom of the Opera* was really a true opera. Kali clung to Matt, digging her fingernails into his leg, clenching his scrubs with her teeth and nearly drawing blood as she panted, screamed and sobbed, then finally begged for an epidural. But it was too late. Her body was a runaway train, over which she had lost all control. It was careening towards the station, turning Kali inside out with the force of it.

"Come on, Kali! Work at it," Matt urged.

"NO!" Kali sobbed, "I can't—I can't take anymore!"

"You've got to work harder!" someone said.

"You can do it, Kali!" Matt said.

"Okay! Kali? Don't push yet!" Dr. Butt ordered. Then, after a few moments, she commanded, "Now! Push now!"

"Work! Work at it! Push, Kali!" It was Matt again.

Kali flailed and writhed, this way and that, as the nurse exchanged eyerolls with Dr. Butt and Matt. "You'd think she was the first woman on the planet to have a baby," someone said.

"Hey! I heard that!" Kali panted, her face contorted with rage and pain. As she screamed that she couldn't survive one more contraction, Harry's head was crowning: a tiny, fuzzy, red dome she could see in the mirror above where she lay, spread out like one of Matt's lab specimens. She was pushing, swearing and sweating so hard that she didn't even feel the snip of the scissors cutting her flesh—the dreaded episiotomy, another thing she had decided not to permit. Matt was busily recording *cinéma vérité* footage of the delivery with his cellphone. "Look at that lovely strawberry blond hair," someone said.

Kali barely had a chance to yell at Matt to get the fucking cellphone away from her crotch, before Harry plopped out, with a lusty primal scream and a rush of body fluids. It would be some time before Kali realized that lusty primal scream and those fluids had been hers. And a longer time before she found out that Matt had been the one who made the 'first woman on the planet' remark.

# Chapter 9

Outside the hospital, the world was too bright, glaring with an intensity that hurt Kali's eyes. As she passed through the revolving glass doors behind Matt, who was carrying Harry in his car seat-carrier combo, she wanted to scurry back into the cozy security of the hospital and the soiled sheets of her unmade bed. She leaned on Matt as they crossed the hot asphalt parking lot, like desert survivors making their tedious way towards a twinkling mirage of parked vehicles, where Matt had parked the Jeep.

Kali and Matt were taken aback by their first look at their tiny newborn son. His tiny head was elongated from the narrow squeeze down the birth canal; he had a few patchy tufts of downy red-blond hair; a large purple bruise on his forehead and one eye had been glued shut by the ointment applied by the nurse. However, by evening, his face had settled into a perfect oval shape as his bright blue eyes looked inquisitively at his parents from beneath the knitted white cap that had been popped on his head to keep him warm.

As they drove south from Torrance and headed back to Long Beach, Kali fretted over Harry's comfort as she fiddled with the sun shades that Matt had stuck to the car windows with rubber suction cups. The shades were a nuisance, tending to roll up suddenly with a *flubbata* sound, or pop off altogether. Even when they stayed in place, the sun always seemed to come into the jeep at an angle that smacked Harry in the face, making him blink, frown and mew in consternation.

Kali was well aware that she looked like holy hell. She was no Kate Middleton, emerging from the hospital cool, collected and beautifully dressed: ready for her close up as she smiled and cradled her picture-perfect baby.

She was exhausted, her eyes burning from lack of sleep, her hair mashed and flattened on the back of her head and sticking up in all the wrong places. Putting on makeup or fixing her hair would have been a monumentally exhausting ordeal. Better to scuttle out of the hospital, hoping that no one saw and remembered her from the labor floor, and get safely home as fast as possible. She was ashamed of the way she had carried on, especially in a hospital where Matt had recently been on rotation and was well-known and liked by the staff and doctors. Okay, she was a woman in labor, who had insisted (for some unknown reason) on a natural childbirth, but still… she should have tried a little harder not to 'let it all hang out' as her mother, Marina, would have put it.

"I've been thinking," Matt said, from the front seat, "about Britta."

"What about her?" Kali was in the back seat, her hand protectively on Harry. Britta should be the last thing on her husband's mind right now!

"We should get her a new TV. The one in her room is pretty old, and there's no cable."

"We don't have money for a new TV, and she can watch Netflix – nobody cares about cable anymore. Besides, she's not our houseguest, she's going to be our employee."

"Uh huh, all true… good point. I just want to make sure she's comfortable, so she'll stick around. You're the one who'll have to start interviewing again if she quits."

"If she quits over something as trivial as no cable, who needs her?" Kali tucked Harry's blanket more snugly around him. The way he was bundled up—a sleeper, a shawl, a blanket, and a lacy crocheted cap and tiny mittens—no one would have guessed it was the middle of summer in southern California. Though he didn't seem to mind, Harry was already a good guy, Kali thought, and living up to his name. He'd hardly cried at all in the hours since he'd been born.

"Oh yeah," Matt said, as if suddenly remembering, "did I tell you she started already?"

"What? Who?"

"Britta."

"Since when?" Kali was stunned.

"Yesterday. She got kicked out of her friend's place early. She said she could find somewhere else to stay, but I didn't see any problem with her starting early."

"But Matt, we agreed we would hire a nanny for September. We can't afford to pay for July and August! Plus, we don't need her now. I'm going to be home with Harry."

"She offered to help out for free, until September, just to have a place to crash, and stash her gear."

"Crash, gear, stash? She used those words?"

"She's young," Matt chuckled, "give her a break. But think how nice it will be for you to have everything clean with meals made, from the minute we get Harry home."

Kali didn't think it sounded nice at all. It sounded more like a horrible unwelcome intrusion. "Is she there now?"

"Waiting with open arms to take Harry and let you get some rest." Matt beamed at her in the rearview mirror; Kali could see his eyes crinkling around the edges.

"I don't want her to take Harry! I don't need any rest!" Kali's emotions were back on the rise; it wouldn't take much to push her into hysteria. "You've only got a couple of days off. I don't want to share this precious time with some stranger!"

Matt sighed, tapping his seldom-worn wedding ring on the steering wheel.

"If that's how you feel, I'll tell her to find somewhere else to stay. But she would have the right to take another job, which she will likely do."

"You could have warned me," Kali said, "you could have asked if it was okay." She was on the verge of tears; this wasn't how the homecoming scene was supposed to go. She wanted a do-over!

"I thought I did tell you. Look, she's a foreigner, and she's our responsibility. I mean, we hired her."

"YOU hired her, Matthew."

"And her room is nice and ready, thanks to all of your hard work fixing it up. Honestly, I didn't think it was such a big deal." As usual, when Matt knew he'd done something wrong, he became defensive. "You must be totally hormonally overloaded, Kali. What woman in her right mind would complain about having free help for two months? I thought you'd be thrilled. It was supposed to be a nice surprise."

"Surprise? You just said you thought you'd told me! I may be hormonally overloaded, but I'm not as stupid as you obviously think." Kali seethed in the back seat, her hand on Harry's steady warmth. She swallowed, self-pity yanking at her, her jaw tightening, a lump in her throat. She had to hold it together, for Harry's sake. "I didn't even want to hire her – we should have interviewed more nannies! This is not fair, to me or to Harry! It's all Sofia's fault that I had Harry so early – that he was, that he is – premature!" She hiccupped.

"He was not premature, or even early. He was right on time."

Kali stared out the window as she struggled to control her emotions.

"Please don't cry, Kali," Matt said. "I'm sorry. You're totally right. I should have asked you. I'll call Britta right now and tell her to pack up and get out before we get home."

"You can't do that!"

"I can, and I will. I just need to pull over, for safety." Matt slowed the Jeep down.

"Don't call her. I can deal with this. We can't throw her out onto the street!"

"I'm pulling over!" Horns blared as the Jeep swerved to the side of the 405 freeway.

Another motorist, confused by the erratic movement of the Jeep, yelled 'Asshole!' out his window. Matt flipped him the finger, put on the emergency flashers, sighed, and turned to look at his wife and baby. Harry, who had been quietly dozing, suddenly opened his eyes, screwed up his face and let out a shriek of rage. His eyes glistened as his face quickly changed from pink to red to purple. "Can't you do something, Kali?" Matt demanded.

"Like what?"

"Nurse him, or something?"

"I can't nurse him! He's in his car seat! We're on the goddamned freeway!" She gasped, realizing she'd just used bad language in front of their newborn son. That would have to stop! "Besides, I fed him just before we left the hospital. He can't be hungry already." Kali watched her son in alarm. He'd cried in the hospital, but not with such intensity. She jiggled his car seat. Harry screamed louder. "He's reacting to the tension between us, Matt. Just get us home, okay?"

After that incident, they made good time on the 405, though its whizzing cars, clattering tractor-trailers, gardeners' trucks and forced lane changes left Kali haggard with anxiety. Everything was moving too fast, careening towards disaster, carrying the three Millers in their Jeep away with it.

47

"We should have stayed in the hospital another day," Kali fretted. "I'm not ready for the real world yet."

"They don't just let you stay there, because you feel like it," Matt said, "it's not a hotel. And Harry will be fine. He's a tough little guy, I can see it already. He'll be a hockey player, just like his papa."

*He certainly will not*, Kali thought. Matt had his nose broken twice, three teeth knocked out, and fifty-two stitches in his face. He was still good looking, in a rugged sort of way, but Kali sometimes wondered what he would look like minus all the scar tissue. The idea of little Harry, with his perfect pink face, adorable nose and sweet little mouth, duking it out on the ice in a bench-clearing, gloves-off, jerseys-over-the-head brawl... well, it was more than Kali could bear to imagine.

# Chapter 10

As they pulled up to the house, Kali could help but notice that it looked shabby, almost menacing, as if not-nice things were going on behind the curtains and blinds. Flies buzzed and settled on the garbage cans on the side and the front walk was more cracked and uneven than Kali remembered it. The lawn was a small carpet of weeds; the front porch on the verge of collapse. Was this the best that they, a doctor and a lawyer, could do for little Harry? The safest, most pleasant environment they could provide? In Belmont Shore, the answer, was apparently, yes.

And things were not right inside the house either. There had been changes. The tea-towels were damply folded on the kitchen counter, instead of hanging over the oven door to dry. The dishwasher was churning away, industriously. Kali never used it in the middle of the day since it made the house too hot and put an unnecessary strain on the air conditioner. In the living room, the sofa cushions had been turned to stand up on their corners, making diamond shapes instead of the neatly-aligned squares Kali liked. And there was an unfamiliar scent in the air: a faint perfume. Kali's house had been personalized in the short time she'd been gone—with someone else's personality. Gripping Harry in his carrier, Kali took a step inside the front door, then froze.

"Has this floor been waxed?"

"Looks like it," Matt beamed. "Britta's been hard at work. I knew you'd be pleased."

"Pleased? That someone booby-trapped our house?"

"What are you talking about?" He picked up her suitcase from the front porch and put it down on the gleaming wood floor.

"Waxed floors are treacherous, Matthew! What if I slip carrying Harry? Or she does? I never put wax on these floors." Kali didn't move, terrified of taking a step. "Britta has to wash it all off, right now."

"But you can practically see yourself in it. It's the first good cleaning this floor has ever had. Come on, Kali, don't be a jerk. The wax will wear off soon."

"Not before someone has an accident!" Kali hugged Harry close. She couldn't believe that Matt, a doctor, no less, didn't appreciate the peril of waxed wood floors. Harry was sound asleep again, snoring with faint wheezy noises, occasionally mewing, or rubbing his face with his tiny mitten-clad hands.

Matt puffed out his cheeks, then let his breath expire with a strained sound. "Okay, Kali. I'll ask her to wash it off, or just do it myself."

"But I have to take Harry to his room right now. He needs to be changed. He'll get a rash. He's been in the same diaper all day!" Kali's eyes filled with tears.

"I'm wearing my runners. Let me take him."

"No!" Kali clutched Harry. He stirred, opened his eyes, blinked once, then wound up and let out a scream of rage.

"See what you've done?" Matt reached for Harry, but Kali pulled him back.

"*Kan jag hjalp dig?*" Britta suddenly appeared, quiet as a cat. Or maybe she'd been there all along, watching them, judging. "Please, can I help?" She was smiling her gap-tooth smile, holding out her arms for Harry.

Kali glared at her, then at Matt, feeling an irrational urge to toss Harry into the air, like a football, to see who'd get him before he landed. "Yes, you can help, Britta. You see," she said slowly and too loudly, as people often did with foreigners, thinking that volume somehow increased their ability to understand, "I want to take Harry to the nursery. The *baby's room*. But you put wax on this floor. Wax!" She tapped her foot for emphasis. "And I'm afraid of falling, because it's so slippery." She shuffled her foot to demonstrate.

Britta looked stricken, her eyes wide with alarm. "*Vaxa? Ah! Jag forstar!* I am so stupid! *Ursakta mig.* I did not think!" There was panic in her blue eyes as she stared at Kali.

Harry was withheld his screams, instead flailing his fists and squirming under his blankets. He was obviously pissed; his cap slid down over one eye, giving him a jaunty, yet disgruntled, look.

"So, I will wash now? The floor?" Britta chewed her perfect lower lip, a charming picture of confused consternation.

"Thanks, Britta, that would be so awesome," Matt smiled. "I'll help you as soon as Kali gets settled."

"The pail? Is in my closet, *ja*?" She turned and hurried down the hallway, not at all bothered by the slippery waxed floor.

Kali watched her go, feeling hot, cross and fat. Cinderella's ugly stepmother, sending the lovely young girl to get a mop and bucket to scrub the floor, because of some hormone-induced, irrational fear of floor wax.

"You don't think you over-reacted, just a bit?" Matt said.

"You're the one who's so big on child safety. I can't believe you let her wax this floor!"

"We wanted you to be pleased with the house, knowing how tired and stressed-out you've been."

*We* wanted you to be pleased? Kali was stunned. Matt was suddenly part of a '*we*.' And the other part was not Kali, it was Britta.

~~~

For Kali, the biggest shock of childbirth was realizing she was just as huge after Harry was born as she had been on the day before. Her weight had dropped a disappointing eleven pounds, out of the sixty she had gained. And whereas before, she'd been firm and smooth and round, like a gigantic watermelon, now everything below her massive breasts was pale, loose and flabby, like curdled cottage cheese. The only permitted exercise (other than rotating her ankles while lying down, to avoid the formation of blood clots) was to sit on the toilet and contract all the muscles between her legs, as if she were trying to hold in a pee – the so-called 'Kegel exercise.' It was hard to imagine working off forty-nine pounds that way.

For her bringing-home-baby outfit, she'd chosen a blue and white checked shirt and coordinating Capri pants. '*Perfect for a new mom!*' it said on Amazon, with a four-and-a-half-star rating. Kali bought the outfit in a size 10, confident it would fit her, since she was normally an 8 (on good days a 6). But as she was dressing to leave the hospital, she found she couldn't pull the pants up higher than mid-thigh. She had to leave the hospital wearing the same outfit that she'd worn going in: an out-of-shape, old t-shirt of Matt's – the one from their honeymoon that said: *'Here Today Gone to Maui!'* on the front, under a voluminous denim jumper: the classic maternity bag.

Had Britta worn *skinny* jeans, with a *tucked-in* shirt, to make her feel bad? To make her look worse? Any considerate person would have realized that the last thing a new mother wanted to be confronted with was some little stick-figure in skinny jeans and a shirt that was *tucked in*.

"I unpacked your stuff," Matt said, as Britta rattled around in her room at the back of the house, probably trying to figure out which end of the mop to use, Kali thought, feeling frumpy and mean and small-minded.

"Well, I can't stand here all day. Maybe you should take Harry. But be careful."

Harry's eyes were closed, and he was breathing gently with rapid shallow breaths. He let out a tiny whine, then a healthy hiccup, before spitting up a stream of breast-milk. Kali watched Matt take the baby down the hall, then skated cautiously into the kitchen to get a glass of water. The Big Gulp cups were not in their usual place in the cupboard. She opened the dishwasher and noticed with surprise that the crystal champagne flutes were in there: two of them, nestled together on the bottom rack. As she stood there staring at them, someone knocked on the front door.

It was a delivery guy, bringing another flower arrangement. How kind everyone was, when you had a baby, she thought, blinking back the tears, as she pulled off the thin florist's paper. More carnations: both pink and blue. Whoever sent them obviously didn't know that they just had a boy. She set the flowers down on the front hall table and took the small card out of its envelope. *'Congratulations!'* was written on the card, in sloppy, fountain pen ink. *'Let's hope you make a better mother than you do a lawyer!'*

Kali was so upset that her question about the champagne flutes flew right out of her head. "Matt?" she called, in a panic, "can you come over here, please?"

# Chapter 11

Harry's eyes popped open. "Ah. Ha-ha!" He reached up his hand – fingers splayed wide apart, a small, sweet, sticky starfish – and tried to seize the mobile that hung over his crib, just beyond reach.

"Dow!" he told it, crossly. A pony, dog and chicken chased after each other, swaying gently. A plush cow with flaring nostrils and a stuffed half-moon between its front hooves hung over the side of his crib. The string that dangled from it was pulled down, with a ratcheting sound, and began to recede into the cow again. '*Catch a Falling Star,*' the tinkly notes played. Harry rubbed his eyes as the blinds of the window were opened and sunshine played across his face.

"Da-day-day," he complained.

"*God morgon*, Harry! You are sleeping so late today! What a lazy boy! *Alskling snuttis.*" The voice was soft but excited. There was another tinkly sound, like tiny wind-chimes from Britta's bracelet of gold stars – as Harry's comforter was shaken out and fluffed.

"How is Britta's little prince this morning? It is a beautiful day! A beautiful day. *En san underbar dag.* Can you say this? *En san underbar dag. Underbar* is wonderful. That's what you are!" The crib's side rails were popped up, then lowered into place. A tangle of blonde hair dangled into Harry's face, tantalizingly close. He reached out, grabbed a fistful and pulled, trying to stuff it into his mouth. "Ah! Harry! No, no. This hurts Britta." Gently, his fingers were pried open, the golden fleece freed. A small teddy, made from a striped sock, was offered as consolation. Here is your bear. *Leksaksbjorn.* In Swedish, this means teddy bear. Is he not the most handsome bear in the world, for the most handsome baby?"

"Woo-chay." Harry stuck the bear's ear into his mouth and gummed it.

"Woo-chay? Is this your teddy's name? This is a funny name. This is not Swedish. Shall Britta teach the prince to speak Swedish? We must call your bear something else. Nils or Oscar. Oscar is good, I think." Harry's fat little neck was covered with kisses, and he squealed and squirmed with delight. "*Pussgurka*," Britta cooed, chucking him under his chin. But then his face clouded over, and he scowled, concentrating fiercely. There was a pause. His face darkened. "What? Is the most handsome prince making the most handsome poo for Britta?"

Obligingly, Harry filled his cloth diaper with a wet, explosive noise.

~~~

"Wow," Sofia said, "he can really let it rip." She was sitting with Kali at the kitchen table, drinking coffee and listening to Britta and Harry on the baby monitor. "I'm glad I'm not the one changing him. Never mind washing all those diapers. I still can't believe you're using cloth. Is it because of pressure from Matt's mother? She's some kind of tree hugger, right?

"Beth has nothing to do with it," Kali said. "It's the responsible choice."

"Have Mom and Dad been by to see Harry?"

"Not yet."

"It'll take them a bit to accept the fact that they're grandparents, again. And I give you a week before you switch to Huggies."

"Not going to happen, Sofia."

There were a lot of amplified rustlings crackled over the nursery monitor, along with Britta's giggling, and Harry's babbling.

Your Swedish nymphet sounds okay, I guess," Sofia said, grudgingly, "but she knows we're listening. Don't kid yourself with that phony little prince routine."

Kali shut off the monitor. "I feel like a sneak, eavesdropping on her."

"You're taking an interest in your son's care-giver, that's all. As his mother, you'd be negligent if you didn't. When do you go back to work?"

"Monday." Kali's heart sank.

"Sneaks up on you fast, doesn't it?"

Kali nodded, a lump in her throat. She'd left Britta alone with Harry, only when she desperately needed a little time to herself, but never for a whole day. And this wouldn't be just one whole day; it would be a series of whole days, stretching on with no end in sight. Even when Matt finished his residency, he still had to spend a year or two doing fellowships, and then a few years establishing a practice. By then, Harry would be in kindergarten, going off to school: the buttons on his overalls twinkling, handkerchief tucked in his pocket, taking an apple for his teacher, his hair parted smartly in the middle, shoes shined. She blinked, her eyes stinging.

Was it possible she'd used up her three months of mat leave already? Stroller wheels had turned endlessly as miles of boardwalk planks (sun and shadow, sun and shadow) had unraveled under her feet. She'd spent long dreamy hours in Harry's room, peacefully gliding in the nursery rocker, feeding him and watching her son change, little by little, day by day. And then there were those diapers. There was always a pail full of them it seemed, waiting to be washed. Every day, the Millers' ancient Maytag squealed in protest as it struggled to spin and agitate the heavy load. Britta always seemed to be busy with something more important when it was time to rinse out and wash the diapers.

"I'll miss the park," Kali said. "I've met some very cool women – stay-at-home moms. They never got too friendly with me, though. I guess they don't think I'm one of them, since I'm going back to work. I get a sympathetic nod whenever I mention that... then they avert their eyes."

"Brain dead," Sofia drained her cup. "I bet none of them has had an original thought in over a decade. What do they talk about? The price of formula at Costco?"

"I don't need to defend them, but I'll miss them, that's all. They've had interesting lives, big challenges. One has Hodgkin's disease and a new baby. She can't breast-feed because of the chemo. Two of them are single mothers."

"They never heard of birth control?"

"You're awful, Sofia. It's horrible what some women have to go through."

"Forget them, Kali. They're not like you. You're an alien being. You'll never be one of them. You work."

"*Outside* the home," Kali corrected her.

Sofia rolled her eyes, clearly not interested in her sister's political correctness or hearing more about the stay-at-home moms in the park. She quickly changed the subject back to the one that was far more interesting. "You shouldn't worry about going back to work, though, Kali. I'm sure Britta's adequate."

"She's better than that. Though maybe not so much with the housekeeping. Or the meals. But Harry adores her. His first real smile was at her."

"That's what *she'd* like you to believe."

"It was. I recorded it with my cell."

"How awful for you."

"I'm glad he likes her. What mother wouldn't want her baby to like his nanny?"

"Oh well, in that case, I'm glad to hear she's so perfect. You're lucky Matt found her and hired her on the spot."

"She's not perfect. I didn't say that. One thing that annoys me is that Harry always smells like her. There's some perfume she wears..."

"Tanis root?"

"It's something Swedish. Loganberry maybe, I don't know."

"So, tell Britta to quit stinking up your kid. Or fire her – that's your best option."

"I just told you, she's good and Harry loves her."

"Kali, I don't know how this could have escaped your notice, but Gisele Bündchen is a hag compared to her."

"Well, I can't fire her because of her looks."

"It's the best reason I can think of, but then, I wouldn't have let Matt hire her in the first place."

"I have no problem with having an attractive nanny for my baby."

"Attractive? You and I are attractive. She's fucking gorgeous."

"Oh, I don't know. With all that shaggy white-blonde hair, she kind of reminds me of an Afghan hound."

"Oh, right, a real dog! A howler. I bet she makes pit stops at every hydrant." Sofia shook her head, pityingly. "And what about little Harry? He's imprinting on her. For the rest of his life he'll want a woman who looks like Britta. His Britta, his beautiful nanny. No one else will ever be hot enough. He'll probably be in analysis for years, forever wanting a Swedish sex goddess."

"Sofia, he's not even three months old. And who says she's a sex goddess? Besides, he sees more of me than he does of her." It wasn't true, but Kali didn't feel like mentioning how Britta seemed to have taken over Kali's time with Harry, subtly nudging Kali aside and leaving her to do the mundane household chores, like the diaper washing, as often as she could.

"But that's going to change, isn't it? Starting Monday. Harry's hardly going to see you at all, is he?"

*Why are you doing this to me?* Kali thought, staring at her sister. And why was she wasting time with Sofia anyway? She should be with Harry, on her second to last day of mat leave. "Well," she finally said, feeling an inexplicable urge to give her sister something to gnaw on, "her personal habits could use improvement. Her toenails are always dirty. I see them all the time because she wears those ugly Birkenstocks. And she has B.O."

"Most Europeans do. It took me a while to convince Bernardo to take a shower every day. They just don't bathe or shower as much as we do."

"And she has hairy legs and pits." Kali's mood lifted as she warmed to the subject of Britta's physical shortcomings.

"But all of that just makes it worse," Sofia said, dashing cold water on Kali's complaint. "Here she is, beautiful but earthy. Attainable. A real woman. Who wants to have sex with a celluloid centerfold?"

"Who said anything about having sex?"

"I only meant, facing up to the fact that she is fashion-model stunning is the first step in dealing with this beast."

"Even if she is so great-looking," Kali continued defensively, "it's hardly her fault."

"Maybe not, since she was born that way, but she could've done something about it. Let herself get fat or dye her hair red or purple – or just brown, like yours."

"I can't fire her," Kali said, ignoring the dig. "Especially now, right when I'm about to go back to work. But I have to admit, when I see some of the other nannies in the park, I wish I'd hired…"

"Someone ugly. You can say it."

"Plus, she yacks on her phone for hours. I don't know how she's managed to make so many friends in the short time she's been over here."

"Maybe she's talking to her fence. Or her pimp. What if she's a porn star or a call girl and just does this nanny stuff on the side? As a front? For her Green card? Have you seen anything interesting when you've gone through her things? Is any of your jewelry or makeup missing?"

"I've never gone through her things!"

"Oh, of course not."

"I might have peeked into her room once or twice. This is my house, after all."

"So? What did you find?"

"I didn't *find* anything. Except a mess. And a Swedish flag on the ceiling. It'll probably take the paint off. She must have used duct tape to stick it up there."

"And of course, if doesn't go with your décor, that Ikea blue and yellow."

"It's red. With a yellow cross."

"That's not the Swedish flag, Kali."

"What?"

Just then, Britta appeared, with Harry in her arms. Kali stared at them, her cheeks flaming. With the monitor off, she'd forgotten that Britta was still in the house. How much had she overheard of Kali and Sofia's spiteful gossip and speculation?

"I will take Harry to the beach now," Britta said. "Is this okay?" She smiled and gave him a big kiss on the cheek, making Harry squeal with delight. "He needs some beautiful California sunshine."

"Don't forget the sunscreen," Kali said.

"*Ja*. Of course!" Britta looked radiantly healthy, and she seemed happy, not like someone who'd just overheard herself discussed as a possible felon or hooker.

She probably hadn't overheard anything, Kali thought with relief, or hadn't understood what she'd heard. "I should get out myself," she said. "I could use some fresh air."

"Come with me and Harry!" Britta beamed. "That will be so nice!"

"Maybe I will. I'll come and find you guys on the boardwalk."

"Don't stay in on my account." Sofia stood up. "I was just leaving. Unless you want me to help you look into that matter we were discussing?" Her eyes flickered towards Britta's room, at the back of the house.

"I don't." Kali took Harry and bounced him on her knee as she waited for Britta to warm a bottle of expressed breast-milk that Kali had labored to produce, using a crude suction pump that seemed to drag the milk out of her more than pump it. Then Britta packed the bottle into the diaper bag, along with extra diapers, a sun-hat and sunscreen. With a wave and a cheerful *"Hejdå"* she and Harry were out the back door.

"OMG, Sofia," Kali said, "what if she heard us?"

"Then she'd quit, and all your troubles would be over."

"They'd be just beginning. The last thing I need is to have to find a new nanny before Monday!"

"How does Matt like having Britta around? They talk much?"

"They have the odd exchange in Swedish, but Matt's is pretty bad."

"I bet he's trying to brush up on it, though. And Britta's giving him all the help she can, in her cute broken English."

"Wrong," Kali said, though Sofia was dead right. "Besides, you know Matt. He works so hard. I hardly see him, so I can't really say how he's reacting to her."

"Well, just as long as Matt's not here when Britta's also not here – that's when you should worry. And I'd get a Swedish dictionary if I were you. Make sure you know what they're talking about. I think it's rude to be speaking in another language when there's someone else in the room who can't understand it."

"I wasn't. I mean, the times I heard them I don't think they knew I was there."

Sofia shot her a penetrating look. "And you're comfortable with that, Kali?"

"Of course, why wouldn't I be?"

"Just saying, I wouldn't be."

As soon as Sofia left, Kali went online and bought a copy of *Swedish in Minutes!* to be delivered to her office on Monday morning. '*Are YOU planning a vacation in Sweden?*' the Amazon blurb read. '*Do YOU want to hook up with gorgeous Swedish girls? Be honest, how cool would it be, if YOU could speak Swedish?*

# Chapter 12

After placing the order for *Swedish In Minutes!* Kali sat for a while at the table, wondering how life had become so complicated, and when it had started to slip out of control. She still had no idea who had sent the malicious card with the pink and blue carnations. It had to be an unhappy client, but which one? It could be any one of them. She and Matt had worked through benign explanations: it was a florist's mistake; it was someone's lame idea of a joke. But they both knew it was neither.

Now that she had Harry, Kali also had full lifetime membership in the paranoid parents' club. She was suddenly acutely aware of the number of twisted psychos (Harry snatchers) out there; the frequency of TV, internet and newspaper stories of child abuse and neglect, and of how often people screamed, fought and smashed beer bottles on Pine Beach Road. She saw how many transients, sociopaths and other undesirables were drawn to the beach. And ever since those carnations arrived, she'd been waiting for something else to happen, some truly awful shoe to drop. It hadn't, yet—but the fear of it stained her lovely summer days with Harry, tinging them with a cold grey fear around the edges.

As for her legal work, once a source of strength and the very thing that defined her, the thought of returning to it filled her with dread. Had her practice been sucked down the toilet while she was away? Had her clients, fickle at the best of times, tossed her aside for some other (probably male) lawyer who was eager to help out while Kali was away? And now she had Sofia's innuendos about Matt and wild fantasies about Britta to add to her anxiety load. A porn star, a thief! Really, she had to laugh! She needed to go down to the beach, find Harry and play with him for a while. It would clear her head and make her happy again. Sofia was absurd, possibly even evil: a truly wicked sister.

Kali rinsed the coffee cups in the sink, recalling those champagne flutes in the dishwasher the day she got home with Harry. She'd never mentioned them to anyone, let alone Sofia, who would seize the juicy tidbit and run with it. So, Matt and Britta had a glass of champagne to celebrate Harry's birth, she thought. Was that SO bad? But who had gone out to buy it? And what had happened to the bottle? Had Matt hidden it? If so, why? How much had they had to drink, and was it right before Matt got into the Jeep to come get Kali and Harry? Had Matt been buzzed when he arrived? Was that why it took him so long to find her room? Had he been wandering drunkenly around the parking lot, or chasing cute nurses up and down the corridors, maybe having sex with them on stray gurneys behind hospital drapes, as a last fling before full fatherhood? And why had he not waited to drink that champagne with Kali—Harry's mother, the most important person in the scenario?

And what if Britta really was up to something illegal? Kali worried. It was not *impossible*. She went out a lot, bought loads of junk food, clothes, jewelry and makeup. Didn't that indicate she had some other, more lucrative, source of income? Maybe her nanny job *was* just a front, for Green card purposes. Maybe, just maybe, Sofia was right. With a creeping sense of shame, Kali made her way to Britta's room, telling herself she was only doing what any good mother would do. She couldn't be expected to go back to work and leave helpless little Harry with a criminal, could she?

~~~

The room Kali had worked so hard to make clean, bright and cheerful for Harry's nanny was now a total disaster: littered with teething toys, dirty diapers and cheesy, forgotten bottles. Britta hadn't bothered to clean up her bathroom either. The tub mat was furry with mold, the sink drain clogged with blonde hair, the water in the toilet scummy. Kali unhooked the child-proof latch on the cupboard, took out a can of drain cleaner and dumped half of it into the sink, the other half into the toilet. The noxious chemicals hissed as the ancient drains moaned and gurgled. Kali shuddered, closed the bathroom door and went back into Britta's bedroom.

The huge red and yellow flag fluttered a little, against the ceiling. Sofia was right again: it wasn't the Swedish flag. So, what was it, Kali wondered?

Framed photos, knick-knacks, a jumble of make-up brushes and pencils, inexpensive bracelets, hair clips and rings littered Britta's dresser. Kali picked up one of the photos. It wasn't a very clear picture, but it was of Britta, herself: dressed all in white, with a crown of burning candles on her head. Some Swedish tradition, Kali supposed. It looked like a fairly hazardous endeavor. Don't try this with Harry, she thought, not on my home.

She put down the picture and picked up another. Britta again, this time leaning against a sports car – one hand on her hip, the other resting on the hood, one foot up on the front fender and an amused smile on her lips. She was pleased with her photographer, whoever they were. Kali felt sure it would have been a 'he.' Probably, they'd just finished having sex when the picture was taken, in that little sports car, perhaps.

Odd, she thought, that Britta would display framed photos of herself. It wasn't as though she would forget what she looked like, was it? Wouldn't it be more natural to put out pictures of her parents, her cat, her boyfriend or her home in Sweden? Britta didn't have any siblings, she'd told Kali sadly. Maybe that's how it was with only children—they became self-absorbed, selfish and vain. Kali didn't want that to happen to Harry. She and Matt would have another baby, or maybe two, eventually. She looked around the room fearing, but at the same time hoping, that she would see something shocking, off-putting or dramatic: a reason to fire Britta. But the only thing she could place into any of those categories was the mess. Britta's trash can was full of Marabou chocolate bar wrappers from Ikea, and crumpled nacho bags. Nothing interesting at all.

Kali peeked into the closet to see piles of clothes, half on and half off their hangers. Other things weren't hung up at all but had been dumped on the floor in a tangled heap of shoes, boots, belts and bags. As with most people who acquired something at no cost, Britta was careless with her looks. She didn't seem to own any nice, good-quality clothes, but women who looked like Britta, especially at her age, didn't need to spend a lot to look great. It didn't matter what junk she hung from her ears or around her neck or wrists, what rag she threw on, what ugly shoes she wore: she always looked amazing. If Kali put on Britta's shapeless sweaters, thin cotton T-shirts, grungy windbreaker and Birkenstocks, she would only look like a middle-aged woman who shopped at the Goodwill. But Britta, in Kali's clothes, in the expensive silks and fine combed cottons that Kali wore to work, that would be something—something Kali really didn't want to see.

She shut the closet door and, hot with shame, pulled open the dresser drawers, one by one. They were mostly empty but for a few stray socks, some greying bras and lace panties, and a hairbrush clouded with blonde hair. The bottom drawer was crammed with paper: dozens of letters and postcards tied in bundles with ribbons. Well, she might be a snoop, but she drew the line at reading someone else's mail. Never mind that it was in Swedish, so she couldn't read it, even if she wanted to.

At the back of the drawer was a wad of printed pamphlets, bound with a rubber band with a yellow cross on a red background: a miniature version of the ceiling flag. *SKANEH!!* it screamed on the front, followed by dense-printed text replete with the tiny circle accent marks of the Swedish language. There were lots of exclamation marks, too.

Whoever had authored the pamphlet had been pretty fired up about something; there was a strong political flavor to it. Could Britta be a communist? A religious fanatic? An illegal immigrant or political refugee? Had she faked her work visa? Another thing to worry about, Kali sighed. There were a lot of pamphlets, so Britta would be unlikely to miss one. Kali reached out to take one then pulled back her hand and ran out of the room as Britta's light step sounded on the deck.

# Chapter 13

At 7:30 on the morning she was due back at work, when she should have been on the 405, chugging bumper-to-bumper towards her office on Santa Monica's Promenade, Kali was lurking in the Millers' garage, spying on Harry's nanny. There was no nicer way to put it. The window that looked from the garage into the kitchen was dusty with cobwebs, so Kali cleared a clean patch with a tissue, then peered into the house. As she stared at the kitchen window, the scene slow-dissolved into a fine spring day, in her imagination, where the Dean of some famous university (Harvard, probably) was addressing the rows of seated, well-dressed, proud parents.

'And now,' the Dean said, 'it is my great pleasure to present this year's valedictorian, recently accepted to Harvard Medical School, the debate team captain, champion rower, and editor of our magnificent year book, Harry Matthew Miller!' There was enthusiastic applause as a handsome young man approached the podium and shook hands with the Dean. On stage, he turned to speak into the microphone. It was a grown-up Harry! Kali was seeing his future! And hers!

'Thank you, Dean, for those very kind and generous words,' Harry said, looking around, totally at ease and enjoying the moment. "You know," he continued, 'I wouldn't be here today if it were not for my father, the great humanitarian and surgeon *par excellence*, Dr. Matthew Miller!' There was more applause as a much older, but still handsome Matt stood up, smiled and waved to the crowd.

'And of course,' Harry continued, 'my wonderful, impossibly gorgeous, nanny—now my wonderful, impossibly gorgeous Mom, Britta Edvardsson Miller!'

'MOM?!' In the garage, Kali's eyes went wide, as her jaw dropped.

Then Harry was applauding, along with the audience as the (indeed) impossibly gorgeous Britta stood up beside Matt, smiling shyly. Matt squeezed Britta's hand as he looked adoringly into her eyes. 'As for my birth-mother?' Harry said, 'well, what can I say?' Kali cringed, from her spot in the garage. His birth-mother!? 'Kali, I know you're out there somewhere, and... well, this is kind of hard...' His voice cracked as conflicting emotions played across his handsome face. 'You had to work, I know that, and not for the money. We had plenty of that, or at least enough.'

In the front row, older Matt nodded. 'You got that right, Son,' he said, as Britta blinked rapidly, squeezing his arm in sympathetic support.

"Not true!" Kali protested, from the garage. But it was true, and she knew it, and some day, so would Harry. As a surgical resident, Matt made enough for them to survive on. Maybe not in their own home, and maybe not with a top-of-the-line Perego stroller and a live-in nanny. But certainly, the three of them could have survived well enough without Kali going back to work. Matt would have been fine with it. It was Kali who wanted it all: a house by the ocean, two cars, expensive clothes, groceries from Whole Foods, walking-around money, restaurant meals on occasion.

'You had to work,' Harry continued. 'You needed to work. Your self-esteem, your ego, demanded it.' He blinked rapidly, overcome with emotion, then paused to collect himself, as Kali cringed in the dilapidated garage. 'Work, the practice of law, defined you. Not having a baby. Not raising me. I understand. And I forgive you... Wherever you are.'

*Wherever I am!?* Kali's eyes filled with tears, her heart aching as though a knife had been plunged into it.

'My one big regret?' Harry continued, as Kali's stomach churned with anxiety, 'I only wish you could know, somehow, that I turned out all right, that everything worked out great for me, and for my Dad.'

The audience applauded. Then, Kali saw herself: Old Kalinka, at the back of the Harvard crowd, trying not to attract attention, hiding under a tree. With a sob, she turned away, pushing her rickety shopping cart stuffed with bags of God-only knew-what. Apparently, Old Kalinka still had enough marbles to know better than to humiliate Harry with her disgraceful presence and was moving along before someone called Security to escort her off the campus.

"Birth mother," Kali repeated as she stood, still peering through the cobwebs of the garage window. She could see Britta now, moving around in the kitchen, dialing someone on her cell. Who could she be calling? What could Britta possibly have to say to anyone so early in the morning – that the coast was clear? The old witch was FINALLY packed off to work? And what was Harry doing, while Britta was phoning her fence or pimp or whoever it was? If Harry were safely in his swing or Jolly Jumper, why wasn't Britta unloading the dishwasher, doing a load of diapers, or any one of the many other things that needed to be done?

Kali had left the house in a frenzy, several outfits, complete with accessories, scattered in her wake and a pile of cosmetics and appliances crowding the bathroom sink. Nothing she tried on fit because she hadn't lost all her pregnancy weight –barely half of it! During Kali's frantic and frustrating wardrobe malfunctions, Britta watched with an expression that alternated between puzzled and frightened, jiggling Harry in her arms as they tried to stay out of Kali's way. Kali could see herself through Britta's eyes: a muttering madwoman storming through the house, pulling laundry out of baskets, sniffing before discarding it, and then scrambling to iron something else, before finally staggering out to the garage in her too-tight Hillary Clinton-style pantsuit, fumbling for her keys, her lunch bag clenched in her teeth, eyes wet with guilt and sorrow over leaving Harry.

Now, attractively framed by the kitchen window, Britta casually pushed her back her long shag of hair before reaching into a cupboard for a snack. Nachos or taco chips, probably. For breakfast! What sort of slap-dash nutritional habits was she likely to instill in Harry? She had to go back in there immediately, Kali decided, and find out exactly what was going on.

As she was about to exit the garage, Britta disappeared. Though relieved that she'd probably gone to check on Harry, Kali continued to stare into the kitchen, feeling depressed and anxious. Harry was going to grow up without her, starting today. In a flash of time he would be a man, with a family of his own. Kali might not live to see any grandchildren.

If Harry waited until he was thirty-five to start a family, as Kali and Matt had done, she would be seventy before she saw a grandchild. Seventy! A wheezing, rattling hair's breadth from eighty! What possible use would she be to him then? Harry and his wife would never trust her with babysitting; they would be afraid she might keel over or fall down the stairs while carrying their baby; break her hip and never get up, unable even to crawl across the floor to reach her phone to call for help. She would be a liability, of no possible use to them. Unless she were dead. They would wait impatiently for her to croak, to collect whatever money she hadn't squandered by then. 'How much longer is the old bag going to hang on?' Harry's wife would whine. (Kali disliked her already: some snooty sorority girl with a name like Ashley or Brittany or Meghan, who would never be good enough for her son.)

Or maybe they would keep Kali prisoner in her own home, locked in the attic, tied up with skipping ropes and fed cat food: elder abuse, it was called. Matt, of course, would still be alive and just nicely into his prime: a vigorous sixty-five. He would have moved into a swanky condo in Venice or Malibu, driving a racy high-end convertible to take his grandchildren to the zoo, or to visit Kali in the nursing home...if they bothered to put her into one. If they bothered to visit. If she were even still alive. Matt would outlive her, Kali was sure of it, even though men had shorter life expectancies than women.

Here she was now, closing in on forty, and not even a partner at Biltmore, Durham & Spears. The rising stars at the firm (all men) got their partnerships early, by mid-thirty. There were only four women attorneys, including Kali. Jada had just turned thirty-one and supposedly had partnership in the bag.

And then there was Gillian – the tattooed patent lawyer that everyone avoided because she was so bizarre. Gillian did that stuff with wingnuts and widgets that no one else could, nor was willing to, do; but it was work that had to be offered by a 'full service' business law firm. Plus, her uncle was a highly-respected Federal Court judge. Generally, the other lawyers just averted their eyes when Gillian was around, or whenever her name came up.

The only other woman attorney was the first-year lawyer, Brianna. She was loosely tethered to Alex Spears in a supporting role, doing entertainment law, the only problem being that the firm never seemed to get much of that type of work. Alex refused to take ownership of Brianna's career, so no one really expected her to be around much longer.

Finally, there was Kali, hanging in at thirty-five, in a panic that her short maternity leave (not nearly long enough to create a lasting bond with Harry) might still have been enough to sabotage her partnership chances. Serious women lawyers, those who had some clearly understood future at their firms, worked right through labor, their assistants trotting files and phone messages in and out of the delivery room. Leaving the hospital after a day, they worked from home for a few more, cellphones cradled under their ears, baby in one arm, so as not to miss a beat in the forward stride of their practices. They were back in the saddle within a week, pushing plants or chairs across their office doors to keep out intruders, while diligently pumping breast-milk behind their desks.

Hideously depressed now, Kali forced herself to get into her car and back out of the garage. She pulled around the corner and stopped in front of the house, letting the engine idle. Maybe she could just stick her nose in the door, see what Britta was up to and give Harry one last teary kiss and a squeeze. She'd pretend to have forgotten something. Or would her sudden reappearance be nothing more than a cruel and self-indulgent act, upsetting Harry's precarious equilibrium?

As she sat there, worrying and debating with herself, Britta opened the front door. Startled, Kali beeped the horn and waved. Equally startled, Britta returned her wave, then stepped out onto the porch, looking puzzled. Feeling like an idiot, Kali waved again and pulled away from the house. Britta would now realize that Kali could pop up unexpectedly at any time, Kali congratulated herself; she would be on her best behavior, and Harry would be safe. Or would the idea that Kali was spying on her only make Britta more devious and cunning? And resentful? Maybe vengeful as well?

Kali stopped for the light at the corner of 2nd Street, wondering why Britta had opened the front door, and why she had left Harry alone while she did it. She glanced back at Pine Beach Road, her throat tight. All she would see of Harry now was on weekends and during the dreaded night shift. Sofia had once described her daughter, Ariana, waking up in the morning as 'unfolding like a flower.' But Harry had quickly zoomed past the unfolding-flower stage.

After two months of relative docility, and occasionally sleeping through the night, he'd undergone a radical personality change a week before Kali's scheduled return to work. He now awoke by exploding with a pterodactyl shriek of rage; hot, sweaty and pissed off at the world in general, and his mother in particular. And he didn't wait until morning for those scenes.

Even wearing earplugs, with a pillow over her head, Kali would be yanked from the edge of sleep with every little whine or whimper, after which she would then stagger into the kitchen to get a bottle of formula from the fridge, where she kept several lined up like a row of sentinels. Once the bottle was warmed in the microwave, she would stumble into Harry's room, on feet thick and clumsy as tree stumps, shaking the bottle and slopping formula onto her arm to ensure it wasn't too hot.

By the time she got back to bed, she was awake and would finally drop off to sleep, just moments before Harry's next outburst. Completely neurotic now, she doubted she would ever sleep properly again. In desperation, she'd begged Matt for sleeping pills. She now had an arsenal of Ambien, Xanax and other hypnotics in the bathroom cabinet. All of them stunned her into a dreamless stupor but left her irritable and woolly-headed in the morning. Not a good look for a lawyer trying to claw her way up the partnership ladder.

There would be no more afternoon naps for her, she thought, no lying on the couch with a cold cloth over her eyes to ease fatigue. It would be business as usual at the office. Her clients didn't care that she'd been up all night, and she wouldn't dare tell them, or anyone else. They would worry about her competence, her response time. They would think about finding another lawyer if they hadn't already.

Matt had offered to share the night shift with Kali or take it over entirely when he wasn't on call at the hospital. But it was more work trying to wake him than to just get up herself. Even if Kali turned Harry's monitor up full blast and attach it to Matt's head with duct tape, he was usually so exhausted that he responded only to the beep of his hospital pager. Britta, too, slept like a stone—in a tousled blonde coma deep in Matt's old waterbed. She was never bothered by Kali's nightly routine thumping around the house, the beeping of the microwave or Harry's impatient cries.

# Mulholland

Tired, cranky, and still in a state of high anxiety over Harry, and everything else in her life, Kali slipped into her law firm's underground parking lot at a quarter to ten: well past midday for the hard-working, dedicated attorneys at Biltmore, Durham & Spears.

# Chapter 14

Once on the fourth floor of the Promenade office building, Kali slipped into the Ladies' to take some deep breaths and study herself in the mirror, bracing for the return to her office and the onslaught of questions and complaints from the long-suffering Alicia Martinez. An exhausted, middle-aged woman in a navy-blue pantsuit that bunched and strained in places it had never bunched and strained before, looked back at her. "You're back," she said to her reflection. "You should feel terrific!" And she did... terrifically miserable.

Eventually, she ventured out of the Ladies' and scuttled along the carpeted corridor, hoping no one would see her. She needed more reorientation time: a chance to remember where—and who—she was as a lawyer and get back to charging every six minutes of her time to a seven-digit file number. But her office was not where she left it. Or, more accurately, it was in the same place, but had shrunk. Her nose was assaulted with the heavy chemical smell of carpet glue and fresh paint.

"They moved your wall," Alicia complained, following Kali into what used to be one-half of her formerly nice big office.

"They, who they?"

"Management. We got in two new attorneys, plus a paralegal, so they had to make room for more offices without paying for more space, the cheap bastards."

"Why didn't you tell me?" Kali put her briefcase down and turned around, trying to orient herself. Her furniture was all there but had been squeezed into half the floor space. And she had only one window now, not two.

"I was told, very rudely, not to bother you with calls."

"Who told you that?"

"Your husband, Doctor Miller. He said my calls were bad for your blood pressure."

Kali sat down behind her desk, feeling light-headed from the carpet and paint fumes. "Well, I suppose, if they needed the space…"

"No one else had their office re-sized, only you." Alicia was holding a bulging accordion folder full of papers and a wad of telephone message slips, clearly anxious to get back to their normal pre-Harry routine. "And I had to float for the last three weeks, for your information."

"Oh, Alicia, I'm so sorry! I didn't know. I thought you could just keep on doing my work, for whoever took over to manage my files."

"Not how it happened. Oh, and your voice-mail overflowed last week. That's why we're now back to using these stupid message slips."

"What do you mean it overflowed?"

"Ask Tech Support. It backed up, like a toilet. A lot of messages were lost. These are the new ones, along with your mail and some draft affidavits. You're supposed to review them for one of Rick's clients, he said you'd know—they're about trademarks or something. Rick's the new Managing Partner, big surprise. The announcement's in your e-mail somewhere. Mr. B. is staying on as Counsel. I had to work for that senile old bastard for two weeks. Well," she looked at Kali, her eyes bright with pent-up anger and frustration, "as you can see, there have been a lot of changes around here, since you've been away." She dumped the file folder and messages onto Kali's desk. "A lot of changes."

"Could you give me a minute to get settled? I need to call home, see how Harry's doing."

"Did you not just leave there?"

"It's not that simple."

Alicia shrugged, muttered something in Spanish, and left, pulling Kali's door closed with more force than was necessary. A few seconds later, she was back. "This just came for you." She handed Kali an Amazon package.

Kali looked at it, at first confused, then remembering: *Swedish in Minutes!* It might as well be porn, for both the shame and attraction she felt as she turned it over in her hands. "Thank you, Alicia," she said, trying to sound all business.

After Alicia had gone, with another slam of the door, Kali swiveled in her chair, flipping through *Swedish in Minutes!* and debating whether to call home. What would she do if there was no answer? Panic. All reasonable explanations—Harry was being bathed, Britta had taken him to the beach—would fly immediately out of her head. She could call Britta's cell, but Britta could always lie and say she was in the house, even if she wasn't, though Kali would probably be able to tell if she was outside from the ambient noise. Better not to call, Kali decided. Not yet. No matter how desperately she wanted to.

She regarded her newly down-scaled office, thinking that Alicia had done a nice job of reorganizing everything. There might be chaos lurking below, but on the surface, things looked good. Through her one and only window, Kali could see a scrap of ocean between two glass and concrete towers. She was lucky to have a window at all, she realized: the junior lawyers all had stuffy little cubes. She began to relax, enjoying the silence of her office's, the privacy and the feeling that she was once more in control. Maybe being back at work wouldn't be so bad.

She took some time to arrange the photographs of Harry that she'd brought in with her. The cutest ones she set on her desk, so she could gaze at them all day. The others, she put on her bookcase, relegating the lone photo of Matt at his med school graduation to the bottom shelf. Her door suddenly opened, after a short sharp knock.

"All good in here?" It was Helen Sharpe, a tiny barrel of a woman who patrolled the office like a Sherman Tank. She was famous for showing up at a person's desk, armed with a cardboard box and security guard—to escort a miscreant quickly off the premises when they were being fired without notice. California was an at-will employment State, she liked to remind all staff, associate lawyers included. No good could come of a visit from Helen Sharpe.

"All great here," Kali said, managing a smile. "It's good to be back."

"Sorry about your office," she said, not sounding at all sorry at all. "Always have to keep our eye on the bottom line, as we all know and must remember." Kali nodded, still smiling, though she had started to sweat. "I'll let you get back to work, then," Helen added, pointedly.

After she left, Kali took some deep breaths, turning her thoughts to Harry: something pleasant, after that brief unpleasant exchange with the HR manager. What was he doing now, she wondered? Was he happy? Did he miss her? Could a three-month-old baby truly miss anyone? She took her cellphone out of her bag. She needed a reason to call. The hair-dryer! She might have left it plugged in by the bathroom sink!

She dialed the home landline and listened anxiously to the succession of tiny beeps, then four rings and her own voice, apologizing for not being able to answer. They must have gone out. It was a nice, warm day but would it be windy by the water. Would Britta have the sense to put a hat on Harry? To bundle him up properly? She dialed Britta's cell, but it immediately went to voice mail. Had Britta turned it off, so that Kali wouldn't bother her? Or was the phone lost or damaged? Kali called back on the landline and left a message about the hat; called again to add another about the hair-dryer. Then she called Britta's cell to leave the same messages but got a 'this mailbox is full' message.

Determined to push all worries out of her head and concentrate on work, Kali pulled the accordion folder towards her. Maybe, she thought, she should just drive home, unplug the dryer and check on everything else. She could be there and back in an hour or two, depending on the 405. But if Britta and Harry were outside, he wouldn't be anywhere near the hair-dryer. She would just keep calling, every fifteen minutes, until she got through, she decided. She forced her attention back to the file folder.

The first document was a memo to all lawyers and staff announcing Rick Durham's elevated status in the firm. Kali had known it was in the works, but she hadn't expected it to happen so fast. At times, her lack of awareness of what was going on in the firm amazed her. Two lawyers or staff (or a combination of same) could be having an affair right under her nose: they could fornicate on top of her desk while she was sitting there dictating something, and she would later be dumbfounded to find out about the liaison. 'No kidding,' she would say, standing by the coffee machine, 'who knew?' The answer would be 'everyone but you.' Alicia was the intuitive one. She could pick out in a crowded room exactly who was having an affair with whom, with a sort of x-ray eye for infidelity. Jada Tyler had a similar uncanny prescience, and it was Jada who opened the door of Kali's office, after a very quick knock, a moment later.

"Back in the harness already?" she cried. "Wow, Mama, stand up! Let's see how you look! Are you skinny again? Come on, come out of there! You can't hide behind that desk forever." She wagged a finger at her.

"I don't see why not."

"I can already tell you look a-mazing! Come on, stand up. Flaunt it, Girl!" Irritably, Kali stood up, sucking in her stomach as much as she could. "Wow. You got your figure right back," Jada said, though it was not true and they both knew it. "That's unbelievable! Have you been working out?"

"Hardly. I haven't had a second to spare." Kali sat down again.

"Well, you don't just zap back into shape like that without trying. And it's a good thing, since it's a squeeze in here now, isn't it? I thought it was uncool to cut your office in half, but you weren't here to object." She shrugged. "That's how it goes at B, D and S, right?" Jada's hair had been freshly styled, her nails perfectly manicured, and she was wearing a high-end, custom-tailored suit with a sexy slit up one side of the skirt. Kali hid her own ruined nails under her desk, along with the rest of her anatomy she didn't care to display again. "Must have been delicious to have had the whole summer off."

"It's hard work, having a new baby. It wasn't exactly a vacation."

"You mean you didn't get in any tennis? Or golf? I thought you and Matt hired a nanny?"

"We did, but she sulked if I didn't let her take Harry, so I ended up doing everything else, like the diapers, the grocery shopping, whatever. But is that the attitude around here? That I had a three-month paid holiday?"

"Whoa, relax, nobody thinks that." Jada paused. "There's some envy in the air, that's all, mostly from the men—mainly the golfers." Another pause. "That book looks interesting," she tilted her head to read the title. "You and Matt going to Sweden?"

Kali shoved *Swedish in Minutes!* into her desk drawer. "We were thinking about it," she lied, aware that she was blushing.

"Nice! Oh, I wanted to let you know there's a memo in your e-mail that you won't like much. You have to do a seminar this week—a freebie. Word's came down from on high, for a couple of Durham's clients—big boys."

"A seminar on what?" Kali was horrified. She wasn't ready to put herself out there like that!

"Marketing, trademarks, advertising law—your usual shtick. Since you've been away, Rick figured you wouldn't have much on your plate for the first couple of weeks. Besides," Jada grinned, "you weren't there at the meeting to say no, were you?"

Kali would later wonder if Jada, with that prescient ability of hers, could have known that the day of the seminar would turn out to be the worst day of Kali's professional life. But the sudden news that she would have to prepare and present one, on such short notice, for some very important clients, completely erased the worries about Harry, Matt and Britta that had been weighing on her mind.

# Chapter 15

"Good morning, gentlemen." Kali beamed at the suits around the granite boardroom table. Not a woman among them, of course, but that was fine: she knew the drill. "As you know, I've been asked to quarterback this seminar." Male clients loved sports metaphors, she'd reminded herself as she'd thrown together the presentation. The reports she began passing around were slick, blue-covered and glossy. The firm's printers had done a nice job, on very short notice. Never mind that the reports didn't say anything meaningful or useful, since that was the usual message conveyed by any law firm's seminar material: 'call us and let us bill you for it!'

Kali experienced a heady surge of self-confidence. She really was back! Back in her world, in total control. This wasn't so bad after all; she could see getting used to it again, then becoming a partner, being able to afford the best for Harry and other Miller kids to come. "So, I ask you all to please tee-off by turning to page one, to the recent case law summary, where you'll note that..." She paused, stricken. It wasn't there! Not only was the first page missing, but page two had been inserted upside-down. "Sorry," she said. "Looks like we have a couple of fielding blunders here."

The clients chuckled, but Kali knew they were not really amused. Not a bit. She noticed a few checking their watches, others their cellphones. Kali cleared her throat. "Let's just go straight to the visuals," she said, recovering well, she thought. "Could someone dim the lights, please?" No one moved, so she just smiled brightly as she walked over and hit the light switch herself. It was then a bit of a challenge finding her way back to her seat, as her eyes adjusted to the darkness.

Without missing a beat, however, Kali reached her laptop and clicked open the presentation images. A gasp of shock and disgust swept through the room. On the boardroom screen was one of Matt's surgical reconstruction studies: a man's face, mid-surgery, the skin peeled back over the skull, the eyeballs dangling from venous threads—a leering grotesquerie. Horrified, Kali quickly shut off the screen. "That was one of our clients who didn't settle his account," she said. Silence. "No, I was just kidding. That was the FDA Commissioner. So, the moral of our story is, don't try this at home, folks. Call Biltmore, Durham and Spears!" Her light (fake) laugh echoed in the totally silent room.

~~~

An hour later, Kali was standing in Rick Durham's office: an overly-decorated corner suite with a private bathroom, complete with shower. Rick was a litigator, the crowned prince of the permanent injunction. His wife, Leighton, liked to dabble in interiors. He was leaning against his bleached oak desk, arms folded, legs crossed. He was a handsome man, Kali had to admit, grudgingly. He looked like a young *Dos Equis* 'Most Interesting Man in the World' before the guy was fired and replaced by a younger 'Most Interesting Man in the World' who was not as good-looking.

Rick's brass blazer buttons had fox heads on them—a Waspy classic; Kali had read about them in a men's magazine once. Rick belonged to a mysterious world where men wore argyle socks, penny loafers and amusing suspenders. The ones he had on today had an abstract piano key design on them. The pennies in his loafers glinted as he began to pace. Though she was in big trouble, Kali couldn't help wondering if Leighton buffed Rick's pennies and fox head buttons, and selected his suspenders, every morning. On a small oval table was a photo of Rick's five children in their private school uniforms, and another one of some Old Boys doing Old Boy things. Kali frowned, trying to make out what those Old Boys were doing. Yachting... punting... putting?

Rick seemed in no hurry to say anything, preferring to let Kali stand there uncomfortably, sweating it out for a while. He could at least have offered her a blindfold, she thought, shifting from foot to foot. He picked up a silver putter from where it leaned against the wall in one corner. Kali wondered, with a tingle of fear, if he intended to whack her with it. Litigators were famous for going berserk when the pressure got too great. But Rick merely aligned himself for a shot at an imaginary golf ball. He swung his putter delicately, but with  confidence.

"Fore?" Kali ventured weakly.

Rick gave her a peeved look. "You seem to be somewhat confused about why you're here, Miller." Old Boys always called other Old Boys by their last names. Kali supposed the rule now extended to women at work, so that the Old Boys could not be accused of gender discrimination.

"Here in your office?" Kali asked, apprehensively. "Or here at the firm?" She tried to look politely interested in what he was about to say next, but her knees were shaking. She desperately wanted to sit down!

"You're here so I can tell you how pissed off I am with you. If Mr. Biltmore had been in that room, you wouldn't have a job right now." Rick's face had turned brick red. "If there was ever a scheme designed to make our firm look bad in front of clients, this would be it."

"It wasn't a *scheme*, Rick! It was a bizarre accident. My husband has all these surgery slides—"

"And that crack about the clients' accounts? Way out of line."

"It was a joke. Come on, Rick. I was as embarrassed as anyone else. More!"

"Why don't you have a chat with our Accounts Committee to find out how funny they think receivables are? Especially yours, which are through the roof. And that remark about the FDA." Rick shook his head, fuming. "The FDA is no joke to any of our clients, especially the ones you had there in that room."

"I didn't know what else to say," Kali protested. "It was a major upset in the first period. I have no idea how that image got into my presentation. It was one of my husband's slides. I was putting the visuals together last night, pretty late. He needed a laptop for something... I guess maybe he borrowed it – and somehow...I don't know, maybe things got mixed up..."

"The firm's laptop? With sensitive client material on it? That one?" Rick scowled at her. Kali gulped, then nodded, shamefaced.

"Sounds like you need a refresher on legal ethics and client data security. This just gets better and better, doesn't it?" He scratched the top of his head as he waited for an answer to what Kali thought was a rhetorical question.

"I can't remember when he borrowed it, or even if," Kali admitted. Add that to everything else she couldn't seem to remember anymore! "Anyway, then Harry, our son, kept me up the rest of the night." She paused. "He's started teething. It's very early. Normally, it's nine months or even a year before they start. Teething. Babies." She drew in a deep breath. "I'd say I had everyone's attention though, wouldn't you? And the rest of the presentation went off well. It wasn't a hat-trick or anything, but I toughed it out to the final whistle. It's just rough when your fourth line generates the most action in the other team's end zone."

Rick examined his putter, looking perplexed. "You know, Miller, sometimes I have absolutely no idea what you're talking about."

"I can see that." Kali nodded. "You're a golfer. I tried to include a golf reference or two. But I get all my coaching from my husband. He played semi-pro hockey for a while."

"No kidding." There was zero interest in Rick's expression.

"Years ago," Kali nodded. "In Europe." She didn't bother to bring up Sweden.

"Speaking of travel—"

"I wasn't, actually."

"Have you considered taking some time off?" Rick gave his putter a final caress with his thumb, then replaced it in the corner. "I think you may need it, Kali. For your sake. For your family's sake."

"But I just came back from maternity leave," Kali laughed, nervously. "What is this? The big heave-ho?"

"Of course not. You've always been an important part of our team. But lately, to be honest, you're not being much of a team player. Understandable. We, the firm, we get it, okay? Times are changing. So, we could arrange a sabbatical for you, for as long as you need. HR is aware of this situation—"

"Wait. I'm a *situation* now?"

"I have the green light to offer you the sabbatical, Miller. Practicing law can get to a person after a few years."

"But I was just off for three months!"

"Don't you want to spend more time with your new baby?"

"We have a nanny, a good one. And I'm a lawyer. I like what I do. I love it, in fact. I don't think I could stay home." She had to tread lightly here, since Leighton stayed home, took care of the kids—with a full-time super-nanny to help—and did her interior design on the side. She was the supportive and self-sacrificing wife, present at business dinners, forever entertaining  clients, showing up at every firm function early to help set up, then staying late to help with the clean-up.

Rick stroked his beard—so clipped and shaped and trimmed it reminded Kali of a topiary. She knew what he thought of her; she could read it in his dark brown, bottom-line eyes. She was a hormone-crazed, breast-feeding, neurotic *elderly primigravida*. Unbalanced. A liability. Someone to be 'handled' and 'managed.' "Well, I'm not prepared to push the issue," he said, "as long as you can assure me that you're not going to make mistakes, that could be costly to the firm."

"Of course not," Kali said, flushing. "I've never made a mistake." That I'm aware of, she added, mentally. "I've never been reported to the State Bar or filed an insurance claim. I haven't ever notified them of a potential claim. You won't see any mistakes coming out of my office." Small though it is, she thought.

"Atta girl," Rick said. But he didn't seem convinced.

# Chapter 16

Having no appetite for lunch and shaken by her presentation and Rick's questioning of her competency, Kali scurried back to her tiny office, slid into her chair and put her feet on a cardboard box of dead files to do some deep breathing and Kegel exercises. Alicia was still at lunch, and would be for another ten minutes, thank God. She was still trying to sort out her feelings about everything that had happened when her telephone twittered. She looked at it, apprehensively. She could understand how lawyers could come to dislike what they did for a living. It was often unpleasant and usually stressful. Much of her work involved play-acting: puffing herself up like a porcupine or an alley cat, to appear fierce to the lawyer on the other side or pretending to her client that she knew the answers to their 'intriguing' legal questions, when she really had no clue.

"I want you to know that you lost me the deal," said the voice on the phone. "The big deal with the fried chicken chain. For my software? Remember how you promised they would come crawling back to offer me a better deal? Well, they didn't. They walked. They're going with the competition. And expanding into Mexico, Canada and the EU. They said I was too greedy." He sniggered unpleasantly. "I guess I should expect a big bill for this, right? A real whopper. A zinger. Or maybe you lawyers don't charge for ruining a person's life. Maybe you just do it for fun."

"I'm sorry?" Kali cleared her throat. "Is this Mr. Potochnik?"

"Bing! Potochnik the *schmuck*. Remember what you told me? You don't need a lawyer to sell yourself down the river?"

It was one of Kali's favorite lines for clients who wanted to jump on any deal that came at them too fast and were easily dazzled. Mike Potochnik had written software for fried chicken restaurants, and he was good at what he did. His product could log sales of thighs, legs, breasts and wings like nobody's business. It could convey to the cooks the exact timing needed to produce an entire order, garlic bread and salad included, fresh and finished at precisely the same moment: the bread piping hot, the salad crisp and cool. But the chicken chain had been playing hard ball, trying to blindside Potochnik and get everything for nothing. They had practically demanded his first-born, served up on a Styrofoam tray with a side of 'slaw.

"Well," Kali cleared her throat and shifted in her chair, "I may have said something along those lines, but I did not sell you out, Mike. I simply advised you that, in my opinion, it was not a good deal. You would have lost control of your intellectual property forever."

"No, not *something along those lines*. You said exactly that. And I'm never going to forget it, believe me."

"All right, so perhaps I did say that. When did all this happen?"

"Just after you left for your summer off. I haven't heard from them, or you, since. But I don't need to tell you that, do I?"

"So it was you who sent me that malicious card."

"Malicious? I merely expressed my best wishes for your new career as a mother."

"Thanks for ruining my summer."

"A ruined summer is not much compared to an entire life, is it?"

"I did not ruin your life, Mike."

"Well, I want to complete that excellent bit of legal advice that you gave me."

"Okay," Kali hesitated, "I'm listening."

"The way I see it, you maybe don't need a lawyer to sell yourself down the river." He paused. "But it sure as hell helps!" He gave a short, ugly laugh and hung up before she could reply.

Kali stared at the receiver for a few moments, her heart thumping unpleasantly as she struggled to rein in her wildly galloping fears. An unhappy client not only meant bad press around the firm and with other clients—if word got out—but she could expect the Accounts Committee on her back, since he certainly wouldn't pay her last bill; and maybe the State Bar, too. A complaint to the Bar meant endless paperwork: letters documenting the problem from the client's often muddled and overwrought point of view and the attorney's butt-covering response. All of it non-billable, dead, wasted time.

But worst of all, what if Potochnik was right? Did she sell him out? Been too impatient to negotiate the terms properly, and do the best she could? She'd been seven months pregnant, and it was hideously hot during the weeks over which the negotiations had taken place. She remembered how irritable she'd been, unable to sleep at night or concentrate during the day. Potochnik had been a pest, the way one-file clients tended to be: calling her several times a day, demanding an explanation and re-explanation for every phrase, word and comma in the thirty-page document prepared by the dozen in-house attorneys at the chicken chain's head office in Texas. It was no good telling him she had no patience for fine print: fine print was her job description.

As she sat there stewing over Mike, Harry popped back into her mind. She pressed the speed call button on her phone, needing to hear his endearing babble, and Britta's assurance that he was safe. No answer. Again. It was 2:15, Harry's nap time. As she puzzled over where they could be, her desk phone rang with a blocked number showing on the caller ID. Potochnik, probably, with more accusations and insults he had forgotten to throw at her before. With a weary sigh, Kali picked up the phone.

"*Hjalp!*" It was Britta. "It's Harry!"

"What's wrong with him?" Kali struggled to breathe, so scared she couldn't take in enough air. This was it: a mother's worst nightmare! Harry was dead or had been kidnapped by some twisted child molester. She would see his sweet little face stapled to every lamppost and bus shelter poster in Belmont Shore, on the local cable news, his name—and the make of the car—maybe that old red Mustang—that the cops were looking for, on Amber Alerts throughout the State. Until they finally found him...

"He's in hospital!"

"What? Why?"

"Is his – his *blindtarm!* They say is his *blindtarm!*"

"*Blindtarm*? What do you mean? His arm? He's blind? What? What are you trying to say?"

"No, no, *blindtarm. Blindtarm!* In the stomach!"

Kali took a deep breath, though her head and heart were pounding, and her mouth dry as sawdust. Harry wasn't dead, he hadn't been kidnapped. He would be all right. He had just swallowed something that disagreed with him. They were probably pumping his stomach now. She had to try to be calm, understand what Britta was saying, and take control. "Okay, Britta? Now, listen. Tell me which hospital you're at."

"The big one—for the children!"

"Okay, good. That's good, Britta. Have you paged Matt?"

"*Ja.*" Pause. "He's here."

"Matt's there? With you at the hospital? Why can't he talk to me? Put him on the phone. Britta? Go and get Matt!" There was a muffled, scuffling sound, then a clunk, as if the receiver had been dropped. Kali pictured it hitting the wall, then dangling from its twisted chrome cord as her own voice bleated helplessly in the pale green vacuum of the hospital corridor. "Britta? Britta, come back! Britta? Get Matt! Please! I need to talk to Matt!"

"He'll be fine," Matt said, shortly, a moment later. He'd called back on Kali's cell as she was darting frantically around her office, bouncing off the walls in a confused panic, unable to think even how to get to the hospital. "I can't talk right now. They're doing a work-up on him."

"*A work-up?* What does that mean?"

"Some blood tests, urine samples. Routine stuff."

"Blood tests for what?!"

"I've got to go—I'm being paged. Harry's out of danger. You don't need to come over. It's just a hernia. His balls were purple, so Britta panicked, of course. He'll be fine." Then the line went dead.

"Out of danger, purple balls, but Harry will be fine," Kali repeated to herself, as her breathing started to return to normal. There was a knock on her office door. "I'm busy!" Kali snapped. Then, whoever it was, mercifully went away. Kali put her head in her hands. This was it: the real world. Welcome back!

~~~

"My God, Kali," her mother, Marina, said later, when Kali called her with the news. "How did he get a hernia? He's a goddamned baby. Was he doing some heavy lifting? Jesus."

"It was an inguinal hernia, Mother. Nobody knows why babies get them. He was born with it. It was painful, so that's why he's been screaming so much. Poor little guy."

"Is he out of the hospital?"

"The hernia's been repaired, and Harry bounced right back, according to Matt. He doesn't even have to stay overnight. I'm waiting for them now. But I'm a wreck. Especially after the way Britta carried on. I was scared to death."

"Wow... Bad trip." There was a short silence on the line. Marina cleared her throat. "But I wanted to ask you about something else, Kali."

"If it's Mike Potochnik, now is not a good time."

"His mom is totally freaked out by what you did." Marina continued. She was an old hippie from the Haight, who'd never moved on from the way she talked in the 'sixties.

"What I did? I merely pointed out to him that what he was being offered was a bad deal. It's my job to tell hard truths to clients when it's warranted."

"But do you have to ruin their lives?"

"I did not ruin Mike Potochnik's life. I wish he'd stop saying that."

"His old lady wants to split, take the rug rats with her."

"If that's true, it's not because of me. If you knew Mike better, you'd realize there are probably a dozen reasons why his wife might want to leave him. But the fact that he didn't sign a terrible deal for licensing his software is not one of them."

"His mom says he would have been a millionaire by now. That chicken chain opened thirty new restaurants here, and twenty more in Mexico and Europe. It was on CNN. Your dad told me."

"He wouldn't have been a millionaire. It's not possible under the deal he wanted to sign. I've never seen such a one-sided agreement. I know my business, Mother. He would have had marginally more money than he does now."

"They were going to pay him two hundred bucks for each chicken joint."

"Well, that's chicken *feed*. They should have offered him ten times that amount."

"Two hundred times fifty is a lot of bread to Mike right now."

"If Mike had taken the two hundred, he'd be suing me right now—that's where his money would be going. His program is good. Tell his mother to let it go. Tell everyone to stop panicking. Chill out. He'll get another offer for it."

"So, there's nothing you can do for him? Zip? Diddly? Squat?"

"I sent him an e-mail asking him to meet for lunch. Maybe we can figure something out." It was blind optimism. All Kali was going to do was let Potochnik take shots at her for an hour, then try to convince him not to take his complaint to the State Bar or the firm's Executive Committee.

"But you won't zing him with a bill for that?"

"No one's going to get a bill. Why should I send him one, anyway? He didn't pay my last one. Tell his mother I'll even buy his lunch."

"Try to be cool with him, Kali. The Potochniks have hung out with your dad's family since way back in the Old Country. "

"If I can get through natural childbirth, Mother, I can get through lunch with Mike Potochnik." It was a definite 'maybe' she thought, as she finally clicked off her cell.

# Chapter 17

The Pysanka Cafe was a small, cafeteria-style restaurant in West L.A., owned and operated by three generations of the Smychych family. The food was basic Ukrainian, modified to appeal to vegans, the gluten-free crowd and those other unfortunates of the world not lucky enough to have been born Ukrainian. The restaurant choice was Potochnik's. He was sick of Santa Monica and especially the Promenade, and doubted he'd ever have a good enough reason to go there again, after the way he'd been mistreated by Kali and her firm.

Kali arrived fifteen minutes late, in no mood for Ukrainian food or humoring Mike, but he was nowhere in sight. The cafe wasn't busy, so he obviously hadn't been turned away for lack of a table. Maybe he was in the men's room getting psyched up for a fight. Or perhaps her lateness had pissed him off so much that he'd been and gone already. The more likely scenario was that he'd read somewhere about getting the upper hand in business meetings, and how being late was a good way to start: signaling to your adversary that you were busy with more important things. That source would also have advised him to meet on his own turf, thereby doubling his upper hand. Potochnik had an apartment around the corner from the Pysanka. Since he lived so close, was unemployed, and had requested the meeting, his lateness was insulting on several levels. But Kali knew it was her job to suck it up.

She chose a table near the back of the restaurant. If Mike was going to make an embarrassing scene, maybe dump sour cream on her head or throw a cabbage roll at her, she wanted as few witnesses as possible. She sat down, facing the door, to be prepared to see and greet him: to head him off. The last thing she wanted was for him to creep up behind her. Ten minutes later, as Kali was scrolling through adorable pictures of Harry on her cell, Mike entered, looking flustered and angry.

"I'm a bit late," he said, as he sat down.

"That's okay, Mike," Kali smiled.

"It wasn't an apology. And I'm going by Mykhail, not Mike."

"Okay, then... Mykhail, would you like something to drink? Go ahead."

The fluorescent lights overhead caught the lenses of Potochnik's wire-rimmed glasses, turning them into flat Orphan Annie disks. With his high forehead and perfectly domed, shaved head, he looked like an egg with glasses. "I might have a beer," he said, sourly. "I don't have to worry about drinking and driving since I can no longer afford a car."

"And you live right around the corner, so that's good.".

"Oh, so I don't need a car? I have nowhere to go anyway? Is that what you mean?"

"No, of course not. I was just—it was just small talk." As he sat there, scowling at her, Kali realized, with a shock, that it had been Mike who'd been sitting in the red Mustang outside the Millers' house the day Matt hired Britta. "Well, go ahead," she said, pleasantly, "order whatever you want. You know the menu, I'm sure. It's on me."

"I guess it would be." He settled back in his chair, and tilted his head, studying her. "You know, I'm intrigued as to why you insisted on this meeting."

Kali looked at him in surprise. Of course, the mothers were behind all this, making Kali think Mike wanted the meeting, and vice versa: throwing them together in the hopes they would work things out, once they were face-to-face. "Well, of course. I mean, you have an issue with something I allegedly did, or failed to do, so a meeting seemed like a good idea, and—"

"I mean, there I was," he continued aggressively, cutting her off, "sitting at home, not doing much of anything, waiting for another big offer to come in, or for my food stamps and Medicaid card to drop through the mail slot, and I get this e-mail from the famous lawyer, Kalinka Wolaniuk – oh, sorry, *Kali Miller* – wants to have lunch. With me! With a small-time computer programmer who can't even sell his software! I was impressed, let me tell you. I called my mother to ask for advice. I hope she doesn't want to see me just to collect her bill, I said, because I don't have any money. But that should come as no surprise to her, I said, since she lost the software deal for me."

"Forget about our account. I've written it off."

"What?" Potochnik slapped his forehead and threw himself back in his chair. "Did I really hear such blasphemy?" He pretended to clean out his ears, then shook his head. "From the big-time Santa Monica lawyer with a tiny office view of the Pacific Ocean? What would your boss Rick Durham say if he heard this?"

Kali stared at him, her lips frozen into a vague smile. He was an unhappy client, no more, no less. She had expected him to be angry and even insult her. But his reference to both her office size and to the Managing Partner of her firm was deeply unsettling. "Why don't you have that beer, Mike? Let's try and be civilized about this."

"Civilized? You need to say that? What am I? Some country bumpkin just fallen off the cabbage truck, with manure on my boots?"

Kali looked around, anxiously, to see who might have overheard. The restaurant had gone completely silent. Even the cashier was leaning on her register, watching them, listening, her eyes wide. "Maybe we should take a walk, Mike, get some air."

"A long walk off a short pier?" Mike sneered. "Isn't that how the expression goes? Maybe Santa Monica pier?"

"That's not what I meant," Kali said, thinking, however, what an excellent idea it was. "I only meant that if you're going to get so angry, perhaps it would be better not to disturb other people."

"I'm not going to assault you," he said. "Why don't you give me a little credit?"

"Then please, have a drink, some food." Kali was desperate to take the tension down a few thousand degrees.

"I notice you're not ordering," Mike said, sullenly. "Ukrainian food not good enough for you anymore?"

"I'll have something. I was waiting for you, being polite."

"The *studinetz* isn't half bad here. Why don't you try it?"

Obligingly, Kali looked briefly at the menu, but she had no appetite for *studinetz* – jellied pigs' feet – or anything else, Ukrainian or otherwise.

"My mother tells me you had a boy," Mike said.

"I guess you didn't know that when you sent me that mixed floral bouquet." Kali held his gaze.

"No. I didn't. In retrospect, I suppose it wasn't a very nice thing to do—writing you that card. I should have handled my complaint more professionally, as I'm doing now. But let's not get off topic. Tell me something about this baby of yours."

Kali frowned, concerned by this sudden change in tactics. She didn't want to go off-topic, especially if that meant discussing Harry. She preferred being openly abused to answering questions about her son.

"You got a picture? Of your kid?" Mike leaned forward on the table.

Reluctantly, Kali took out her cellphone and scrolled through the photos to find a picture of Harry that she felt like showing Mike. The one she chose was an early one, taken at the hospital the day he was born. Potochnik would have a hard time identifying him from the picture.

"Cute." Mike said, after a cursory glance. "He gets the red hair from your husband, I suppose."

"It's blond now, actually. No one seems to know where he got it from. But I don't see why you want to talk about him, Mike." She quickly put her cell away.

"What's his name? Your kid?"

"Harry."

"Pretty Anglo isn't it? Harry. Do you call him Hal? Like in Shakespeare? "

"Henry," Kali said, "Prince Hal was Henry. Not Harry."

"There's a difference?"

"Of course, there is."

"It's not Zynovoy or Lubomyr is my point."

"And your name's not Mikhail," Kali bristled.

"It is, actually. I shortened it—trying to get ahead in this country. It doesn't help, having a name like Mykhail Potochnik. And with the legal representation I got, being called Mike didn't help either. I don't know why I should be surprised that you called your kid Harry. Anti-Ukrainianism runs in your family."

"That's ridiculous and unfair. Also, untrue."

"So, are you going to send little Harry to Ukrainian summer camp?"

"I hadn't thought about it. He's not even six months old." Kali tried to picture Harry in an embroidered shirt, plucking a bandura—but failed.

"There's a waiting list," Mike sniggered. "You can't get him signed him up too early."

"Well, Mike—I mean Mykhail—my husband isn't Ukrainian. Neither is my mother, as you know."

"Of course not." He smiled unpleasantly.

"But if Matt were…"

"Sure, sure. You don't have to explain."

"Did you go to Ukrainian summer camp, Mike?"

"Every year until I was sixteen. I had to learn the dancing—that Cossack bullshit—all that jumping around in boots and baggy pants."

"Really? And that scar on your cheek—sorry, but I couldn't help noticing—I don't mean to embarrass you, but is it from a saber?"

"A zit," he said sourly. "When I was fourteen. I never should have picked it. Anyway, getting back to the dancing, the girls always pissed me off, you know? They had it so easy. Just a little hopping and skipping around with flowers and ribbons."

"I've always admired that dancing by the men. It looks awfully difficult. You must have been in terrific shape."

"Oh sure, my knees will never be the same. I need a double knee replacement, but I can't afford one. Not now."

"Well, I'm glad you brought that up, money, I mean. I invited you to lunch to talk about your software, and about how we can get you a really good deal, make you tons of money." She hesitated. "Failing that, we could discuss finding something for you at my firm."

"Finding something?"

"A job is what I was thinking."

"Like what? Janitor? That's usually where people like your Rick Durham would expect to find Ukrainian immigrants, isn't it?"

"I meant in computer systems. Programming. We employ a couple of guys in IT, but they're not that great. We could use some real expertise. I mean, my voicemail backed up and overflowed, can you believe it?" She faked a laugh. "There's a person you could talk to—Ross Owen—the firm's information systems analyst, also an attorney, and a super nice guy. I'd be pleased to give you his number, and a referral."

"I don't need your job creation program. I'm keeping myself busy. I've written a book on programming and I'm trying to get it published – that's a full-time job in itself."

"Wow, that sounds great!"

"Know why I'm having trouble? Because of my name. No one wants a book on computer programming written by a guy named Mykhail Potochnik. They figure it has to be forty years out of date already."

"I'm sure that's not true."

"That's what an agent told me. But I refuse to change my name, unlike *some* people. You think *Kalinka Wolaniuk* would be working in a swanky Santa Monica firm?"

"Of course. Why not?"

"Don't kid yourself. You'd be doing labor law somewhere, or collection work for the Ukrainian Credit Union. Thanks for your"—he made air quotes with his fingers—"offer. But to tell you the truth, Biltmore, Durham and Spears would be too big a change for me. My program is for chickens. You can't expect me to switch over to rats."

"Well, I guess we don't have anything else to talk about then." Kali reached for her bag and stood up, her cheeks flaming.

"I still intend to write to the State Bar about you, make no mistake. I might even sue you. I haven't decided. I'm not sure I want to make that much of a time commitment."

"You do what you have to do, Mike. But I gave you good representation. I even came up with a trademark for your program, for free, when you couldn't think of anything."

"Good name? *Road Runner*? That was half my problem. Who wants to buy a fried chicken program called Road Runner? Might as well call it *Road Kill*."

"It's better than *Speedy Chicken*, which you thought up, and sounds like roosters on crystal meth." Kali immediately regretted the comment. It was not the professional way to handle an unhappy client, by insulting his ideas.

"I'm not going to continue this silly discussion." Potochnik glared at her.

"Well, I gave you excellent advice, Mike."

"It's *Mykhail*. And your heart wasn't in it, *Kalinka*. Your mind was on other things. I wasn't a big money-maker for you. You didn't want to waste your time."

"That's not fair. Most of my practice is individuals or small companies with untested and innovative products, like yours."

"Well, I'm going to teach you to take greater care with those clients. If you have any left, that is."

"I really wish you wouldn't do this. You will sell your program, I'm sure of it. It's awesome and you know it. I'll even review your next agreement for no charge or write one up for you myself. And I'll come up with a new name, too, if you want."

"No thanks." He laughed shortly, unpleasantly. "You've done enough already, my *Kalinka*, which, by the way is a Russian name. I don't know what your father was thinking." He scowled. "Russian! He was never much of a patriot, Boris. I'm sure he's even worse now."

"Well then, speaking of my father—think about our families," Kali pleaded. "They've been friends forever. Why do you want to start a feud?"

"I know," Potochnik said sadly, "this will probably kill my mother. But sometimes one must put personal feelings aside. I'm a man of principle. Besides, I didn't start all this. You did. And you will have to pay for that."

Kali had to get out of the Pysanka before she burst into tears. Or maybe that was what she should do: throw herself at his feet, sobbing, admit he was right, that she was losing her mind, was hormonally overloaded and psychotic from sleep deprivation, with a nanny who looked like a young Uma Thurman, was some kind of political activist, and engaged in private jokes with her husband using words and phrases Kali couldn't find in *Swedish in Minutes!* And that if the firm fired her, she and Matt would have to sell their house and move into an apartment. They wouldn't be able to afford Belmont Shore or anywhere else in Long Beach, or L.A. They might have to move to the Valley! Harry would never again have a daily stroll along the boardwalk where he could to grin and point at the seagulls. She looked at Potochnik, her eyes filling. "Please," she squeaked, not at all above groveling.

Mike avoided her eyes. "You go back to your fancy law firm and make some more money off clients who stupidly trust you."

It was no use, Kali realized. With a strangled sob, she rushed out of the Pysanka Café. She was so distraught that she headed east on the 10 Freeway, instead of west, and was almost at the Staples Center in downtown L.A., before she realized her mistake.

# Chapter 18

Every year, Kali became infected by the Christmas spirit in early November, just after Halloween. Halloween itself had been a bit of a bust, at least where her expectations for Harry were concerned. She had looked forward to it as the first year she didn't want to turn out all the lights, close the blinds and pretend no one was home. This year, they had Harry, a house in a friendly upscale neighborhood, and an adorable, almost painfully cute, cow costume that Kali had bought on Amazon. Of course, Harry was far too young for trick-or-treating, or to eat any of the goodies Kali and Matt collected on his behalf, but he was not too young to be shown off to their friends and neighbors.

The cow suit had stuffed horns on the hood, and a swishy tail dangling from the rear. Harry, however, had been less than impressed with it. He had a cold, for one thing – the snot from his running nose mingled pathetically with the black and white grease-paint that Kali had carefully dabbed onto his face. He'd whined at the first house Matt carried him to, whimpered at the second, and by the third was screaming miserably, flinging his small decorated paper bag of candy on the sidewalk as he struggled wildly to get the cow costume off. Later, the sight of other children crowding the front steps in brightly-colored costumes and often terrifying masks had pushed him over the edge into sheer hysteria. Matt had made up a bottle for him and hustled him off to bed, leaving a discouraged Kali to distribute (or eat) all of the miniature candy bars by herself.

Christmas, however, was sure to be a big success. Even though Harry was too young to get much out of it, it would be terrific fun: their first Christmas together as a family!

# A Nanny for Harry

A few days before the 25<sup>th</sup>, Kali found herself in Santa Monica Place on a grey and rainy afternoon, taking a break from the office as she tried to find some cute clothes for Harry in Nordstrom. She was sure it had recently been rearranged for the sole purpose of confusing her. Jazzed up 'Jingle Bells' was blasting everywhere, jangling her nerves. Suddenly, she heard a *'Ho, Ho, Ho'* so genuine and profoundly merry that she thought, for a moment, it must be Saint Nick. She followed the sound until she found him, sitting on his throne, all alone, during a lull in the photo-taking. This Santa was as perfect as his laugh.

His hair and beard were real—long and silky white—not that fake cottony stuff typical of department store Santas. He looked a lot like Jerry Garcia. Kali wanted to call her mother to give her the good news: Jerry's alive and well, working at Nordstrom's! He seemed so patient and kind that Kali decided to go right up to him and tell him what a superb Santa he was, and how he had made her day, just by being there. He winked at her and gave another bowl-full-of-jelly chuckle.

"Why don't you come sit on Santa's knee?" he said. "No one's ever too old for telling Santa what they want for Christmas."

Kali studied him for a moment, uncertainly. The only one around was one of his helpers: a very attractive young woman in a red velvet mini-skirt and fake fur-trimmed jacket who smiled and jingled a ring of bells, encouragingly, at Kali. Oh, why not? Kali thought, as she stepped up onto the platform and settled gingerly, on the edge of Santa's lap. "So," she said, coloring a little, "what do I want for Christmas?" She drew in a deep breath, let it out slowly. "How about time? Can you get me some more of that? I want to bake Christmas cookies with Harry, my son, this year. But I've been so busy at work..."

"Time is something Santa cannot bring you, I'm afraid."

"You're right," Kali sighed, "it's my own fault. I waste way too much of it shopping for one thing, but being a Nordstrom employee, I'm not sure you would agree." Santa said nothing, but his eyes twinkled. "Well, how about giving me ten years of my life back?" Santa shook his head, sadly.

"Take a year off my husband's residency? Or even six months? How about three?"

"Ho, ho, ho," Santa said, without enthusiasm.

"What about energy? Or make me a better mother. More patient with Harry." Santa stroked his beard reflectively. "Okay," Kali sighed, "just bring me a new nanny. Maybe one of your elves wants to be retooled, needs a career change? But not that one over there with the bells." No response, this time, from Santa. "Can you at least bring me some more hair?" Kali said, finally. "Mine fell out, and it's not coming back anytime soon."

With that, Santa put so much energy into his "*Ho, Ho, Ho!*" that Kali almost fell off his knee in fright. "The wig department is on the first floor!" he boomed, loud enough for all other shoppers and sales staff to hear.

The resulting keepsake photo didn't show Kali with the impish, devil-may-care expression she'd hoped to see. Instead, she looked tense and pale and pinched, sitting edgily on that creepy Santa's knee, as if afraid he might have a hard-on beneath that expanse of cherry-red velvet.

# Chapter 19

Matt, along with the other residents, was expected to take part in performing some Christmas entertainment for the staff at his hospital, squeezing in some time to get it together when he wasn't polishing his research paper for presentation early in the new year. As a result, Kali saw even less of him than usual in December. He would arrive home very late, grouchy and haggard, spend a few minutes playing with Harry on their bed, then hunker down to go through his slides, or work on the script for a silly hospital skit, in which all the staff surgeons were to be mercilessly roasted.

Kali still hadn't asked him how one of his horrifying slides got onto her laptop presentation for Rick's clients. He would see it as *her* lack of professionalism, not *his* fault, and he was so stressed out, the conversation was in no way worth having.

The organized holiday festivities, from Kali's end, consisted of a party for the entire firm at Shutters, on the beach – to which no spouses or significant others were invited – and a smaller party at Jada's condo, where only the lawyers and significant others were invited.

On the morning of Jada's party, Harry sat in his high chair by the kitchen window as Britta bustled about, feeding him cereal and mashed banana, treating it as a special occasion: his mother was staying home for the day! '*An act,*' Sofia would say it was, but Kali had no interest in that sort of joy-sucking cynicism today. She felt cozy and companionable, as she enjoyed the feeling of being safe and warm in the happy little seaside house. With a surge of good will and Christmas spirit, she realized that she liked Britta, truly liked her.

Britta would be spending Christmas with some friends in Burbank, which meant there would be less picking up after her for Kali to do. That alone would be a holiday. And even better, Kali would finally have Matt and Harry all to herself.

"Do you have Santa Claus in Sweden?" she asked Britta.

"*Nej*. We have Lucia. The girls dress in white, with candles on the head. There is Lucia in every school, every town, every church. There is one for all of Sweden. It gets a bit ridiculous."

"Oh, Lucia," Kali nodded. "Like in that picture you have? That's you as Lucia, isn't it?"

"My picture?" Britta looked at her, eyes wide in surprise.

"I had to take a man in there, to read the meter, in your room," Kali said quickly, hoping Britta would not press her on that, since the gas meter was clearly outside, on the side of the house, for anyone to see. "Don't worry," she added, lamely, with a short laugh, "I wasn't snooping." Though that was exactly what she been doing, and she and Britta both knew it.

"Yes," Britta said, frowning, "that is Lucia. She was an Italian saint. We aren't even Catholics, in Sweden. Lucia is for light – the festival of light. Because it is so dark in winter."

"But isn't it dangerous, putting lit candles on your head like that?"

"They use electric lights, not so much candles now."

"Do you miss your home, Britta?"

"Some things. The food. There is not so much junk food in  Sweden."

She was one to complain about junk food, Kali thought; it was all she ate.

"So, what else is different there?"

"We don't have so much sky-scraping buildings. And there is more space. The houses are not so crowded together, with the tiny backyards like you have."

*Well, I asked*, Kali thought. She could hardly blame Britta for being honest.

Then Britta was lifting Harry out of his high chair, calling him *pussgurka* and giving him noisy kisses. Jealousy washed over Kali, her jolly mood fading. She reached into the cupboard above the stove and took out the green tin recipe box that had been her grandmother's. "Why don't you make some Christmas cookies, Britta? While I take Harry out for a walk?"

"*Nej*. I am not so good, making cookies. I will take Harry out. But he should be changed now. He has a wet diaper. His pants too, they are wet." She kissed him again. "Is better you make cookies."

"I don't want to," Kali said, feeling cranky and a bit childish. "I mean, here I am with one precious day off to spend with Harry. I'm not going to waste it by rolling cookie dough." She was suddenly, unreasonably, angry. Why couldn't Britta make herself scarce for once? Why did she have to be so clueless? Couldn't she sense that Kali desperately needed some time alone with Harry?

She shoved the recipe box back in the cupboard. She would just buy the damned Christmas cookies, like any other working mother. Harry wouldn't know the difference; he only had one tooth, for heaven's sake. Next year would be the year to start on Christmas traditions with him. She wouldn't waste a single second more on housework or cooking or other drudgery. Today, until Jada's party at least, she belonged to Harry... without Britta.

# Chapter 20

Jada, looking stunning in a sheer black blouse over a velvet bustier with silver-sequined harem pants, directed Kali and Matt towards the dining-room, which had been set up with a full bar and a tuxedoed bartender. One of the senior partners, Alex Spears, was standing morosely in the foyer, glowering into his single malt. He looked and sounded like Eeyore at the best of times, so Kali was not surprised by his glum demeanor, despite the holiday season.

"So, Alex," she said, as Matt quickly headed over to the bar, "you seem lonely out here. Didn't you bring anyone?" He was notorious for appearing at firm functions with a good-looking woman –never more than half his age - on his arm.

"My girlfriend's back at my place," he said, sourly. "With the fucking dog."

"You got a dog?"

"*She* got a dog. I said no for three months, but in a single moment of weakness, I broke down. She's going to have to look after it. I told her I wasn't going to do it." He tinkled the ice in his glass, aggressively. "And I meant it. Not a damn thing."

"Oh, I didn't know you were ... living with someone."

"At the moment," he said, drily. "For allowing that dog, I should be shot and pissed upon."

"Well, if it's piss you're after, I'd say a dog is heading in the right direction. Or you could try a baby."

Alex nodded, with no trace of humor. "So, how's the kid  anyway?"

Kali hated it when anyone referred to Harry as 'the kid'. But Alex was a name partner, so it would not be smart to critique his terminology.

"Harry's doing great," she said. "And I'm finally feeling like my normal self again." She looked into Alex's eyes, seeking affirmation that she looked like her normal self—maybe even better? But he only nodded and tinkled his ice cubes again.

"That dog will live forever," he grumbled. "It'll live to shit on my grave. It ate a sock the other day, then vomited it up. The sock couldn't be saved. And it was a favorite of mine. I had to throw the whole pair our, of course."

"Ouch, that must hurt." Kali was trying to think of a more pleasant topic. "I don't see Brianna—is she here, or still stuck back at the office?"

"How should I know? I'm not her nanny."

Kali looked around for Matt to help ease her out of this unhappy conversation, but he was securely cornered by Jada and three other women. Everyone loved to talk to doctors, especially young, cute ones. The only thing anyone ever asked, after discovering that Kali was a lawyer, was 'criminal law?' Their eyes would light with momentary interest. Then the light would die as Kali admitted she only did business law, the boring stuff, just another paper-pusher. Maybe someone should write a thriller about the gritty realism of a true legal practice, she thought: *The Vengeful Client, Continuing Legal Education Nightmare! Receivable Over Ninety Days!* "Well," she finally said, anxious to get away from Alex and his negativity, "I better go check out the buffet before there's nothing left."

Alex neither objected to, nor acknowledged, her leaving. Such a rude man, Kali thought, her cheeks hot. Why did she even bother trying to make conversation with such an unpleasant person? She wandered over towards the piano, listening to snippets of other people's conversations.

"How's your nanny working out?" Jada was suddenly in Kali's face. "I hear she's drop-dead gorgeous."

"Who told you that?"

"Oh, a little bird."

"A little bird named Matt?" Kali managed a condescending smile, to indicate she wasn't threatened.

"Not saying. But it wasn't him."

"Well, she's not gorgeous. She's attractive. And great with Harry. That's what really matters."

"Harry. He was so awesomely cute that day you brought him in to the office!"

Kali didn't care to remember the day she'd brought Harry in to show him off. It seemed hardly anybody was in that day, and those who were seemed too busy for even chucking Harry under the chin or making an admiring comment. Alicia had trailed after her, even to the restroom – where Kali changed Harry's diaper – relaying a long list of grievances and barely acknowledging Harry. Kali felt offended and insulted by everyone on Harry's behalf. In addition, she's been exhausted by the effort of wrestling Harry into a cute outfit, and driving him all the way to Santa Monica, as he fussed, whined and shrieked in his car seat.

"Is he getting any serious hair yet?" Jada was asking. "Your kid?"

"His name is Harry."

"My bad. I meant Harry."

"He's got a bit more hair, not much."

"Not living up to his name then?" Jada popped an olive into her mouth.

"It's Harry. Not Hairy." If Jada was trying to goad Kali for some reason, it was working.

"Where did he get the blond hair from, do you think?" She munched her olive, then delicately removed the pit from her mouth.

"I don't know, Jada. But people *do* keep asking us that."

"Everyone's going to think your nanny is Harry's mother."

"I guess they might," Kali smiled, as if she found the idea  amusing.

Far from being amused, she was remembering one afternoon when she was reeling from a particularly bad sleepless night and had come home from work early, hoping to steal a nap before dinner. She'd been surprised to see Matt's Jeep pull up a few minutes later. His case had finished early, and he'd come home to take Harry down to the beach, maybe for an ice-cream, before his bath. Kali didn't feel like going, but Britta did.

Together, Matt and Britta wheeled Harry towards the beach as Kali watched from the kitchen window, noting the air of easy intimacy between Matt and Britta. With Harry, they looked like a charming little family. Was that what Matt hoped? Kali had watched until they dwindled into tiny specks, feeling like a dried-up, cast-away husk; an old brood mare put out to pasture, with nothing to look forward to but the glue factory. They were gone for almost two hours. Kali never did get her nap.

"You should see our nanny," Leighton Durham, ahead of them in the line for food, chimed in. "She's homely, to put it kindly, but so great with the kids. We interviewed a Danish girl first – stunningly beautiful, like yours, Kali. She seemed nice, and I would have hired her – I actually would have – "

"No, you wouldn't," Jada poked her. Kali winced, but Leighton merely laughed. "Absolutely, I would have! But Rick said no way. He didn't need that kind of temptation in the house."

"Didn't it bother you that he would admit it?" Kali was shocked.

"Not at all. He's a man who understands his own weaknesses. It's better that way." Leighton tilted her head and studied Kali, waiting for her reaction.

"Wow, I'm starved," Kali said. "This food looks amazing. We get fish sticks, three times a week. Microwaved."

"Our nanny cooks, too," Leighton gushed. "She could do a spread like this without any help at all."

"Britta's great with Harry," Kali repeated, feeling defensive, "and that's what counts, isn't it?" She wished Leighton would go away, but she had to be pleasant to her. She was, after all, The Managing Partner's Wife.

"The chicken is to die for." Jada squeezed Kali's arm. "Talk to you girls later. I have to go do my hostess thing." Though she wasn't feeling the least bit hungry and would have preferred to spend the rest of the evening getting drunk, Kali piled some chicken, rice and salad on her plate, remembering how much she used to enjoy entertaining: all that fussing over menus, the shopping and cooking, the decisions over centerpieces, flowers and candles. No time for any of that anymore. And why couldn't Britta cook, anyway? Anyone could read a basic recipe—and Britta had more than enough English to do that. Or she could just cook in Swedish—make Ikea meatballs or whatever.

She carried her plate back into the living room, exchanging scraps of small-talk and polite smiles here and there, heading for the only vacant chair. Rick, the man who couldn't trust himself with a Danish nanny, was standing beside it, talking to Pete Johnson and Ross Owen: two other partners.

"Kali." Rick pressed his lips together, drawing them out at the sides in what was probably intended to look like a smile. "We were just discussing the

Potochnik situation." He was wearing red and green suspenders with Santa heads all over them.

"Really?" she said, wondering who had told Rick. Had Mike finally gotten around to sending out his hate letters? Kali had almost forgotten about Mike. "I've been meaning to talk to you about him," she said. "I'm sure I can handle the situation. I just haven't had the chance to get to it, what with the holidays." In truth, she'd been hoping Mike had dropped his idea of filing a complaint with the State Bar, or of suing the firm for malpractice.

"Family friend, I understand?" Rick said.

"My parents are friends with his parents, but the family connection goes way back—to Ukraine."

"Well, that helps."

Was he serious? Kali wondered. It made everything so much worse! "I'm confident we'll get it sorted out, no worries," she said.

"My door is always open, as you know." Rick studied her for a moment. "It's going to mean a lot of extra work for you. Most of it non-billable." A money bleeder, a time suck, which was exactly how he thought of her as well, Kali imagined.

"Word's out you're speaking Swedish now," Pete said, munching around a canapé. "What's that all about?"

"It can't be an easy language to take on," Ross added, "this late in the game." The three partners studied Kali, eyebrows raised, waiting for her answer.

But before Kali could come up with one and endure the tedious questions that were sure to follow, Leighton grabbed one of Rick's suspenders and pulled him over to join the carol sing. "No shop talk, Rick, you promised." She was wearing a set of Christmas-light earrings that flashed on and off, alternating from side to side, as she led her husband away. At that moment, Kali liked Leighton Durham... a lot. And Jada Tyler, a lot less. For who but Jada could have been going around the firm telling everyone that Kali was trying to learn Swedish from a phrase book she kept hidden in her desk?

She wandered around, listening in on more conversations. Someone was bemoaning the fact that his sister-in-law had threatened to buy a bathroom mirror for his family for Christmas. Behind Kali, someone else was saying: "Shit and puke. Years of cleaning up shit and puke –that's what you sign up for when you have kids."

"And don't forget the screaming and the tantrums, and years without sleep," someone chimed in. "And then there's the nightmare of the teenage years!"

Kali decided to forget about making conversation and take her food into Jada's home office, to eat in peace. There, she could gather her thoughts and calm down, after that discussion about Mike Potochnik. Inside the office, she sat down in a comfortable chair and ate steadily, in silence, listening to the sound of her chewing for a while, then slurping some wine. Matt would still be out there, mingling in the crowd, giving surgical advice and generally being witty and charming and the life of the party.

"*Dot var en utskt maltid.*"

"What?" Kali practically choked on her chicken! It was Gillian, the patent lawyer, sitting on the plush velvet loveseat, her feet up on a matching ottoman. "Gillian, hey, how's it going? I didn't see you there in the dark."

"Staked out this room as soon as I got here. It's mine. Don't get any ideas."

"What was that you just said?"

"I said that was a good meal. Somebody told me you were part Swedish."

"Oh, for Christ's sake! We have a Swedish nanny, for our baby." Irritably, Kali pushed the rice around on her plate. "Why is everyone so obsessed with our fucking nanny? Damn. Anyway, are you Swedish too?"

She didn't need a reason to dislike Gillian; she hardly knew her, hardly knew anything about her, though they had worked together at Biltmore, Durham and Spears for several years. Gillian was tall and awkward, with short, straight white-blonde hair and yellowish eyes, like those of an Alaskan Malamute. Her clothing was always unconventional—to put it kindly. She never wore makeup, had a pierced nose and multiple tattoos on her arms and neck—one reason the partners discouraged her from ever meeting, face to face, with clients, which by all accounts was fine with Gillian. Tonight, she was wearing a black satin jacket, patterned with giant pink cabbage roses, over a long floaty chiffon skirt, and an incongruous pair of heavy, black, army surplus boots.

"One of my grandmothers was Swedish," Gillian said. "I only learned enough to compliment her cooking. House rule. She's passed now, anyway."

"I'm sorry," Kali said. Gillian shrugged. "So," Kali continued, "how's the patent business?" She could listen to Gillian rattle on about patents for a week straight, even a month—anything but talk about Swedes, Sweden or nannies.

"All good. Never have to meet clients, people leave me alone. Some might think it's boring, but I don't. I probably should have gone into engineering, I'm such a geek."

"No, you're not," Kali said.

"Isadora's doing better, thanks for asking. She's out of rehab now. I think she might make it this time. Fingers and toes crossed."

"Oh, that's such great news!" Kali said. Gillian had a young teenage daughter who was always in some kind of trouble, so there was a lot of drama swirling around in Gillian's life. No one knew where Isadora's father had gone, since no one ever asked. He wasn't there, and could not be reached or found, was all Gillian ever said about him.

"Yep," Gillian said. "Here's to miracles." She raised her glass.

"Your tattoos are cool," Kali said, to change the subject. "What do they mean?"

"Nothing. My tattoos don't mean anything. I wish people would stop asking."

After that, they ate in silence for a while, occasionally commenting on the décor, or Jada's book collection, until finally Kali excused herself to go find Matt, exhausted by the effort of trying to make small talk with her colleague.

~~~

"I can't wait to get away to San Fran," Matt said, leaning back on the head-rest as Kali pulled her car out of the driveway in front of Jada's building. "How 'bout you?" He patted her knee.

"Right now, I'm more concerned about getting home safely." Kali had only had one glass of wine, and was, as usual, the designated driver. She took the responsibility very seriously, especially now that she and Matt were parents.

"You'll manage—you always do." Matt yawned and closed his eyes. "San Fran's going to be great. I just want to get away from the hospital and be alone with the woman I love."

"I thought you had to present your big research paper."

"That's only for one hour. The rest of the time, I'm yours. Think you can handle me?"

"I ought to be able to do more than that." Kali tried to ignore his hand on her knee, paying full attention to her driving.

Much as she wanted to continue bantering with Matt, Rick's reference to Mike Potochnik was bothering her a lot. She hadn't told Matt about him, and normally would have asked his advice. But he was so busy, preoccupied and tense lately, she didn't want to add to his load. Besides, what could he do about it? How could he help? It was her practice and her problem. If she couldn't handle it, she wasn't much of a lawyer. And what if Matt thought less of her if she told him? Maybe he would side with Potochnik, and agree that she really was incompetent, or had been careless or negligent.

"I had a good time tonight." She looked sideways at her husband, disappointed to see he'd already fallen asleep. There would be zero possibility of sex after they got home. San Francisco was going to be her chance to revive their sex life, as well as their marriage.

# Chapter 21

Since Matt had the luxury of being off-call on both Christmas and New Year's Eve, he was expected to make it up by being on-call on Christmas and New Year's Day. Kali spent both days wheeling Harry up and down miles of hospital corridor on stray gurneys or wheelchairs. She hung around in the hallway with Harry as Matt checked on patients, answered interns' questions, and popped into the operating room to give opinions to junior residents. *My child is going to grow up playing with hospital waste the way other kids play with Lego*, she thought, steering Harry away from a cart full of used latex gloves and dirty linens that had attracted his interest.

A few times, Matt took her and Harry around to various nursing stations to show them off. 'Where did that blond hair come from?' the nurses would *always* ask, looking from Kali to Matt and back again. Whatever answer she came up with: her sister was a blonde, one of her uncles had sandy-brown hair, Kali always felt they suspected her of lying—that Harry wasn't really her son, or that Matt wasn't Harry's father.

Kali ate Christmas lunch straight from a vending machine. Harry loved the coin slots, automated claw and bright glow of the machine, so he was hugely entertained as Kali slurped microwaved soup from a plastic cup. *As good as a home-cooked meal*, she thought wryly. *All I need are a couple of fiskpinnar.*

By the time they got home, it was almost six. Britta had left earlier in the day, after a prolonged and tearful goodbye to Harry, to stay with friends over the holiday. Harry was cranky and tired, and it was too late to cook the turkey. Matt and Kali each had a glass of wine, then gave Harry a bath together. They agreed that what was important was not the turkey, stuffing and cranberry sauce, but that they'd spent Christmas Day together: their first as a family.

Matt made Kali wait until Christmas night to give her his 'significant' present. As soon as Harry was asleep, he presented her with a small, blue velvet bag. Inside was an elegant oblong box, and inside that was a heavy gold link necklace: sixteen inches long, eighteen carats.

"Wow," she breathed.

"Like it?"

"I love it! But can we afford it?" It was bad enough that Kali was a hopeless spendthrift. Matt was the one who could be counted on not to spend a dime unless absolutely necessary.

"Don't worry," he chuckled, obviously pleased with himself, "It's paid for."

"How could you possibly afford this?"

Did he hesitate, just for a moment? "I got five hundred bucks for publishing one of my papers, and I did a seminar for a drug company, on wound dressings. Plus, I got food money reimbursement from my last rotation. Satisfied?"

"I'm sorry. Don't be mad."

"Well, if you don't try it on soon, I'm going to have to conclude that you don't like it."

"How could anyone not like this?"

"I was going to get you pearls, but I couldn't believe how much they cost. I could only have bought you like, five, and no string or clasp." He laughed.

"It's so gorgeous!" she said, fondling the heavy gold links.

"Yes, you are." Matt said. "My beautiful wife. Mother of my beautiful son."

Kali blinked, misty-eyed. His food money! He'd spent his food money on a necklace for her jealous, ungrateful, suspicious neck.

"Nothing's too good for my woman." There were spots of pink high up on his cheeks and a stray lock of dark hair curled down over his forehead. He looked unbearably attractive.

"Help me put it on, please." Kali waited while he put the necklace on her, watching the flickering lights of the Christmas tree. She thought about the night they'd trimmed the tree: she and Matt... and Britta. Then she remembered something she'd tucked away in a back corner of her mind, afraid of examining too closely. She'd gone into the kitchen to get some eggnog and returned to stand in the entrance to the living room. As she watched, Britta passed a glass ornament to Matt, with a murmured comment, in Swedish. There was something going on between them! At that moment, Kali had felt it with a near certainty. She hadn't joined them in decorating the tree after that, but had sat in a corner, sulking and drinking. Soon after, she went to bed. Alone.

"Did you get anything for Britta?" she asked. She had given Britta flannel pajamas from Victoria's Secret along with matching bed socks. Practical, not exactly sexy. but on Britta, even that would look amazing.

Matt kissed the side of her neck, then got up to fiddle with the lights on the tree. "A stupid thing. I gave it to her the other day, before she left for her friend's place. Why?"

"Just wondering."

"It wasn't much. A joke, really." He got down on the floor and reached in behind the tree. "The green string is burned out. I better unplug the whole thing before I try to change it. I don't want to electrocute myself on Baby's First Christmas." The tree lights blinked out, and he and Kali were suddenly sitting in darkness. "I guess that wasn't very smart." A few of the glass ornaments tinkled as he sat up, brushing the lower branches.

"So, what did you get her?"

"Who?"

"Britta."

"A gag-gift. You know, the kind that make you gag." He grinned, his teeth shining in the dim light from the streetlight in front of the house.

"I thought gag-gifts were reserved exclusively for me." Kali's eyes were getting used to the darkness. "You know, like a thing we have, just between us?"

"You've moved up a couple of rungs in my esteem. You've given me a son. Now I don't have to have you beheaded."

"I'm the dowager queen now, is that it?" Other terms sprang to her mind: *kicked upstairs, bought off, given the golden handshake.* She fondled the smooth, heavy necklace.

"You could put it that way," Matt said. "But I don't know why you'd want to."

"I just feel sort of hurt that I didn't get a joke gift, that's all. Silly, I guess."

Matt put his face in his hands. "What do women want, Lord?"

"I only meant that it's a sort of tradition with us, right? That you give me a funny gift?"

Before he could answer, Matt's pager beeped. Clearly relieved, he got up and turned on the living room lights. He spent the next twenty minutes on his cell, arguing with an ER doc about whether a drunk with a broken hand should be admitted by the plastics or orthopedics department, and whether Matt had to go into the hospital to admit him. Kali watched from the sofa as Matt, still on the phone, leaned his head back against the wall. Feeling guilty and full of remorse, she noted the frustrated hunch of his shoulders, and his exhausted face.

She never did have get a chance to make amends or find out what he'd given Britta for Christmas, since he left for the hospital a few minutes later. By the time he returned, well after midnight, she had already knocked herself out with sleeping pills.

# Chapter 22

Kali was lying on her stomach stretched out on their bed, watching Matt pack. Beside her was a pile of clothes that she might take to San Francisco. "The way men pack is so unfair," she complained. "Men put one suit in a garment bag, toss in a couple of shirts, a couple pairs of socks and boxers and they're set. You don't even need to remember your razor. You can always pick up a disposable somewhere."

"If it's so annoying, don't watch." Matt was preoccupied with sorting through a cigar box that housed his meager collection of jewelry: his dad's Rolex, his college ring, and the wedding ring he seldom wore because he had to scrub in so often for surgery. Kali would have enjoyed buying him some jewelry, but she'd given up on shopping for Matt. If she bought him something, she could hardly hide it, and he was getting so cranky about her spending that the pleasure she derived from buying was almost entirely erased.

"When are your folks blowing in?" he asked.

"Tomorrow morning."

"You know," Matt said, after a moment's hesitation, "we do have another solution to the Harry problem."

"I wasn't aware we had a Harry problem."

"I meant, the babysitting issue. We could take him with us, for free. The airline doesn't charge for infants."

"But Matt, we need some time alone together. How are we going to go out, if we have to look after Harry?"

"We could take Britta. She could get a room with Harry."

"Are you insane?"

"Why? Lots of people take their kids and nanny when they go on holidays."

"Maybe rich people!"

"Just think about it. I've checked with the airline and there's still a few seats available. And the hotel has a single room available for her, believe it or not."

"You called the hotel and the airline?" There they'd be in the hot tub, happily drinking champagne and getting to know each other again when they'd hear a tapping on the door. Kali would look up and see Britta in a white terry robe, loosely belted, with Harry in one arm. *'Kan jag komma* over?' she would ask, pouting prettily, 'my room has no *varmt bad.'*

'Hey, Britta, come on in! Shove over, Kali,' Matt would say, effusively. 'There's even room for Harry! Isn't this the life, girls?'

Britta would be there at breakfast, and lunch, maybe dinner as well. They could hardly be rude and not ask her to join them, could they? And she would be at the pool, toweling her yards of blonde hair as Kali struggled up the pool ladder, her own mousy hair plastered flat to her head, or wearing an ugly rubber bathing cap. "Of all the idiotic ideas you've ever come up with—"

"Hey! Hold on. You don't have to pop an aneurysm. I thought you'd like the idea. We wouldn't have to worry about Harry."

"I don't want Britta with us on our vacation! *Forstar ni?* Or do I have to spell it out for you? In Swedish! I can do that, since it seems that's all you understand these days."

Matt held his breath and squinted at her, obviously planning his next words carefully. "Okay. Forget it. It was an idea, maybe a dumb one. But I still don't know why we need your parents here. Britta can look after Harry on her own for a week."

"After that *blindtarm* incident? No way. She's too short on common sense."

"It was no *incident*. She just got scared when she saw his purple nuts."

"Well, she didn't have to overreact. Calling me at work, screaming *'hjalp!'* over the phone. Especially since you were already there! I almost had a heart attack!"

"She did a great job that day. She took him straight to the children's hospital and paged me immediately. I'd rather have someone overly cautious than someone who tries to treat Harry herself."

"I thought he was dead or poisoned and having his stomach pumped. And I'll never understand why you couldn't have given me the full story over the phone. *Blindtarm* means appendix. His appendix wasn't even involved! Neither was his stomach—which Britta was yelling about over the phone." Kali jumped off the bed and started angrily throwing clothes into her open suitcase. Almost five months had passed since the day of the *blindtarm*, but she and Matt still argued over who was the best or least able to deal with an emergency. It was a sort of miserable '*Good Parent-Bad Parent*' contest, that Kali invariably lost. "You're lucky I didn't fire Britta," she muttered.

"If you want to fire her, go ahead. Break Harry's little heart."

"As if he knows the difference. All he cares about is that someone feeds him and wipes his bum."

"That just shows how little you know. Why don't you try reading a book about babies sometime? You might learn something." Matt was tossing things into his suitcase as fast as Kali. "Fire her if you're so anxious to. Just make sure you get a good replacement. I'd like to hear one of your friends' nannies try to tell you over the phone that Harry needed a hernia repair, if you think you had trouble with Britta. Some other nanny might have tied a tourniquet around his nuts and permanently ruined his sex life. Or done some faith-healing number on him. You should try another nanny, then maybe you'll see how lucky we were to have Britta. But by then it would be too late. Someone else would have snapped her up and we'd never get her back."

"Sofia thinks she might be a hooker or maybe a drug dealer. We both think it's odd that she spends so much, on what we pay her."

Matt stopped his packing. "You know what's odd? How much time you two spend sniping and yammering about her. It's sick. Is a beautiful girl so threatening that you need to find something wrong with her? Make her into a whore or put her down in some other way?"

"She's hardly beautiful." Kali was ashamed to hear herself say something so obviously untrue. "More like cute. In a way, with those buck teeth."

"Not beautiful? Really? She worked as a model in Stockholm, modeling underwear. Duh."

"Oh, a Swedish underwear model? How funny you didn't mention that to me when *you hired her*. I thought she was a gangly kid with braces." Did he hesitate, just for a moment, before answering? Kali's eyes met his.

"She grew up, obviously," Matt said. "And no one said anything about braces—that's your fantasy. And the modeling gig wasn't during the time I was over there. She just mentioned it to me recently."

"Oh, she just casually mentioned that she professionally modeled underwear in Sweden? How did that subject come up, I wonder? And what else came up with it?"

"You're disgusting, Kali."

"I didn't realize 'underwear model' was part of your Swedish vocabulary. How would you translate that? Would it be in my *Swedish in Minutes!* phrase book? The Hotel Services section? Excuse me, bellhop. Could you recommend a good underwear model? Why yes, ma'am. We have a few on call here at the hotel, and you can find the correct term right after *var ar kontakten for rakapparat.*"

"What are you talking about?"

"Where is the plug for the razor? I know some Swedish too, see? So, you two better watch out when you're canoodling!"

"You really are losing it, Kali, if you have to snoop through a Swedish phrasebook for kicks."

"Why? Because I want to talk to Britta and make her feel at home? Just like you do?" Kali opened the door on her side of the closet, raked a few hangers along the pole, yanked off a sweater and threw it into her suitcase. "Maybe Britta didn't actually tell you about her underwear modeling days. Maybe she just demonstrated, with body language! Simple Swedes are supposed to be so good at that."

"When did you become such a jealous threatened bitch?" Matt's brown eyes had a yellow look. If he were a cat, he would have laid his ears back too, Kali thought, feeling a bit afraid of him.

"And don't give me this crap about how you want to make her feel at home. She knows you don't like her. She's told me that much, *i engelska.*"

Abruptly, Kali sat down on the edge of the bed. "Look, maybe I shouldn't go to San Francisco with you. If we're going to fight the whole time, I'd rather stay home. At least we'd have some relief from this constant bickering. We've been at each other's throats since Harry was born." More accurately, it was since Matt hired Britta, but she didn't feel like getting into it now.

"So, stay home if you want, Kali. But, hey, stupid me—I thought it would be a good chance for us to get away and get to know each other again."

"Oh sure. That's why you wanted to bring your Swedish underwear model along."

"The way you've been acting lately, I'm not sure I want to know you any better. And what the hell. Your plane ticket was only four hundred bucks and we're loaded, aren't we? We can afford to just throw it away."

"But we could afford another four for Britta's flight? Plus, the cost of a hotel room for her? Or maybe you intended for her to just sleep on a rollaway bed beside ours? On your side, of course. Just economizing, right?"

Matt checked over the contents of his shaving kit, his lips pressed together, then stuffed it into his carry-on bag. What right did he have to be enraged? Kali thought. Because she wouldn't agree to take a Swedish underwear model, who was also probably his mistress, along on their trip? Or was she really losing it, as Matt said?

She watched as he continued his packing, his face furious. Was he, could he really be, only concerned with Harry's well-being? Perhaps he honestly didn't want to leave their son. And if that were true, shouldn't Kali be grateful she married such a caring and concerned man, instead of reacting like a spoiled neurotic nit, throwing a tantrum because of her own pathetic insecurities? When was it that they'd both lost their sense of humor, she wondered, as she watched Matt zip up his suitcase, then place it along the wall of the bedroom.

"I'm going to wake up Harry," he said. "We can't let him sleep all day. I'll take him for a walk. Alone."

He left the bedroom and was soon in the nursery entertaining Harry, talking in that squeaky, all-purpose falsetto he used to amuse his son and to imitate the women in Kali's family, including Kali herself.

# Chapter 23

Kali sat slumped on the bed, trying to sort out her feelings over the trip that was supposed to function as their second honeymoon. Not only were she and Matt quarreling constantly, but Matt was right about not wanting to leave Harry. She totally panicked about it, when she let herself think about it.

Her parents were coming to stay with Harry and help Britta manage. They were kind, well-intentioned and adored him, but they were getting older and could probably sleep through a sonic boom. Plus, Kali's mother was a bit of a whack job, and Boris was... well, Boris: never having had much tolerance for, or interest in, children, Kali and Sofia included.

And Britta was Britta. Who would hear Harry when he yelled in the middle of the night, wanting a bottle or needed to be changed? Would the three of them have enough common sense to deal with diaper rash, let alone a real emergency? Would any of them notice that an emergency was even happening? And was it fair to ask her parents to be responsible for Harry in the first place?

From San Francisco, Kali would be reduced to frazzled impotency, as on that day of the *blindtarm*: a faint frantic voice over the telephone, only this time hundreds of miles away. Matt wouldn't be there either, to shepherd Harry to the right hospital department, to use his connections with the doctors on call. She had tried to tell Matt about these feelings the night before, when they were in bed.

'If we don't go now, cut the strings, we'll never go anywhere,' he'd replied. 'Are you going to wait until Harry's twenty-one before you'll leave Long Beach? Apart from your plane ticket, this is a free trip, covered by the hospital. We can party all night and get in the Jacuzzi. I can tie you up with surgical dressings, like in the bad old days. Hmm? Remember?'

Compelling arguments, Kali thought. But now that leaving Harry was an impending reality, wasn't Matt changing his tune? Wasn't he just as worried as she was? Perhaps that explained this bitter argument they'd just had—the worst Kali could remember.

Nobody warned them that having a baby would eliminate any easy-going tendencies they each had; that they would never again sleep or get up whenever they wanted to. Never lounge in bed on a Sunday morning or spontaneously go out for a beer on a hot summer night. 'Enjoy your freedom while you can,' was the only pat piece of advice they got, from all directions, while Kali was pregnant: as if they should go out every night, party 'til dawn and somehow bottle every moment to savor later when they were stuck in the house with a cranky baby and no sitter.

For all her expressions of love and affection for Harry, Britta never lingered in the evenings, usually making a face when asked to stay late or babysit on a weekend. Usually, Kali came home to find her standing by the window, jiggling Harry as she waited impatiently, jacket on, bag slung over her shoulder, ready to bolt out the door.

Since Christmas, the feeling of being trapped had hit them hard. Kali and Matt seemed to turn on each other, hurling accusations of incompetence or gross negligence when it came to Harry's care. *Somebody* left this switch plate uncovered; *somebody* didn't wash this bottle properly; looks like *somebody* forgot to buy more formula. That somebody was almost always Kali.

And no one had told Kali that she would start fantasizing about sleep the way she once fantasized about sex: anticipating it, hoping it would just naturally happen; never getting enough; daydreaming about being able to sneak in a quickie some afternoon. Worst of all, the things that had once appealed most to her and Matt about each other had become the greatest sources of irritation: Kali now viewed Matt's youthful energy as silly juvenility; her sophistication, he saw as cranky middle age.

Kali went down the hall and stood watching Matt playing with Harry in the nursery, holding him up to bat at the Little Bo Peep mobile. The sheep, three white and one black, were light and fluffy. Each time Harry grabbed for one, it bobbed up and away out of his reach. He made excited gasping sounds, undaunted by the futility of his efforts. Kali had to smile.

"Matt?" she said.

"Hmm?" He didn't turn around.

She felt like apologizing, but she didn't know for what. For memorizing innocuous Swedish phrases and hurling them at him in a jealous rage? For suggesting that Britta was a prostitute? For being herself? "If you're going down to the beach," she finally said, "would you look at the retaining wall? I think we've got a problem with it."

"Great," Matt said, "just what we need. Another money-sucking *Proctor*." He held a squirming Harry up against his chest and riffled through the bureau drawer to find a sweater. He obviously wasn't going to invite Kali to join them for a walk. "See you in a bit," was all he said.

Kali gathered up the toys littering the floor of Harry's room, then went into the bathroom. Through the small window, she could see their sad little garden below, and the sludge of grey ocean beyond. Matt already had Harry in the stroller and was struggling to maneuver it over the uneven ground. Britta hadn't been much help with that garden; in fact, Kali had been shocked to see how little she knew about nature and making things grow. Britta was an expert on things like Instagram and Tinder, and all varieties of American junk food. So much for the nurturing-Swede theory. She wouldn't know a loganberry if one hit her between the eyes.

Wishing she hadn't bothered to allude to her recent forays into *Swedish in Minutes!* Kali watched Matt jab his foot into the crumbling mortar of the retaining wall, shake his head, then lift Harry in his stroller over the top and onto the sand below. The boardwalk didn't reach as far as Pine Beach Road, so they had to drag, push or carry Harry in his stroller through the sand for a few hundred feet to get to it.

Never had the five-year age difference between Kali and Matt seemed as glaring as it had over the months since Harry's birth. At times, Kali imagined what it would be like to find someone her own age, or older. Someone who had confronted his own mortality, but bravely struggled on, tinged with sadness, waking every day as she did, in a panic over the passage of time, wondering which part of the body was going to give out next, and how much the damage control would cost. Maybe it would be a tendon, shot like an old bra strap; a tooth that was chipped or cracked; perhaps a mysterious, alarming lump that had suddenly popped up in a groin or armpit or appeared as an ominous shadow on an x-ray.

So far, Kali hadn't had anything serious go wrong, but there was always something niggling and incurable: back pain, headaches, a sour stomach, diarrhea. Like their house, Kali's body was brimming with *Proctors* that lurked below the surface. Matt, on the other hand, was still young enough to deflect the thought of death with some glib saying like, 'when your number's up, it's up,' and believe he meant it.

If Harry ever had to choose between them, he would be better off with Matt, Kali knew. Matt was the one who could save Harry in an emergency: perform CPR, the Heimlich maneuver or a lightning-quick tracheotomy. He had the youth, the energy, the strong back; plus, he was a 'fun dad'. Kali was just an *elderly primigravida*, and lately, a pill-popping insomniac. Now that she was no longer needed for breast-feeding, she was the one who could easily be replaced. Sofia was probably right: it was only a matter of time before Matt left Kali for a younger woman.

She turned away from the window and left the bathroom to deal with the mountain of clothes on the bed and finish packing. All things considered, their second honeymoon was off to one hell of a lousy start.

# Chapter 24

"I miss him already, don't you?" Kali asked Matt as they were finally airborne on their way to San Francisco.

"Like a cluster migraine," Matt said.

"Seriously?" Kali was shocked.

"Sure, I miss him. Harry's a great baby. But he *is* a baby. We need some adult time, alone."

Kali had left her car, with Harry's car seat installed, pointing out of the garage so her parents wouldn't have to take needless risks by backing out, and had attached a diagram to the car seat, illustrating how Harry was to be safely buckled in. She'd posted signs all over the house for the enlightenment of her parents: MAKE SURE TO KEEP CRIB RAILS UP; CAREFUL OF HOT COFFEE!!; DO NOT USE FRONT BURNERS ON STOVE; KEEP BLIND CORDS TIED UP!!! Matt had notified every resident at the children's hospital, so all were poised to receive a frantic call from Boris or Marina—ready to bump Harry to the front of the line in the emergency room.

They could have brought Harry with them, without Britta, but Kali's imagined air travel horrors were worse than those she concocted for him at home. There was Harry, being torn from her arms as the plane plummeted towards earth, seconds before it burst into flames; Harry being shunted down the escape chute—a shrieking, terrified bundle; Harry's oxygen mask failing to drop down from the compartment when the cabin depressurized and Kali losing consciousness before putting hers on; Harry being snatched by a psycho at SFO while Matt and Kali searched for their bags. No, Harry had to be better off at home, with Kali's parents... and Britta.

"Well, I miss him a lot," Kali said. "I need to drown my sorrows in drink. Let's get some booze as soon as they start the service. How 'bout champagne?" She turned to Matt who was intent on reading something he'd taken from his carry-on bag. "What are you doing? This is supposed to be fun time."

"I guess you'd take it personally if I spent half an hour reviewing my paper?"

"Considering this is our first time away together since Harry was born, yes." She called for the flight attendant and ordered champagne for two, recalling those crystal flutes, nestled together in the dishwasher. Now was not the time to ask Matt about those. She didn't want to spoil their flight and possibly their entire trip after hearing his explanation. Perhaps it was one of those questions best left unasked. When the drinks arrived, she turned to her husband. "Now, drink up, so I can take advantage of you."

"Up here? At a cruising altitude of thirty-thousand feet?" Matt licked his lips and chuckled a little. It was his 'turned on' chuckle; Kali remembered it well.

Kali hesitated. "Sure. Why not? We haven't had any turbulence. We need to shake things up a little."

"You're on, Baby!" They clinked glasses and knocked back the champagne. "Okay, so…" Matt put his hand on her knee and massaged it, "what exactly did you have in mind?"

"I don't know." In truth, Kali didn't know what she had in mind. Nothing, probably.

"If you don't want me to work on my paper, you're going to have to come up with something pretty diverting." He leaned over and nuzzled her ear. "How about we do it in the john?"

"What? Seriously? There's no room in airplane bathrooms. Besides," she craned her neck to see over the seats behind them, "look at all the people waiting to get in."

"Sure, they're all lining up to do it in there too. We just have to wait our turn. And be resourceful. Creative."

"What if they flash the 'Return to your Seats' sign while we're in the thick of it? What if we get trapped in there and the plane goes down?"

"I can't think of a better way to go, can you?" He nuzzled her ear again, tickling the inside of it with his tongue. It made the roof of Kali's mouth tingle. She shivered. "All we have to do is wait for a break in the line." His fingers inched up from her knee, tracing circles on Kali's thigh.

"Well, I'm not really sure I'm that kind of girl," Kali cleared her throat, nervously. She was feeling the buzz from the champagne and the altitude. "What if we get caught? Maybe I'll just read the airline magazine instead." She took the magazine out of the seat pocket. "There's an article on Napa Valley wines that looks interesting."

"Kali, you're at your sexual peak. You're supposed to be able to wear out guys my age."

"Is that why you married me?"

"What do you think?" He put the magazine back in the pocket, took her hand and placed it on his crotch. Matt could get an erection over just about anything; he seemed to have a hard-on more often than he didn't. And it was true that when he met Kali, he'd been thrilled by her sexual appetite, her willingness to experiment, even with some rather offbeat 'variations' involving ties, surgical dressings and spatulas. Now, six years later, he had to be feeling swindled. And she couldn't believe she had ever been such a sexual adventurer.

"Well, okay. I'll go first. You wait about three minutes, then follow me. Just bang once on the door and I'll let you in."

"I'll be banging more than the door."

They sat together in silence, feeling warm and agitated, sipping their champagne and anticipating the completion of their outrageous plan, as if they were the first couple to ever conceive of the idea.

"So, what should I do when I get in there?" Kali asked, as she struggled out of her seat and climbed over his knees.

"I'm sure you'll figure it out." Matt patted her on the backside as she stepped into the aisle.

~~~

Kali's progress towards the rear of the plane was unsteady. She wondered if she'd lost her mind or was really and truly this desperate for Matt's attention. She half-hoped there would be a long line of people waiting to use the facilities.

125

But there was no one back there. It wasn't a full flight and the back few rows were sparsely populated. The flight attendants were busy with the food service. The jump seat was empty.

Kali stared at the brightly-lit VACANT sign on the lavatory door, before opening it, feeling weak-kneed and woozy. Once inside, she studied the layout of the cramped cubicle, genuinely puzzled about what, exactly, she was supposed to do. Matt seemed to think she should know. Was it some kind of test? If she failed, would it mean she was hopelessly repressed, a failure as a woman in her sexual prime? A missionary-position flop? The space didn't seem to lend itself to anything more involved or long-lasting than *coitus interruptus* of the most unsatisfactory kind. In fact, it was hard to imagine the two of them fitting into that space together, let alone doing anything more acrobatic than breathing.

Were the three minutes up? She should have made it five… or ten. Or never. What would Matt think if he arrived, primed and raring to go, and found her standing there, peering into the mirror above the basin, or just washing her hands? She'd better do something to look interested in this venture, and she was… sort of. It was going to revive their marriage, wasn't it?

Slowly, Kali turned around in the cramped space, trying to work out the various possibilities for coupling. There weren't many. Vertical was the way to go, obviously. She could try and sit on the narrow sink counter, but then her butt would rest in the wash-basin, probably overflowing it. AS A COURTESY TO OTHER PASSENGERS, PLEASE WIPE THE BASIN AFTER USE, it said, faintly disapprovingly, on a sign beside it.

She assessed the toilet seat next, marveling at how casually she would have plopped herself down onto it in her younger years, uncaring about how many of her body parts came into contact with it. Now, it seemed to swarm with bacteria, microbes, viruses. Feeling a sudden urge to pee, she lifted her skirt, pulled down her panties and squatted uneasily above the toilet seat, quads protesting. She pulled her panties back up, flushed the toilet, and felt a small surge of panic as the blue water was sucked noisily away. Matt would be there any second, she had to get busy!

There wasn't enough room to do it doggie-style. She tried to bend over the small counter. Her expression, reflected in the mirror, didn't show sexual excitement but instead acute embarrassment. She couldn't go eyeball to eyeball with herself for the duration of the act, with Matt reflected over her shoulder, his face contorted by ecstasy and exertion. She started to sweat. The things some women would do to pump some sexual adrenaline back into their marriages!

She then tried leaning with her back against the door, putting a foot up on first the toilet seat, then the basin counter. She imagined Matt puffing and banging away, oblivious to the thin door that would be trembling under the strain. The sign on the outside would flash from VACANT to OCCUPIED, then back again as Kali's backside bumped against the latch.

Maybe Matt could sit on the toilet, and she could sit on his lap, facing him? He wouldn't care about microbes, not this time. But wasn't there some type of danger associated with airplane toilets? Kali recalled something about suction, about a tremendous vacuum being created under certain conditions. DO NOT THROW OBJECTS INTO THE TOILET warned the sign above it. She and Matt were obviously too big to get sucked out, but—infinitely worse—they could get stuck there, wedged in the bowl, like two humping dogs she'd seen welded together for hours in front of the house. They'd have to wait until the plane landed to be freed. It would probably make the six o'clock news across the country! There was a muffled thump on the door. Matt already, and she had done none of the things she was supposed to do to prepare for their adventure, whatever those things were. Hyperventilating slightly, she unlocked the door to let him in.

"You're not ready," he said, looking disappointed.

"I wasn't exactly sure what to do."

"Christ, Kali. It isn't that complicated."

"Well, it's a bit hard to lie back naked under satin sheets in here, or maybe you hadn't noticed. And it's bright enough to do brain surgery. I'm having a bit of trouble getting into the mood."

"I'll get you in the mood." He pulled her close, breathing hard. He reached a hand up under her skirt, then drew back and looked at her in amazement. "You've still got your underwear on."

"Well, duh."

"Take it off, Kali. That's pretty basic, isn't it?" He started fumbling to undo his belt, then pushed his jeans and shorts down to his knees.

"But where should I stand?" Mortified, Kali slipped her panties off and, not knowing what else to do with them, stuffed them into the waistband of her skirt. Then she hiked her skirt up. "This is so romantic," she said.

"It will be," he said, "in retrospect. You'll get hot over this memory for years. Lean up against the door."

"I thought maybe I could sit up on the counter."

"Forget it. No room. No time." He seemed to know what he was doing. Had he done this before? Not with Kali. "Put your arms around my neck, then wrap your legs around my waist."

"You've got to be kidding."

"Just do it, Kali. There are two guys out there with exploding bladders, desperate to get in here. If you keep playing around, they'll break down the door."

Kali put her arms around his neck, then, using what was left of her stomach muscles and wishing she'd done more of those Kegel exercises, she gave a little jump and managed to get her legs up around Matt's waist. Almost immediately, they began to slide down again. He grabbed her under the thighs and hoisted her back up into position. "Nobody said this would be easy," he grunted. "Grab onto me with your legs. Use your  muscles."

"I'm no Olympic gymnast!"

"Well, I can't do it all." He fumbled around, and after a lot of rather comical struggling, managed to stuff himself inside her. "Man, you're dry. You could have brought some gel or something."

"I don't normally carry lube in my purse. And you'd be asking a ton of questions if I did."

"Let's not fight, okay?" He winced as he thrust harder.

"So, do you want to forget about this?" Kali said.

"No way. This is great." Another dry thrust. Then he stopped, his head on her shoulder, his hands digging into her thighs.

"Now what?" she said.

"What do you mean, now what?"

"I can't stay like this for long."

"It won't take long."

"What if they hear us outside?"

"Then they're lucky—we won't even charge them." His eyes were closed, his brow creased with concentration as he labored to get some in-out action going. "This is wild. You're awesome."

Kali arched her back, trying to relieve the pressure on the door, afraid it would pop from its hinges and they would tumble out into the aisle, bare-assed, and glued together, like those two dogs Kali had seen on the front lawn of 67 Pine Beach Road—stuck together for three hours. Matt opened his eyes to look at their reflection in the mirror. "Hey, check us out. We look great! Too bad we can't see more!"

"Yeah" she said, pretending enthusiasm, "this is so hot!"

"Damn right," Matt panted. "Doesn't get much hotter."

What if he really did enjoy it? Kali worried What if it led to more of such things, and he insisted they start 'doing it' in all sorts of high-risk public places: shopping mall restrooms, hotel lobbies, underground parking garages, park benches? She clung to him, sweating with the effort of keeping her legs around his waist. The muscles of her inner thighs, long since atrophied from lack of exercise, trembled uncontrollably. Kali leaned her head back, trying to look sexy and squeeze some pleasure out of the experience. Maybe Matt was right: it would be a lot more enjoyable in retrospect. FOR YOUR PROTECTION THIS LAVATORY IS EQUIPPED WITH A SMOKE DETECTOR met her eyes.

"Christ, it's hot in here." Matt thrust and pumped, thrust and pumped. Then he laughed abruptly.

"What's so funny?" Kali tried to smile into the forest of his thick dark hair.

"That plug on the wall, beside the mirror."

"What about it?"

"Look at the sign under it. FOR YOUR RAZOR."

"So?"

"What was that Swedish bit you said yesterday?" He pushed deeper into her, as Kali's smile faded. "What was it?" he demanded. "That phrase?"

"I can't remember," Kali said. "Why?"

"Where's the plug for the razor? Say it."

"No, really. I can't remember."

"Come on," he panted, "it was funny!" He was perspiring heavily, pumping harder, working frantically.

"*Var ar kontakten for rakapparat,*" Kali finally said, through clenched teeth. "Again!"

"No!"

"Please!" The sweat was trickling down his forehead as he thrust faster and harder. The door of the cubicle shook; the mirror trembled.

The intercom system beeped. "Does someone need assistance in the lavatory?" inquired a voice.

"Say it again!" Matt whispered, fiercely, "I'm almost there!"

"But what if the whole plane can hear us? What if we're being broadcast through the intercom?"

"Just say it!"

"*Var ar kontakten for rakapparat!*" Kali felt like pushing him down onto the toilet in case some turbulence would create the necessary suction to catapult him out into the stratosphere.

"Oh! Oh, Kali! Oh, my God!" He was kissing her, hungrily. Then he collapsed, his weight slumped against her, breathing hard, moaning.

A man was pounding on the door. "What's going on in there? Do you need help? Are you okay?"

"More than okay, buddy!" Matt pulled out of Kali, dropped her, then struggled to get his pants up over his sticky thighs. "That was amazing. You're absolutely the best."

"How do we get out of here now? With all those people outside?" Frowning, Kali wiped the insides of her thighs with a piece of paper towel.

"I'll tell them you've been airsick and need a few more minutes to get cleaned up."

"Oh, nice!" Kali pulled her underpants out of the waistband of her skirt and stepped into them. She was trembling violently; her legs felt like Jell-O. "I'm supposed to let everyone think I've been in here puking all over myself?"

"If you've got a better idea," Matt said, "let's hear it."

# Chapter 25

When Kali returned to her seat a few minutes later, Matt had his chair back in the reclining position, earbuds in, eyes closed. He was smiling dreamily. Kali climbed over him and sat down, sulking and leaking body fluids, badly wanting another drink, and at the same time fantasizing about strangling her husband with his headphone wires. She reached over and yanked out one of Matt's earbuds. There was no sound coming out of it. He'd only been pretending to be listening to something! "So, what was all that Swedish bullshit about?" she demanded.

"Nothing. You're funny, that's all. You're a constant amusement. A turn on. An amazing woman."

"That so?"

"Yup." He gave her hand a vigorous pat.

"I'm not sure that's a satisfactory response."

"Why don't you just sit back and relax? Think about what we just did, feel wild and sexy and alive?" His eyes were still closed. "That was just like the bad old days, wasn't it?" He put the earbud back into his ear.

Kali sat for a moment, then pulled it out again. "There's something I've been meaning to ask you about, Matthew."

He looked at her, exasperated. "Okay, shoot."

"When I gave my presentation at work—for Rick's big clients—one of your surgery slides was on my laptop. A really horrible one—a man with almost no face. It was projected all over the boardroom wall."

"Are you kidding? That's insane!" He laughed. "But I bet it livened up your presentation. So, what did you say?"

"I can't believe you think this is funny!"

"What did you say? To the clients? Come on, Kali, I've got to know!"

"Oh, I don't remember," Kali sighed. "Something stupid and lame, like don't try this at home."

"You said don't try this at home? Seriously?" Matt then laughed so hard he had to gasp for breath, his eyes watering. "To Rick's biggest clients?" He put his face in his hands. "Oh, I'm sorry, Kali. Oh my God!" His shoulders shook, as he laughed harder, on the edge of hysteria.

Kali jabbed him hard in the arm. "Matthew, I was totally humiliated! It could have cost me my job! And I'd like to know how that slide of yours got in there."

"How should I know?" Matt wiped his eyes with his sleeve, still chuckling. "Are you suggesting I sabotaged your talk? Why would I do that? I don't want you to get fired." He laughed a little more. "We need your pay, Babe."

"It was the very first image that came up," Kali sulked. "So embarrassing!"

"Tough act to follow," Matt nodded, struggling to hold back more laughter. "Well, there has to be some reasonable explanation. Maybe Harry was crawling around and dumped out a tray full of my slides, and Britta got confused and didn't know where they should go."

"Oh, sure. That must be it. Why didn't I think of that?"

"Maybe he grabbed my thumb-drive and stuck it in your laptop."

"Yeah," Kali nodded, "like any other baby would do. Please don't laugh anymore."

"Sorry," Matt said, but his lips were still twitching.

"And even if that did happen, if you can somehow blame poor little Harry for this, why wasn't Britta with him, while he was doing all this crawling around, dumping out your precious slides and jamming thumb-drives into laptops?"

"She can't be expected to watch him every second."

"Why not? That's her job. That's what we're paying her for."

"What if she was just putting in the laundry or something?"

"She never does the laundry. That's my job, according to her. What if Harry stuck a pair of scissors into an electrical outlet, while she was so busy doing something else? Would that be excusable too? Would you overlook that so easily? Would you laugh then?"

"This is a stupid hypothetical argument, Kali, and I'm not going to get dragged into it. You just feel like fighting, for some unknown reason."

"Can't imagine why. After being so sexually satisfied." Matt gave her a look. She had his attention now. "And while we're on the subject of Britta…"

"Oh, God. How did I know we would end up on that subject?" Matt sighed, running his hands through his hair.

"I'd like to know what that big flag on her bedroom ceiling is about. It's not Swedish, is it?"

"I never said it was."

"So, what is it?"

"It's from a region, in the south of Sweden, called *Skane*." He looked uneasy.

"*Skane*? Isn't that where you lived?"

"For a while."

"So, this region has its own flag?"

Matt shrugged. "I guess so. You sure know how to spoil a great mood."

"You guess so? Why do I get the feeling you know more about it than you're telling me?"

"I don't know. Why do you?"

"Because you do."

Matt shook his head. "Okay," he sighed, "there's a movement—they're sort of separatists. The people in Skane feel they're more Danish than Swedish. They wanted to separate from the rest of Sweden at one point. The flag is a combination of the two countries' flags. The red is Danish, the yellow cross is Swedish."

"Wait a minute. Here's this country with one of the highest standards of living in the world, and some whacko group wants out?"

"You'd understand if you lived there. Swedes can be pretty dour."

"Ingrid Bergman, Britt Ekland and Uma Thurman are dour? Give me a break!"

"You can't judge a whole country by a few movie stars."

"Dour," Kali snorted.

"Anyway, as I was trying to say, it's the Danes who have the *joie de vivre*. It all boils down to the strict drinking laws in Sweden. People in Skane got fed up with having to take the boat over to Denmark to do any serious boozing."

"You've got to be kidding."

"I'm not."

Kali didn't say anything for a moment. "So, Britta's one of these heavy-drinking Skanish separatists?"

"I don't think so, no," Matt said. "Actually, I have no idea. Why don't you ask her if you're so interested in Swedish politics? Anyway, there was a Scania right wing political party, but it dried up over the years, so it's really a non-issue now."

"Not to her, apparently. So, let me get this straight. Harry's nanny is some kind of anarchist, living in our house, maybe organizing political rallies, planning some violent protests? Maybe there's some rally going on there right now. They're doing all that wild drinking, thrashing each other with birch branches."

"It's the Finns who do that stuff with the branches. And now you're just talking crazy. Crazy paranoid Kali is back."

"Crazy paranoid Kali? Is that what you and Britta call me?"

"Of course not." Matt ran his hands through his hair again. "Just quit worrying so much about Harry, okay? Your folks are there, remember?"

"They're probably tied up with duct tape by now!" Kali clutched his arm. "We have to go back! Britta's got political pamphlets in her bedroom. In her dresser drawer! Dozens of them!"

"You went through her drawers?"

"I had to! I had to find out what was going on, for Harry's sake."

"No. For your sake. And I bet Sofia put you up to it."

"She did not."

"I knew it." Matt shook his head. "You two are pathetic, you know that?"

When they got off the plane, an hour later, they were still arguing about whether Britta should be expected to watch Harry every second, whether she was an anarchist, why Kali thought she should be entitled to go through Britta's drawers, and what business any of it was of Sofia's.

# Chapter 26

Things improved after Kali and Matt got to their hotel. Their room overlooked the atrium: an enormous vaulted space meant to evoke a tropical greenhouse, interspersed with fountains and pools on different levels. In the middle of the largest pool was an island of glass blocks where a pianist, in tie and tails, played Gershwin on a white baby grand.

For the first day, Kali luxuriated in having nothing to do but relax and enjoy the obscenely thick towels and complimentary bathrobes that were supplied, fresh and warm, anytime they asked; in having their bed turned down, and in the gold-wrapped chocolate truffles, like the droppings of a tooth fairy, left on their pillows. For the first night in months, she slept without pills.

In the afternoon of the second day, Kali went down to the hotel spa for a massage, then sat in the steam-room, suddenly finding it hard to relax as she worried about how they were going to pay for all the hotel extras. The massage had been sixty-five dollars for a half hour. Hopefully, Matt wouldn't blow a gasket when he was handed the room bill for the 'incidentals.'

After that, she tried the sauna for as long as she could stand it: barely ten minutes. Matt could happily cook in a sauna for hours—a passion he'd acquired when he lived in Europe. The German saunas were the best, co-ed being the norm. How often had Kali heard the story of his startled delight when three long-legged *frauleins* walked in on him and casually dropped their towels? Britta, Kali imagined, would be a big fan of saunas, too.

There were brief periods of time in San Francisco when she managed not to think about Harry. But the instant she did, it was with a surge of guilt and a quickening of alarm. She called home first thing in the morning and as late at night as she dared, aware that she was probably waking up her parents. As she dialed the home number, or her Mother's cell, she would brace herself for impact. When there was no answer, she panicked; when there was, she struggled to decipher her mother's code language, which had become worse as Marina got older. Kali didn't remember being unable to understand her mother, when she was a child. When Marina said everything was *copacetic* what did it really mean? When she said everything was *hangin'* was that better or worse than *copacetic*? What did it mean when Kali could hear Harry wailing in the background? What did it mean when she couldn't?

Only once, did Britta answer the phone. She was friendly enough but didn't seem eager to chat. 'I will get your mother,' she'd said. 'Mrs. Wolaniuk?' she called, 'it is the *satkäring*. Your daughter!' Kali meant to look up *satkäring* in *Swedish in Minutes!* when she got home. She didn't dare bring it along on their trip, certain it would have led to another heated argument with Matt. It probably meant something like 'worrier' or something to do with being a mother. Perhaps, *käring* was Swedish for 'caring.'

Meanwhile, Matt was busy at the conference. There were some big names at the meeting: top surgeons from all over the world, and he wanted to circulate and meet as many as he could. The dinners Kali had with him took on a definite pattern, inevitably shared with some tag-along, spouseless surgeon whom Matt, with his usual gregariousness, had urged to join them. All this bustling glad-handing was an investment in his future, their future. Kali should get to know some of the wives, he said, there were bound to be some interesting women there, or why not take some of the courses organized for spouses?

Though skeptical that there would be anything of interest to her, Kali dutifully got the spouse program from the 'gosh-great-to-see-you' girls at the information center. There was a *Breakfast at Tiffany's* event where champagne and chocolate-dipped strawberries would be served, and where a complimentary appraisal of one's own jewelry could be obtained. Later on, the *chef de d'hôtel* would demonstrate how to turn at-home entertaining into a cordon bleu event. Kali considered going to both: the first to see if her hundred-dollar wedding band was still worth as much now, six years later; the second to see what the hotel chef had in mind for her to do, creatively, with fish sticks.

Also scheduled, a day-long trek to several California vineyards, a Christian Dior cosmetic makeover, a harbor sail where a line of designer cruise-wear could be purchased at cost. There were a number of 'Spouse in the Office' courses for women who wanted to get more involved in their husbands' practices, with breakaway focus groups on income taxes, investing, and fee-billing software.

The remainder of the spouse programs were designed to present the surgeons' wives on a platter, ready for carving up by the high-end local merchants. There were daily cocktail parties, luncheons, fashion shows and shuttles with the wives herded onto luxury coaches, plied with more champagne and bussed to the most exclusive shopping centers in Northern California.

Kali went to one of the fashion show luncheons, but it gave her a headache: too much rich food, over-amplified music and flashing lights that hurt her eyes and made her feel panicky. Daywear, cruise wear and sportswear zipped by at a frenetic pace. There were outfits to wear while shopping, for afternoon tea, twin-sets for your husband's office. There were society fundraiser ensembles, togs for the beach, and foul-weather gear for the yacht. During dessert, the cocktail gowns swished past Kali's table: a parade of jewels and shiny sequins that made her think of fishing lures. She couldn't have afforded so much as the earrings on one of the women modeling those outfits.

# Chapter 27

The last day of the conference was the one on which Matt was to present his research paper. Out of six thousand delegates, only twelve hundred had signed up to hear his talk, and Kali could tell he was disappointed. Every single butt in a chair counted, he told her, even hers. Of course, Kali would be the supportive wife and cheer him on at his presentation.

While she waited for his talk to begin, she wandered around the Exhibitors' Hall, looking over the displays of glittering scalpels, scissors, tweezers, gelatinous tactile implants, luminous-colored cold packs for post-surgical swelling and all sorts and styles of wraps and bandages. A strolling violinist and accordion player were doing a rendition of '*Spanish Eyes*'; at one of the booths a lab-coated man was cauterizing a chicken breast while another performed laser surgery on a slab of meat.

Matt's presentation was a great success. He was confident enough to lead in with a joke and lucky enough to get a laugh. Not once did he have to recover with a lame remark like: 'don't try this at home, folks.' Kali had sat patiently in the back row, trying not to gape at the terrifying images being projected. She watched her husband's dark head bobbing at the lectern while twelve hundred surgeons—a sea of surgical genius, the heal-with-steel set—stared with finger-twitching interest.

Afterwards, she had lunch with Matt in the hotel restaurant, though he was flying high with his success and they were constantly interrupted by other surgeons wanting to talk to him about his research. Kali listened with a politely fixed smile for as long as she could, then excused herself to find other diversions.

It was Matt's moment—she needed to let him run with it, and just get out of his way.

She didn't have much enthusiasm for the Cable Car Museum or the simulated earthquake on Pier Thirty-Nine. And she'd been warned away from a nostalgic return to Marina's old haunt, Haight-Ashbury, which wasn't what it used to be of course. She passed some time at the Disney Store, waffling over whether to buy Harry a talking tree stump, a set of wind-up dinosaurs or all the animal friends of Pocahontas, until the endless loop of '*It's a Small World*' drove her back out into the street. She strolled up and down San Francisco's windy hilly streets for the rest of the afternoon, looking for something else to buy. Eventually, she ended up at Nordstrom, circling four floors of merchandise on the spiral escalator. At the end of the day, all she bought was a musical miniature cable car for Harry. She was definitely losing her shopping mojo.

~~~

"Come over here and see this view, Matt."

"You mean, see this view and come." He followed her to the window and slipped his arm around her waist. Since their inflight adventure, and now that the boiling debate over Britta had settled to a simmer, Matt had become quite amorous: the proverbial octopus-man, lunging for Kali when they were alone in elevators, sliding his hands over her thighs in the hotel Jacuzzi, groping her boobs in the back of Ubers. It was a lot like the first days after they met, but she was a bit suspicious as to the source of this sudden *amour*. She imagined herself being interviewed on some daytime talk show. 'What is the secret of my successful marriage to a younger man?' She would smile cryptically and say: 'I know how to ask for a razor outlet, in Swedish.'

On their last night in San Francisco, the Millers lay in bed together, being spoons, after some mind-bindingly great sex. Matt was the greatest spoon in the world, Kali thought happily. She loved his smooth, solid body; he was always warm, like a trusty furnace. It looked as though things were going to be a lot better between them. And, until they opened the front door of 67 Pine Beach Road later the next day, there was no reason to think otherwise.

# Chapter 28

*'All happy families are alike, but an unhappy family is unhappy after its own fashion,'* wrote Tolstoy, at the beginning of *Anna Karenina. 'Everything had gone wrong in the Oblonsky household.'* Kali would have occasion to recall and ponder these opening lines many times after she and Matt returned to Belmont Shore.

"Now, before you totally freak out," was the first thing Marina said, heading them off at the door, "remember that I was just trying to do my best for your kid."

Kali held Harry tightly in her arms: a hiccupping, sniffling bundle of misery. He'd come down with chicken-pox while they were in San Francisco, but Marina and Boris didn't want to worry her, so they didn't mention it when Kali called. Harry's eyes were crusted over, and his little face so obliterated by the oozing pox that there wasn't a clear spot to plant the many kisses Kali so desperately wanted to give. As soon as she saw him, she'd burst into tears. Matt immediately got on his cell to the children's hospital, demanding to talk to the medical resident on call, and then an ophthalmologist.

"Where's Dad?" Kali asked, as she jiggled Harry in her arms.

"He's out driving around, letting off steam. This whole scene really messed with his mind. He was having flashbacks."

"What messed with his mind? Harry's chicken pox?"

"Oh, no, that's just a bummer. He loves the little ankle-biter." Marina avoided her daughter's eyes, fiddling with her reading glasses, then pushing them up on top of her head, and into her long grey hair. She sniffed.

"Do you have a cold, Mother?"

"No. It's been hot as hell here this week, that's all. My nose is stuffed."

"I don't get it, not any of this." Kali sighed. "And where's Britta?"

"Don't freak out, okay? Everything's totally cool." Marina didn't look like it was cool, whatever 'it' was. "We had a difference of opinion, that's all. She had some sort of meltdown, flipped her wig and split."

"She left? Went out? She went to the store? Down to the beach?" Kali stared at her mother.

"Oh, I don't think she's out shopping. She's been gone for three days."

"What? Why didn't you didn't tell us!?"

"We didn't want to spoil your vacay. Your dad and I handled it. Both you and your sister had chickenpox, and you two survived."

Harry was looking up at Kali in silent misery. "Cookie," he said.

"Did you hear that?" Kali looked at Harry, amazed. "I think he said cookie." She looked up at her mother. "Is that all that you and Dad fed him, by chance?"

"Of course not." Marina looked away, not meeting her daughter's eyes.

Kali didn't press the point, grateful that at least her parents probably hadn't given Harry pot, or smoked up around him. Although poor Harry looked terrible—he even had chicken-pox inside his tiny ears—he didn't seem all that uncomfortable and had settled into Kali's arms, resting his head against her shoulder, hiccupping occasionally.

"So, what was the argument about? With Britta?"

"Your goddamned cloth diapers, that's what. She wanted to use disposables the minute you guys were out of here. But I said, hey Britta, that's not cool. You can't sneak around behind my daughter's back. You know Kali wants you to use cloth diapers, though God only knows why. And who's going to pay for disposable diapers? If you want to use them, you can pay for them yourself. Me and Boris are on a fixed income.'"

"So, what did she say?"

"I don't know, something in Swedish. Might as well be Swahili, for all I know. Rude, for sure. She's really something, that chick. Where did you find her?"

"I didn't find her. Matt did."

"She's *kurva*, know what that is? Ask your dad. His mother used to call me that. She was a real piece of work, your grandmother."

Kali knew what *kurva* meant, in Ukrainian: a slut.

"Well, anyway," Marina continued, warming to the subject of Britta, "at first she used the cloth diapers on Harry, bitching and moaning the entire time. She didn't do a single load of laundry. Well, those dirty diapers were starting to stink, and I wasn't going to wash them. I had four years of washing cloth diapers for you girls and I still can't wrap my head around that. So, I told Britta to give her melon a shake and go do the fucking laundry. That's when she packed her bags and split, calling me rude names in Swedish."

Matt came in, to start digging through his medical bag. "Where's Britta? I need her to pick up a prescription for Harry's eye infection and we need calamine lotion for his pox." He found what he was looking for and screwed together the parts of his ophthalmoscope.

"She's gone," Kali said, wincing as she waited for his reaction.

"What do you mean gone?" He flicked on the light of the ophthalmoscope, then peered into Harry's eyes, gently pulling up one eyelid, then the other.

"She quit," Marina said. "Skipped out. No notice, nothing."

"They had an argument about Harry's diapers," Kali said. "Britta wanted to use disposable ones, and Mom told her she couldn't."

"All I said, was that if she wanted them, she could pay for them herself." Marina folded her arms, defensively. "The diapers were just an excuse. She likely found another gig, for better bread."

"Well, somebody has to go out to get this medication for Harry," Matt said, all business-like. "Let's get him into a bath. Poor little fellow. When did the pox come out?"

"The day you left," Marina said. "He's been up all night, every night. Boris is whacked out. Me too."

"Well, we need to find Britta," Matt said. "We can't just let her wander around the streets."

"Don't kid yourself," Marina said, "that girl knows how to take care of herself."

"It's not only that," Matt said irritably, "we can't manage here without a nanny. We've both got to work tomorrow." He gave Marina a look indicating that he thought all of this was exactly what he had expected to happen, with her in charge. He then started bustling around, getting baking soda for Harry's bath and phoning the pharmacy to get someone to deliver Harry's eye ointment.

Marina settled down on the sofa, obviously relieved that the house, Harry and Britta were no longer her problems. "So, Kali," she said, cozily, "what did you score in San Fran? Anything groovy?"

"Just a music box for Harry. It plays *It's a Small World*."

"Nothing for yourself?"

"I'm still too fat to look at clothes. And I don't need anything else." Kali was amazed that the conversation was expected to slip so easily into trivialities, after all the drama. She continued to cuddle Harry, but Marina seemed to have forgotten that he was there. Her bag was already packed, waiting beside the front door. "Bet you can't wait to get out of here," Kali said.

"It's been a bit of a drag. But hey, that's babies… tell me about it." Marina checked her cell. "Don't freak out about Harry. He's a tough little fucker. But I wouldn't go running out to find that crazy Swedish bitch if I were you. Oh yeah, there's a leak in the back of your house. How you get water damage in SoCal has got to be one of life's greatest mysteries. The carpet's soggy under the window in what's her name's bedroom, and it stinks in there. It gave her something else to bitch and moan about. She wanted to sleep in your room, but I said no way since I didn't know what personal shit you guys have got stashed in there."

"Thanks," Kali said. "Thanks for everything, Mom."

A car horn sounded outside. "That's my old man!" Clearly, she couldn't wait to blow out of there. Marina got up off the sofa, grabbed her bag and gave Kali a kiss. "When we said we were down with staying here, we didn't know we'd have a sick baby on our hands. But you didn't either—I get that. I just wish you'd given us the 4-1-1 that your nanny was some kind of far-out, wing-nut psycho."

~~~

"The important thing is to get Britta back before she winds up in some kind of trouble, or gets deported," Matt said after Kali's parents had gone.

*Deported? What a great idea*, Kali thought. "Why would we ever want her back, after what she did? Quitting without notice? Abandoning poor little sick Harry while we were away?" she said.

"There's two sides to every story. Your mother can put people off without meaning to, and she's got an attitude. Plus, you never know what she's talking about. If we don't know what she's talking about half of the time, imagine a foreigner trying to understand her."

"Well, she's ten thousand times more helpful than your mother. Beth's seen Harry exactly once since he was born."

"She lives on the east coast, for Christ's sake. Leave her out of this."

"Well, Britta called my mother some kind of bad name."

"Nobody claimed Britta's a saint."

"She sure looks one, in that picture she's got, with the candles on her head and that white dress."

"What picture?"

"The one she had on her dresser. I assume she took it with her when she ran out of here."

"That's not Britta," Matt frowned.

"What do you mean? And how do you know? Have you been in there a lot?"

"Look, let's not fight, please. My point is that Britta may have had a good reason for leaving."

"Dirty diapers are a good reason for abandoning a helpless baby?"

"Kali, we love Harry, and we love his shit. But we can't expect everyone else to. Like I said, there's probably more to it than that."

"I bet she won't even want to come back."

"We should at least give her the option."

"I'll have to think about it."

"It's you who's going to have to find another nanny. My next rotation is going to be a killer. Anyway, I have an idea where she might be. Remember Gosta Lindgren? He was the micro-fellow at Long Beach Memorial last year."

"I don't remember anyone named Gosta Lindgren."

"Anyway, he knows Britta's family. If she isn't staying with him, she probably called him. At least he'll know where she is."

"I can find someone better than Britta, someone who isn't a deserter, who isn't going to bail at the first little problem. There's lots of good people looking for work. We could get someone who could clean up around here, and do some cooking, too."

"You want to spend another thousand dollars on the agency fee?"

"We could advertise, we don't need an agency."

"What? On Craig's list? Hire some whack job?"

"Lots of people I know found good nannies that way." It wasn't exactly true, Kali thought, feeling a bit ashamed… it wasn't true at all.

"Well, it's your decision. I can't take time off to help you interview, but I *will* review all candidates. You'll have to stay here with Harry and work from home until you find someone. But go ahead, it's your law practice."

"You don't think Britta would go to some hostel, do you?" Kali suddenly pictured her stuffed into a dumpster in an alley or being jostled about in a line-up of homeless people, waiting for a blanket, socks, and a bowl of soup. She was some mother's daughter, after all. There had to be a pleasant, gentle woman back home in Sweden looking at the Lucia picture, her eyes filling, wondering why she no longer heard from her beautiful daughter.

Kali swallowed, suddenly overcome with remorse. On the other hand, maybe Marina was right. Maybe Britta was streetwise and cunning and very well able to look after herself. Perhaps right now she was rolling her eyes and telling funny stories about the Millers' small domestic traumas, sitting in a bar in Belmont Shore, surrounded by her Swedish *Meet Up* friends. "I hate to bring this up now, but can you go see about the dampness in her room?" Kali asked. "My mom says there's some kind of leak under the window."

"Leak? It hasn't rained for months." Matt looked so exhausted, Kali felt like crying.

"Never mind, I'll take care of it," she said. "It's not your problem."

"Thanks, Kal," he said, as he gave her a quick kiss. "I'm so tired I can't even see straight, just like poor little Harry. And I've got be at the hospital by five tomorrow."

~~~

At the back of Britta's room, Kali saw what her mother was talking about: a wet stain on the carpet. Not knowing what else to do for the moment, she went into Britta's bathroom for a towel. She searched through the cupboards and grabbed a greying hand towel that she spread out over the stain. Then, she couldn't resist the urge to take a quick peek to see if Britta left anything behind, some clue as to whether she was gone for good or just making a statement.

All of Britta's clothes, jewelry and make-up were gone. So were her photographs, the red and yellow flag, and—Kali pulled open the bottom drawer –so were the '*Free Skane!*' pamphlets and the bundle of letters. Only garbage and dust balls remained for Kali to clean up, whenever she found the time.

She should feel relieved, she told herself. She'd wanted to get rid of Britta from the start. But all she felt was panic. Tomorrow was Monday. Things would have piled up in the office during her week off: faxes, e-mails, memos, voicemails from irate clients who weren't going to get any less irate when they were told that Kali would be out for a few more days to find a new nanny and fix a problem in the back wall of her house.

Well, there was no other solution, Kali thought. She would stay home with Harry and manage her practice from Belmont Shore until they found the right nanny. She was intelligent, strong and capable, and she had an amazing assistant. Harry was just one tiny baby; Kali could handle him without help. She'd had him on her own lots of times: weekends and evenings when Matt was on call. Besides, he was her son; he was part of her. He would intuitively understand her fragile state and make allowances for it; they would communicate without words. A day with Harry would be great fun, even if he had that horrible chicken-pox.

# Chapter 29

"Da da. Da! Da, da... dada?" Harry called, hopefully, from the nursery. "Day." Pause. "Dee." Puzzled by his mother's lack of response, he continued. "Eh? Eh?"

Kali had given him a bottle less than an hour before. He should have finished it and drifted back into a fragrant, milky sleep. She was desperate for another half hour of sleep to shake off her Ambien-induced confusion. She wasn't even sure what day it was.

"EH?" Harry demanded, much louder this time.

Kali still couldn't bring herself to move. She wanted to weep with exhaustion. Her head ached from a night of interrupted half-sleep; she felt blurred, erased, colored outside the lines. But Harry sounded so perky, rebounding quickly from his illness. He wanted to get out and get going! He was not an introspective baby who could amuse himself for hours with a set of nesting toys or just playing with his toes. He was turbo-charged, fuel-injected: a full tank of gas that had to be used up before he would sleep again. As soon as he saw her, he would start shoving toys in her face, expecting her to play with him and repeat rhymes about bunnies, mice and chickens.

Matt had left for the hospital hours ago. As she'd lain in bed, eyes closed, listening to him stumble around to find clean socks and shorts, Kali fantasized about putting his evil pager down on a hard surface and smashing it with a sledgehammer, forever silencing its nattering beep.

"Eh? Ya?" Harry called. "No mo yay ..." he added, mournfully. Then, he was anxious again. "Beebee! Beebee. Bay! Ba-ay? By-eye." His voice trailed off, ending in a sob of frustration.

*Get up!* Kali told herself. She could tell that he was standing in his crib, rattling the rails. He let out a series of pissed-off howls. "Dow! Dow! Ahoo! Ahoo!" This was followed by a single loud squawk of rage, then a few fake coughs. Oh! Oh! Radio!" Kali was amazed. He couldn't have said 'radio', could he?

With a groan, she flung aside the comforter and swung her legs over the side of the bed. She dug a soiled pair of sweatpants (Matt's) out of the laundry basket, groped through the bottom drawer of their dresser for a sweatshirt, not caring whether the top matched the bottom, or if either of them fit. That she could get them on was all she cared about. She couldn't find a bra, so decided that underwear was optional at this point. "I'm coming, Harry!" she called, staggering into the bathroom to splash water on her face and pull a brush through her hair. If she didn't have to go to work, she wouldn't have to do much else in terms of grooming. How much simpler her body maintenance would be! She could let herself go completely, become a total slob. All the of brushing, tweezing, clipping, shaving, softening and dyeing parts of her body rituals would be reduced to two quick brush-offs. Minimalist. A hairbrush and a toothbrush. Simpler than most men, since she wouldn't have to shave.

Avoiding her reflection in the mirror, and knowing she looked like 'death warmed over' as her mother liked to say, she was glad there was no Swedish nymphet there to make her look even worse by comparison. It was a relief that Britta gone. Kali began to feel better, more positive, cheerful even. She was back in control and would be an awesome work-from-home mom! Harry, hearing her in the bathroom, was excited, rattling his crib rails like a convict banging a tin cup along the bars.

"So, what do you want to do, Kiddo?" Kali asked, standing in the doorway to his room. From behind the chicken-pox scabs, he grinned at her so hard it seemed like his round little face might split.

"Up. Up!" He had three and a half milk-white teeth now. He was a chubby, endearing baby, and she should be delighted at having this precious unplanned day with him, which she was! Of course! "Way oh? Eh oh?" Harry grabbed hold of the crib rails, rocking back and forth, impatient with her inertia.

As Kali lifted him—a warm, sodden, smelly bundle—she felt a twang of lower back pain. Since he had already outgrown his change table (what a waste of money!) she lay him down on the carpet and peeled off his soggy sleeper and soaking-wet diaper. As Kali lifted the top off the diaper pail, she was almost bowled over by the stench. Marina hadn't been kidding. What if the ones at the bottom (now over a week old) were mold-infested? Or crawling with maggots? She stuffed the newest one on top, and slammed the lid shut. That particular mess would have to wait.

Harry was crawling happily out of his room, delighted to be free of his sleeper and diaper. "Just where do you think you're going, Buster?" Kali hooked him under one arm and carried him into the bathroom, with another stab of back pain. She put him on the mat beside the tub and turned on the water for a bath. What had happened to her creamy-skinned, silky baby, she wondered? The chicken-pox were everywhere, even in his nose. She dumped half a box of baking soda into the tub and let him splash around for a while before indulging him with an array of squeeze toys, ducks, dinosaurs and frogs, a floating flotilla of small watercraft. She tried not to get irritated by his splashing which increased in intensity until he was sending tidal waves onto the bathroom floor. It was only water, and could easily be cleaned up, she reminded herself. She would let Harry have his fun.

After ten more minutes, she plucked Harry out of the tub, dried him, and dabbed calamine lotion on his pox. He didn't care for the idea of clothes—she had to wrestle with him and finally distract him with a carrot squeeze toy as she got him into a playsuit. Dressing a robust, uncooperative baby should be a rodeo event, she thought, like steer-wrestling or hog-tying. Hogs and steer might be bigger, but they weren't nearly as loud. Size had nothing to do with power.

By nine o'clock, Harry had thrown a waffle, a handful of Cheerios and a sippy cup full of orange juice to the floor—holding his arm straight over the side of his high chair and locking gazes with Kali as he did, as if to taunt her.

Kali called Alicia to say she wouldn't be back in the office for a couple more days, until they found a new nanny. She still hadn't decided what to do. Should she call Gosta Lindgren to find Britta and beg her to come back or start the rounds of agency and internet searches? Alicia made a lame effort to sound empathetic, but there was no way she could truly understand or forgive her. Alicia was clearly pissed. Kali asked her to e-mail over anything urgent or call anytime if someone needed her and couldn't be put off for a few days. Potochnik hadn't called, Alicia assured her. So far, there hadn't been a peep out of him. For this small mercy, Kali was hugely thankful.

Alicia would be bored after a week with nothing to do but filing and would be classifying everything on Kali's desk as 'urgent' and in need of Kali's immediate attention. But Kali wouldn't be able to look at any of it while Harry was awake.

Next, she dialed Matt's pager. She only wanted to say hi and report that Harry was back to his usual energy-level, and that she was doing great herself. A nurse called back immediately. "Dr. Miller is scrubbed," she told Kali, crisply, "was it anything important?" Kali admitted it wasn't, feeling guilty and foolish for taking up the nurse's time when some patient's life was at stake, acutely aware that the O.R. staff regularly made jokes about Dr. Miller's 'domestic trauma pager.' She knew, because Matt had told her. And she suspected he had come up with the term himself.

Kali let Harry empty all the kitchen cupboards, bang the pots and pans around, and try a few on his head. Then she sat him down on the kitchen counter to let him splash around in the sink, then fill his bottles, the microwave dishes and other containers with water, which he then dumped onto the floor. After that, he busied himself with Mr. Potato Head—throwing noses, ears, eyes and lips from the toy basket all over the living room.

Kali mopped up the water from the kitchen counter and floor, collected the parts of Mr. Potato Head, and refolded the clean laundry that Harry had tipped out of the hamper. She struggled to fish the pot lids out from under the sofa with a broom handle, swept up the Cheerios and washed the sticky spilled juice from the floor. It wasn't even ten o'clock and Kali had already she'd run out of ideas for amusing him. She called Harry's pediatrician to ask if it was okay to take him outside. It was bright and sunny, not at all cold. A walk would clear her head and give her a chance to consider what to do about a care-giver for Harry. The nurse practitioner said it was all right to take him out, but to bring him back inside if he seemed bothered by the sunlight. "And keep him away from other children," the woman added, "until all the pox crust over."

"Oh? How long will that take?"

"About two weeks."

Two weeks of keeping Harry in quarantine? Avoiding public libraries, drop-in centers, playgrounds, swimming pools and parks? No wonder Britta had quit! As Kali was gathering up the remaining toys, Matt called to say he would be starting a surgery at four and not to expect him for dinner. She shouldn't bother to make him anything either; he would just grab something in the hospital cafeteria. Make dinner? Right! She barely had time to wipe her ass! Microwaving fish sticks was even beyond her.

It took almost an hour to pack up the bottles, diapers, wipes and everything else she thought Harry could possibly want or need during their walk. Once packed up, Kali struggled to push Harry in his Perego stroller through the mess she had once imagined would be a lovely, bountiful garden. Only a cheerful field of dandelions had popped up, and all the neighbors would be grumbling about their gardens and yards becoming cross-pollinated and infested by the Millers' mess.

Kali hoisted Harry over the retaining wall, as she'd seen Matt do, feeling another stab of back pain—this one deeper and more intense than any so far. The stroller wheels immediately jammed in the sand, jolting Harry, making him whine and whimper. Kali was sweating, desperate to get to the boardwalk.

A mother and her toddler approached, took one look at Harry's pox-riddled face and hurried past. Harry didn't seem offended by the slight, but Kali adjusted his hat to shade his face, and tugged the ear flaps down into place on either side of his head. He pulled at the ties of the hat and whimpered, trying to push it off. Frustrated, he tilted his head back to sniff the beach air, reaching out a chubby finger to point at a seagull swooping and diving overhead. "Baby!" he said. He didn't seem at all bothered by the sunlight, though Kali had brought the adorable Baby Boo-Boo sunglasses, and a bigger hat for him, just in case.

At last they reached the wooden planks of the boardwalk. Sand had blown across the boards, filling in the knot holes and dusting it to look like a sprinkling of cinnamon sugar. Kali's stomach rumbled as a reminder that she hadn't eaten anything, though it was almost noon. She was craving the latte and toasted bagel that she had every morning in her quiet office, with its sliver of ocean view.

This is it, she told herself, this is what it means to be a stay-at-home mom. Wake up, and imagine you'll ever get a chance to even smell the coffee. How did women do it, she wondered—look after not just one child, but a whole bunch of them, clean the house, do all the shopping, make three meals, and manage a horny husband at the end of the day? How had her mother, space cadet that she was, ever managed it all? Kali was developing a growing respect for Marina!

She dug through the diaper bag until she found a teething biscuit—the only food she'd thought to bring—and bit into it. She pushed Harry along the boardwalk, feeling guilty about being there on a Monday, as if she were playing hooky. She was a nine-to-fiver; it was in her blood. The idea of being a slightly wacky, creative, indulgent stay-at-home mother had a lot of appeal, but she knew she would want all that, plus a six-figure salary, and a socially acceptable ATTORNEY label to stick on her forehead when it was advantageous.

Harry seemed to enjoy the bumpy rhythm of the planks as they trundled along, and was soon asleep, his head lolling over the side of the padded Perego, snoring with soft whistling sounds. It was amazing what contorted positions babies could sleep in, Kali thought. If she slept like that, she'd be seeing a chiropractor for months! She stuffed the rest of the teething biscuit into her mouth and took a clean diaper out of the bag to fold into a loose cushion which she wedged under Harry's head to give it more support. As he slept, his lips and tongue moved rhythmically, sucking on a phantom bottle. The diaper bag clanked gently as it dangled from the back of the stroller.

As she walked, Kali's fatigue began to catch up with her. She still felt dim and woozy from the sleeping pills. She'd taken a double dose the night before, afraid she would be up the whole night, worrying over what to do about Britta and about how she was going to take care of Harry, totally on her own.

# Chapter 30

The thought of interviewing nannies exhausted Kali more than the sleepless nights. And there was the fee the agencies charged: the equivalent of a month's pay for the nanny. They'd paid it for Britta, who came to them from an agency, even though Matt had known her family back in Sweden. Money was always a worry, it seemed.

Kali lifted the brim of Harry's hat and peered at his dear little face, smeared with bright pink calamine lotion. He adored Britta, and wasn't that all that really mattered? So what if she was a bit of a slob, and her housekeeping and cooking were less than spectacular? And, with a little more penny-pinching, maybe they could afford a house cleaning service every other week, to help Britta with the daily chores. Wouldn't it be worth it to spend a little more for Harry's happiness? And so what if she was a Skanish separatist? She was in the United States. Wasn't she entitled to hold whatever political opinions she wanted about her homeland? It wasn't as though she would be causing any trouble, was it? Her anger at Britta was fading by the minute. 'Swedes could never be said to be lazy or lacking in entrepreneurial spirit,' according to *Swedish in Minutes!*

'Don't be an idiot,' Kali's wicked side argued, 'now is your chance to hire somebody really ugly! Fat, with warts on her nose, bad teeth, and less hair than you have!' Kali walked on, pushing Harry in his stroller, at war with herself.

All of the boardwalk's benches were occupied by the unemployed, vagrants or homeless, reading, mumbling to themselves, or dozing in the sun. No one was likely to move over to give up a seat for Kali. A group of joggers pounded past, then a woman with a pair of greyhounds whizzed by, followed by a long line of intense, Spandex-clad cyclists.

Kali wheeled Harry over to the edge of the boardwalk, near the lifeguard station, and sat down on the planks, pulling her knees to her chin. Not having anything else to do, and not wanting to rouse Harry with any sudden movement, she scanned the ground in front of her, searching for bits of sea glass. It was one of her favorite pastimes: a totally useless hobby since there was nothing much one could do with it, once collected. There were already three jars of it, lined up along the Millers' kitchen counter.

If she quit practicing law, Kali thought, she would have time to ponder the mysteries of sea glass and a host of other small domestic conundrums, as well. Or would she have time for any reflection at all? She pictured life in a one-bedroom apartment—probably all they could probably afford, in any nice safe part of Los Angeles, without her income until Matt's practice got going. With two or more screaming kids, Matt would be bellowing for quiet, as he tried to write research papers to get his tenure at a teaching hospital. A greasy plastic tablecloth would be on the kitchen table; toys, diapers and cheesy bottles everywhere.

A lifeguard climbed up into his chair to scan the shoreline from behind his Ray Bans. Kali knew he wouldn't even see her, or that she would vaguely register as a middle-aged lady with a baby—nobody worth hitting on. He wouldn't be able to see the sagging boobs, varicose veins or stretch marks from where he sat, but he would assume those. Maybe he would think Kali was the baby's grandmother, if he thought about her at all, which was unlikely. How had she managed to slip so suddenly from youth into middle age? Wasn't there some stage in between? And if so, where had it gone?

Harry stirred in his stroller and fussed a little, rubbing his eyes with his fists. Was he being bothered by the sunlight? Kali worried, as he filled his diaper. She could almost see radiating wavy lines coming from it, like cartoonists used to depict something stinky. But there was nowhere to change him. She could hardly lay him down on the gritty boardwalk or the sand and if she used his blanket, what would she put over him to keep him warm? The nearest public restroom was at least a half-hour walk, and it probably wouldn't have a changing table, and would be filthy as well.

Maybe Harry could be coaxed back to sleep. Without much hope, Kali jiggled his stroller, trying not to seem anxious. Babies were like sharks: once they smelled your fear they'd tear you to pieces, emotionally. The jiggling irritated him. He screwed up his face and let out a shriek, his eyes glistening with rage. Kali hurried to offer him a teething biscuit, but that only seemed to annoy him more. He shoved it back at her, shaking his head and howling. The bottle she offered got the same reaction. He began struggling to get out of his stroller, straining at his seat belt, arching his back and screaming.

Kali stared at him, terrified. He was so loud it made her stomach churn; it made her sweat and grind her teeth; it made her want to throw up her own teething biscuit. "Okay," she pleaded, "calm down. Please, Harry. Don't get so mad." She decided to make a run for home. She took the brake off the stroller and started to walk fast, taking long strides as she pushed it. The diaper bag clanked as it hit the back of the stroller, infuriating Harry even more. She broke into a run, feverishly wheeling her screaming son along the boardwalk, the diaper bag swinging and clattering as Harry flung himself back and forth in a panic to break free of his restraints. Everyone they passed stared, shook their heads, and clucked in disapproval, totally judgmental. Kali wanted to scream at them to mind their own damned business!

The stroller wheels wedged into the sand again, as she finally reached the end of the boardwalk. Ignoring her intense back pain, she bent over and lifted it— Harry, bags and all. Her feet churned up the sand as she plowed along, desperate to reach home. Then, she was abruptly confronted by the Millers' retaining wall. She'd forgotten that she would have to climb back up over it! Harry kicked and waved his arms, hysterical now. Kali fumbled to undo his seat belt, then lifted him out of the stroller which immediately clunked over into the sand.

With Harry flailing like a windmill under one arm, Kali struggled to unhook the diaper bag from the stroller. She would have to come back and retrieve the Perego later; there was no way she could carry everything now. Panting and exhausted, she finally made it to the back door of the house, with Harry still screaming. As Kali charged inside, he projectile-vomited formula all over the floor, the wood molding, the kitchen appliances and the wall.

After hustling Harry into his room, she changed his diaper and squirted banana-favored Tempra into his mouth. Was his fever rising again? she worried. What if the strain of the walk had pushed him over the edge, into a more serious illness? Debating whether this was an emergency that merited paging Matt, she sat in the glider with Harry, making soothing sounds, futilely trying to calm him down and reason with him, until his thrashing and hysterics subsided, and he miraculously fell into a sudden, deep sleep.

Gently, Kali put him into his crib, then crept out to get a bucket and sponge to tackle the formula that seemed to be everywhere and was quickly drying into cement on the walls and floor. That done, she remembered the stroller. Grabbing the nursery monitor, she turned it up to full volume and hurried outside, leaving the monitor on the back step. She plunged through the backyard to discover that, just as she'd feared, the Perego had been stolen. Six hundred dollars! They couldn't afford another one!

Sniffling with self-pity, she hurried back into the house and threw herself onto the sofa. She checked her cell to see there were twelve missed calls from Alicia and seven recorded messages. She grabbed her laptop from the coffee table. It was time to go online and start the search for a new nanny. She hated Britta for abandoning them, after all her pretenses of loving Harry so much—her little cucumber, her little prince! What a crock of shit! As soon as the going got tough, Britta got going. Kali would never take her back. Never! Not even if she crawled up their front walk over broken sea glass or had to stand in-line at soup kitchens for the rest of her life, before (hopefully) being deported. There were some things a mother just couldn't forgive!

# Chapter 31

## Bell

Bell, Matt observed drily, seemed to fulfill most of Kali's requirements. She was an older lady: short, squat and no-nonsense, and she could clean like nobody's business. She began with an attack on the kitchen cupboards, reorganizing them so efficiently that the space that had before been inadequate, now seemed cavernous. With tight-lipped determination, Bell scrubbed the cupboard shelves to a dazzling whiteness, then lined them with cheery checkered shelf paper that she purchased on her own time. Only after a great deal of protest and obvious extreme embarrassment did she finally accept reimbursement from Kali. The Millers' few battle-scarred pots and pans sat mournfully, lost in the vast amounts of gleaming paper-lined storage space

The oven and refrigerator sparkled, inside and out, and Bell fished out the crud that fell between the stove and the kitchen counter. The burners were neatly lined with tin foil to catch any drips and Bell even scoured the kitchen trash can, disinfecting it with Pine Sol and leaving it out on the deck for an afternoon to air.

Next, Bell assaulted the bathrooms and bedrooms. Kali came home from work to find all their towels neatly rolled, tight as yule logs, stacked and grouped by color in the linen closet. The face cloths were formed into mini yule logs. 'What the hell?' was Matt's only comment as he opened the closet door, dripping wet from his shower in urgent need of a towel.

'I think I've died and gone to heaven,' Kali smiled as she unrolled a towel and handed it to him.

In Harry's room, all of his little shirts and sweaters were neatly pressed and hung up on hangers (on hangers!). His sleepers were professionally folded (had Bell worked for a dry cleaner or a clothing store?) and organized in the bottom drawer of his bureau. Like a bloodhound, Bell tracked down every one of Harry's tiny missing socks, neatly balled them into pairs, then lined them up in a plastic tray—that she bought herself—tucked inside his top drawer. Matt's jockey shorts, boxers and briefs received a similar treatment. Bell was Marie Kondo on steroids!

"Why do I need some stranger snooping through my shorts, checking for skid marks?" Matt complained as he undid the rather complicated fold, so he could put on a pair, one Saturday morning. Kali didn't bother to point out that he never would've complained if it had been Britta going through his underwear with such dedication.

There were tight hospital corners on their bed, made with freshly ironed (*ironed!*) sheets; their pillows were plumped, the comforters fluffed and freshened, beaten free of long-accumulated dust and hung out to air in the ocean breeze. Bell chased the dust balls out from under every stick of furniture and assaulted the cracks in the sofas and chairs with the Dustbuster, diligently sucking up ancient cookie crumbs, lint and (mostly blonde) hair. The whole house gleamed... it shone... it sparkled... it smelled of bleach, Vanish, Fantastik and Mr. Muscle. The toilets flowed with efficient gurgling, the drains at last freed of sludge.

And Harry was miserable.

"He hates her," Matt said to Kali, under his breath, watching their son kick and flail as Bell, her face red as a tomato, struggled to wedge him into his high chair and buckle the safety belt across his writhing and arching body. In desperation, she put a plastic bowl on her head and did a clumsy little dance, trying to amuse and distract him. But her performance infuriated him even more.

"She's an honest, decent person. It's the change that's upsetting him," Kali said. "Bell is someone new—he's not used to her. Give it time." They were in their bedroom, having just come home from a dinner given by Matt's faculty in honor of a visiting professor from New Zealand. According to Bell, who was wringing her hands, goggle-eyed with anxiety when the Millers returned, Harry had cried the entire time they were out, then thrown up his dinner, and finally fallen asleep just minutes before they got home.

"Any new nanny is going to be an adjustment," Kali added.

"She's been here for two weeks, and he doesn't like her any better today than he did the first time he saw her."

Matt slid his shorts down, then kicked them up behind him with one foot, deftly catching them in mid-air before tossing them over his head, basketball style, into the laundry basket. "And have you ever asked yourself how does she manage to get so much cleaning done? I mean, what is Harry doing while she's busy tying my underwear in  knots?"

Kali was silent for a moment. "I have to admit, I have wondered about that."

"He's so active, we can't let him out of our sight for a second. So how does she do it? She could be doing anything to him—locking him in a closet or tying him up outside on the deck or God knows what else."

"She wouldn't do anything like that!"

"How would we ever know? It's not like the little guy can tell us."

"I know she's not being cruel to him. She's a kind and decent person. A mother can tell. Look at how hard she tries—putting that bowl on her head."

"That was one of the most disturbing things I've ever seen."

"It's sad, really. She just doesn't seem to have much of a way with babies. Her references were excellent, though. The children apparently adored her, where she worked before. The mother said her son was really upset when Bell left. And she didn't have to admit what happened with Harry tonight. She could have told us that everything was fine. We wouldn't have known the difference."

"Okay, but just think what the house looks like when both of us are here with Harry. Do either of us have time to buff the bathroom  faucets?"

"Maybe we're just disorganized... or lazy."

"And maybe Harry hates Bell for a reason."

A week later, Bell was gone. They didn't have to fire her: she quit, sobbing that she'd never been so insulted in her life. Never had she met a baby who wouldn't let her near him. She didn't know why he didn't trust her. She was deeply offended and disgraced, she said, her eyes full, her hand over her heart. She just couldn't take it anymore!

# Bing

Kali believed that Bing just got off on the wrong foot. They'd hired her, then asked her to babysit on a Saturday night before she officially started the job. She was supposed to be there by seven; by nine she hadn't arrived.

Finally, she showed up at nine-thirty, distraught about the Uber ride, claiming the driver had tried to molest her taking her miles out of her way then threatening her with a knife. She was terrified, she said, dabbing at her eyes with a sodden tissue. She only took the Uber because she fell asleep in the afternoon and forgot to set her alarm, so she didn't have time to take the bus all the way to Belmont Shore. She didn't have a car. The Millers hadn't asked if she even had a license.

Matt answered the door when she finally showed up and explained to her that if she couldn't be on time for a babysitting job and couldn't call to let them know, they couldn't possibly trust her to look after Harry. What was she liable to do? Forget him in the park one day? At that, Bing burst into tears, begging to see Kali to explain. A woman's thing, Kali sighed, coming into the room. She'd been hiding in the kitchen while Matt did the dirty deed of firing Bing before she started. After more discussion and stern warnings from Matt, they agreed to give Bing the job, on probation.

She had a number of personal problems, the root of which was her sponsorship into the United States of her entire extended family, all of it now up in the air. Her father had a job as a school crossing guard while her mother stayed home, hiding out in an apartment in Reseda, and looking after Bing's niece, while the girl's mother worked illegally in a doughnut shop. Bing's brother was in a car accident; her older sister was regularly beaten by her alcoholic husband.

On Bing's third day of work, she called Kali at the office and begged her to come home. Bing's grandmother had jumped off the Veteran's Memorial Pier. They'd pulled her from the water and managed to save her from drowning, but she had a concussion and a broken rib. Bing had to go right away to the hospital, then look after her grandmother full-time. There was no way she could work a full-time job.

## Lavinia

Lavinia was a hairstylist by trade, but she also had been a short-order cook and managed a factory somewhere that produced canvas tote bags. The phone number she gave Kali to call for a reference seemed to be permanently busy; a day later it was out of service. She had a phenomenal number of friends, acquaintances and relatives. At the end of her first day with the Millers, Kali came home to find a dozen cake plates in the dishwasher which were never explained to her satisfaction.

Lavinia asked for the next day off. There'd been some kind of accident in her cousin's apartment: a china cabinet had fallen over with lots of broken glass to be cleaned up and her cousin was afraid of cutting herself. Also, she had to go to Immigration. Unfortunately, it was the Immigration office in downtown L.A., since that was where she had originally checked in, and there was some type of screw-up with her green card. Also, she needed seventy-five dollars for the government fee to transfer her employment contract, and a pay advance. Kali refused to pay the seventy-five dollars. It wasn't her fault Lavinia was changing jobs. But she did give her the pay advance and the day off. She never saw Lavinia again.

Lavinia's friends and relatives called for weeks after, wanting to know if Kali knew where she'd gone. Some of them complained that Lavinia owed them money. Two of those who called were men, both claiming to be her husband. Kali finally had to have her cellphone and the home phone number changed.

## Virgie

By now, Kali and Matt had agreed that more time had to be devoted to the interviewing process, and Matt would have to get involved at an early stage. They were getting desperate, would likely make a serious mistake if 'they' weren't more careful. 'They' were lucky Harry hadn't suffered some terrible mishap already. For the next interview, Matt created a written quiz, which he read from pedagogically, during the interviews.

"Okay, Virgie," he said, looking up from the typed sheet of paper in his hand, "that's your name? Virgie? Is that short for Virginia, or what?"

Virgie beamed at him, nodding.

"Yes. You're nodding," Matt said. "Yes what? It's Virginia?"

A flash of smile was accompanied by a puzzled look in Kali's direction and another nod, this time less confident.

"Okay," Matt raked his hands through his hair, "so your name's Virginia." He scribbled a note on his paper. "Now, what would you do if Harry—the baby—got a cut?"

"Cut?" Blank look.

"Yes, a cut." Matt made a chopping motion with his hand, on his arm.

Virgie's smile faded. She looked confused, then anxious. "Cooking?" she asked.

"No, not cooking," Matt frowned.

How can he stand it? wondered Kali, squirming at the sight of Virgie's troubled expression.

"So, what would you do?" Matt demanded.

"Do?"

Unable to watch the bloodbath any longer, Kali hugged Harry to her and gazed out the front window at Pine Beach Road. That red Mustang was back, she saw with a tingle of fear.

"A cut," Matt repeated, looking frustrated. "Cut. Like with a knife? Or scissors?" He made a scissoring motion with his fingers.

"Ah," Virgie said, "a cut!" She nodded enthusiastically, and smiled broadly, clearly relieved.

"It's not a good thing to happen," Matt scowled, "so I don't know why you're smiling. Anyway, tell me what you would do."

"I think, maybe put some soo-gar," Virgie said, after some thought. "At home, we put soo-gar."

Matt was silent for a few moments. "Well, I don't know what soo-gar is, but it's not what we use here."

"Sugar," Kali said. She couldn't look at Matt or Virgie.

"What?" Matt said, sort of squinting at her.

"Sugar, Matt. She said sugar."

"Yes," Virgie beamed and nodded. "Soo-gar!"

"Isn't there some medical basis for it?" Kali asked, after Virgie had gone, very soon after.

"For what?" Matt said, not even looking up from the textbook he was reading.

"For putting sugar on a cut?"

Matt just sighed, shook his head, and continued reading.

# Edwina

In her office, Kali pressed the speed dial button on her phone to dial their new home number. The phone was answered on the third ring, so Kali was immediately relieved. Third ring was perfect, just the way she liked it. It meant Edwina has busy, but not too busy to take Kali's call. "Hi there, Edwina," she said, "it's Kali. I was just wondering how things were going, since it's your first day, and all."

"Oh, no problem." Edwina giggled into the phone.

"I mean, Harry seemed so upset, when I left."

"Sure." Another giggle.

"Did he settle down right away?"

"Oh, sure. No problem!"

"Is there anything we need? Anything I should pick up on the way home? Formula? Disposable diapers?" Cloth diapers were now a distant, unrealistic fantasy that Kali had finally gotten out of her head, as Mrs. Dalton had predicted.

"Oh, I don't think so," Edwina said. "Everything's okay. No problem."

"Great," Kali smiled, relieved that they finally had someone who could take control: an efficient, kind and sensible woman. "Harry certainly seems to like you."

"Sure, of course he does! Why not?"

"I don't hear him right now, what's he doing?"

"Is that right?"

"No, I don't hear him at all. He's being pretty quiet. What's he doing, Edwina? Having a nap?" Kali swallowed.

"Oh no. No nap." Edwina giggled. "He's in the bathtub. Just playing with his toys in the water."

"WHAT?!"

~~~

"I found Britta," Matt told Kali later that night. "She's staying with Gosta, as I thought. He called me, said he thought it wasn't right that she didn't tell us where she was."

"That's interesting." Kali felt like she'd been punched in the stomach.

"I'm so relieved to know she's safe."

"Uh huh, me too."

"She's looking for another job. Hasn't found one she wants yet."

"Well, good for her," Kali said. "I hope she finds something."

"And I hope you find a good nanny for Harry, before something really bad happens to him."

"How can you say that?" Kali demanded appalled, "or even think it?"

Matt turned out the light. "Goodnight, Kali," was all he said.

# Chapter 32

*'The essence of Skåling – whatever the occasion or setting, whether relaxed or formal – is the making of eye-contact, glass raised, with all other persons. This must be done not only before taking of the first sip, but immediately thereafter, and before and after every subsequent sip.'*

Kali fixed her eyes on Gosta then on Britta, took a sip of wine and looked at them again, each in turn. She'd declined the offer of coffee and cinnamon buns. Strong drink was what she needed, but watery wine would have to do. *"Skål,"* she said, trying to look friendly and agreeable as her eyes darted from Gosta to Britta, then back again. She was feeling light-headed, not from the wine but from the repetitive eye-contact required by Swedish custom. It added to the humiliation of having to come crawling to Gosta Lindgren's house to beg Britta to come back.

Kali had sat in her car on the street in front of his house in El Segundo, wavering over whether to go up to the door. She could already hear Sofia's screams. 'You did *what*? You went after her and brought her back? Do you have some kind of *death wish* for your marriage!?' It was only Harry's whining from the back seat that finally motivated Kali to get out of the car and go up the front walk, holding him in front of her like a talisman.

Kali, Britta and Gosta were now sitting in his living room, the atmosphere strained. "So – *Skål!*" Gosta sipped his wine. Britta, who declined a drink, seemed engrossed by Harry's antics around Gosta's sound system. He was twiddling the buttons and dials, apparently delighted that no one was pulling him away from it.

"Are you sure you don't mind him doing that?" Kali asked worriedly.

"Of course, not!" Gosta chuckled. "In Sweden, children have an honored place in the household. They're not pushed under the carpet as they are here in the United States!"

"They're hardly pushed under the carpet," Kali smiled. "And our Harry is not one to be pushed. Right, Britta? Except maybe in his Perego, which we unfortunately don't have anymore." Britta didn't react to this information, instead, she looked broodingly out the window.

"We don't have enough children back home," Gosta said. "Sweden has a declining birthrate, only 1.7 children per couple. So, you must let your son play. It's nice to have a baby in the house. What harm can he do?"

"Oh, our little Harry can be quite creative, can't he, Britta?"

Britta still avoided her eyes and didn't reply. It was she who'd answered the door when Kali rang the bell. '*Dra åt Skogen*,' she'd said. If Kali hadn't been holding Harry, she was sure the door would have been slammed in her face. As it was, Harry went crazy with joy at the sight of Britta, struggling wildly and reaching his little fat sausage arms out to her. Britta softened immediately, taking him from Kali, smothering him with coos and kisses. A moment later, Gosta appeared and invited Kali to come in, since Britta clearly wasn't about to.

Kali fixed her eyes on Britta, then Gosta again, and took another sip. All this repetitive eye-contact could get tedious, especially if she had to watch Harry, whose personal activity dial was now set on 'Search and Destroy.'

"Well, *Skål*," she repeated, downing the last of her wine. She felt suddenly optimistic that she and Britta would be able to work out their differences and that Harry would soon have his beloved nanny back.

"So, Kali," Gosta said, "it seems you know something of our Swedish customs. Where did you learn about *Skåling*?" He sucked on his pipe, working to get it going. He was the diplomatic type, the picture of patience and tact; next in line for the Nobel Peace Prize, after this challenging negotiation.

"Oh, one picks these things up here and there," Kali said, in answer to Gosta's question, not feeling like mentioning *Swedish in Minutes!* "Matt lived in Sweden for a couple of years, as you know." She looked at Britta for a reaction, but her face was hidden by her hair as she bent over Harry, settled in her lap on the floor. "I don't really know much about your customs," Kali added. The drinking part is about it."

"Some would say, that's most of it," Gosta chuckled.

"Britta?" Kali was determined to get some response from her, or at least an acknowledgement that Kali was there in the room. "I talked to my mother about what happened between you two, with the diapers."

"Ah." It was half-sigh, half-snort. "The *satkäring*." That word again. Kali hadn't been able to find it in *Sweden in Minutes!*

"Yes," Kali said, "my mother can be difficult at times, I guess, but she's a very caring person, as you say. That's why she got so upset with you. She was just worried about Harry... and me."

"*Hall flaben*," Britta said, without expression.

"Britta doesn't mean to be so rude," Gosta said, "she's only unhappy because your mother threw her out of the house. It's understandable."

"*Forbannade satkäring*," said Britta, her blue eyes dark. "*Pattaglytt.*"

Gosta shook his head and worked his pipe. "*Nej*, Britta. That language is not called for here."

"The story I heard is that Britta quit without notice and just walked out," Kali said, annoyed. "No one asked her to leave. Look, we aren't going to get anywhere if Britta keeps saying things about me that I can't understand. I've come here in good will, to see if we can reach an understanding, and put the past behind us. This isn't easy for me. It would have been much simpler to just hire someone else." She looked away, steeling herself for the big lie. "There are lots of great nannies out there looking for work, who would think our job is a very good one."

"*Vadglytting du ar*," Britta said. "*Jakla mog. Javla skitstovel.*"

Gosta sighed, shaking his head again. "*Var sa god.*" "*Jag hatar.*"

"*Vad ar det for felpa er?*"

"Hello?" Kali said. "I don't speak the language, you guys. Please, help me out."

"I'm sure Britta will come around and see your point of view," Gosta said. "It may take a bit of time, that's all. And she says she's sorry if she sounded rude." She said no such thing, Kali thought, but she also knew she had to suck it up. "I'm willing to forgive any insults to reset our relationship. I... we... want you to come back, Britta, to look after Harry again."

"*I helvete heller*," Britta said.

"Britta!" Gosta looked shocked.

"Why did Matt not come?" Britta demanded, flipping back her shag of white-blonde hair.

"Matt? He's in surgery. Besides, this is between you and me, isn't it?" Was she missing something here, Kali wondered?

"I think, I may help with what seems to be lost in translation," said Gosta. "The problem is that Britta believes you and your mother do not like her. She does not feel comfortable in your home, because she is sensitive to this dislike by the women of the household. It would have helped to have Matthew here as mediator, to smooth the waters, as you say. But in his absence, I see I'll have to do." He chuckled in a self-congratulatory way. "A poor substitute for a handsome young hockey player, I confess."

"He's a surgeon now," Kali said, "and not all that young. But I'm sure he'd be pleased that you remember his hockey days."

"Oh yes, we remember Matt. He was a marvel in Angelholm!"

"I've never seen him play," Kali confessed.

"Oh, that's a great pity! His fights were wonderful! The way he would smash other players against the boards. Always a lot of blood when Matt Miller was on the ice!" Britta grinned and nodded vigorously.

"But getting back to our, um… problem," Kali said, not wanting to think about Matt as a hockey enforcer, though she knew he'd been a good one, always up for dropping the gloves and going at it. "I know Britta thinks my mother and I don't like her, but she's wrong. And my mother doesn't live with us anyway. She doesn't even visit much. Besides, I think this business over the diapers was just a huge misunderstanding, that's all. I don't know what you call it in Swedish."

"*Forbannade rora*," Gosta suggested.

"*Sluta tjafsa*," Britta added, looking down again and scowling.

"We use disposable diapers now," Kali said. There was no reaction from Britta to this information. "So anyway, with Harry being so sick with chicken-pox, I think everyone was just under a terrible strain while we were away. So, look, Britta, you can use disposable diapers from now on, okay? And it's not true that I don't like you, I like you very much. We all do, especially Harry."

Britta brightened. "He is a good boy—a little prince. *Alskling*!"

Kali thought back to the thrashing, purple-faced *alskling* she'd dealt with the day after Britta quit. "I'm glad you think so. That's why we really want you to come back, and we hope you will."

Britta hugged Harry tightly, then said something to Gosta in rapid Swedish. "Harry is the first baby she has ever looked after," Gosta translated, nodding. "She is very attached to him, naturally."

"Well, that's great," said Kali. "And he's attached to her. We all are."

Gosta hesitated, listening to Britta. "She is speaking in Swedish now because she is feeling very emotional. There is still this troubling question about her room."

"What about it?"

"*Rummet ar for kallt,*" Britta sulked, "*en lacka.*"

"She doesn't like the room you put her in," Gosta explained. "It's damp, and there is a smell—a bad stink?" He looked at Britta for confirmation. She nodded, her eyes wide. "From some leaking of water."

"I'm going to take care of that," Kali said.

"And she's not too crazy about this waterbed you make her sleep on," Gosta added. "If it's so wonderful, she says, why don't you sleep on it yourself? It makes her seasick." He packed his pipe as Kali watched, annoyed by the complaints Britta suddenly had about her accommodations. "And there is *insekter*," Gosta added.

"*Kackerlacka,*" Britta nodded, looking frightened.

"Pardon?" said Kali.

"Bugs. Cockroaches," Gosta said.

"We don't have bugs in our house."

"*Ja,*" Britta nodded. "*Ach toiletten ar sonder.*"

"Also, there's something wrong with the toilet," Gosta said, "it backs up."

"Oh, come on!" Kali protested. "This is the first I've heard about anything being wrong with the toilet or the room. Well, unfortunately, it's all we have." She stood up. "I think it's pretty clear that Britta's decided not to come back. Maybe she's already found another job. That's fine. There are lots of fish in the sea." She took a step towards her, holding out her arms to take Harry back.

Britta said something in impassioned Swedish, to Gosta.

"Kali, she says she is willing to come back if you could just improve her quarters a little," Gosta said.

"We can't buy a new house if that's what she means. I worked hard to make her room as nice as possible. And clean. If the toilet's broken, we'll call a plumber and get it fixed. All she had to do was tell me. But other than that, there's nothing else we can do to improve her room. Obviously, Britta isn't as attached to Harry as she likes to pretend. Can I have him now, please?" As soon as Harry was in her arms again, he started to whine, struggling to get down, reaching out to Britta.

"*Och spruta mot insekter,*" Britta said, her eyes lowered.

"She only wants some bug spray," said Gosta, "that would be enough."

"If there really are bugs, I'll get an exterminator. Bug spray isn't good for babies, or anyone else. We'll get rid of the bugs, okay, Britta?"

"*Ja.* This is okay."

"Good," said Gosta, happily, "then all is settled!"

"I will go now to pack my things," Britta said. "Can I take Harry to my room?"

"Sure," Kali said. He prefers you anyway, she thought.

After Britta and Harry had gone, Gosta beamed at Kali. "I am so glad this has worked out. We are very fond of Britta, but it's like living with a teenager." He chuckled. "Kali, if I might make another suggestion, perhaps you could do something to make Britta's room a little more upscale? These girls from Europe, they don't like to feel like servants. Most of them, like Britta, come from very good homes. They're not used to dampness and cockroaches."

"Maybe if she kept her room a little tidier there wouldn't be any cockroaches, if there are any, which I have never seen, by the way." Kali tried to sound as though she was working hard to come up with an amicable solution, though she was annoyed and insulted.

Gosta smiled and shook his head. "We could go on and on, hearing your grievances about each other. But what's the point? When the time is right, I will mention to her that she should be tidier. But I think you will agree, now is not the best time. She only wants to feel part of your family. Try to make her feel as though she belongs."

They looked at each other, in silence, for a moment or two. "Just one more thing, Gosta," Kali said, "I want to ask you about Skane."

"Skane?" He looked surprised. "Okay, shoot." He chuckled, awkwardly.

"There's some kind of movement going on there, is that right? To become Danish?"

"Well, it's a little more complicated than that. But things have settled down in recent years." He seemed uneasy. "And Britta is a peace-loving person, as are most Swedes." Then he laughed suddenly, awkwardly, showing all his teeth. "*Skynda pa!*" he called, sharply, over his shoulder. He turned back to Kali. "She should hurry up, not be so rude. There is no need for her to take all day. All day is what it will take my poor wife, to clean up after her!"

It was obvious, Kali thought, that the Lindgrens couldn't wait to get rid of Britta.

# Chapter 33

By the time they finally left, the sky was a dense, bruised purple, deepening to black along the horizon. Kali had just enough time to pack Harry and Britta into the car before the first raindrops squeezed out of the constipated sky. As she pulled the car away from Gosta's house, the raindrops were plunking onto the windshield and bonking the roof of the car, heavy as water bombs. It hardly ever rained in Southern California, but when it did it was like Armageddon.

Kali was glad she had to concentrate on navigating the 405 through the storm: it gave her an excuse for not talking to Britta. She needed time to sulk over the litany of complaints about Britta's room and bathroom, and to contemplate the number of aggravating phone calls, estimates, and the troops of tradespeople she would have to deal with (and pay) to fix the toilet, track down the (phantom?) bugs and dry out the carpet. Then there was Matt's mother, Beth, and all the fuss she would make about the disposable diapers if she ever visited or called, if Matt or Britta let it slip somehow.

Britta insisted on sitting in the backseat with Harry, seeming to have forgotten the entire discussion at Gosta's or that she'd ever walked out on the Millers, leaving Kali in the lurch. She was babbling cheerfully to Harry, alternating between Swedish and English, calling him *snutiks* and *askling* and other terms of endearment and generally acting as though Kali was not even in the car with them. "So, what have you been doing for the past two weeks?" Kali finally asked, over the slap and thump of the windshield wipers. The rain was so heavy she could hardly see the road, and traffic had ground to a halt.

"Just on holiday," Britta said, "I needed to rest. *Jag kanner mig frisk.*" She kissed Harry, with a loud smacking sound. "But I am okay now."

So much for Britta getting snapped up by another family, Kali thought. She hadn't even been looking for a job. "Holiday," she said, "that must have been nice."

"*Ja.* Was very nice."

"Also, I'm just curious, but you asked about Matt. You know what long hours he works. Why did you think he should have come to Gosta's?"

Britta didn't answer immediately. "Matt is my friend," she finally said. "I know him for a long time."

"But I'm your friend too, Britta. I hope you believe that."

"That is also nice. But Matt, he is very good to me."

"Oh?" Kali glanced at Britta in the rearview. "In what way?"

Britta shrank down behind her hair and cuddled Harry. "Just nice, he is very nice with me."

"Well, he's a good guy," Kali said, "nice to everyone." Then she added, "and a really great husband, too." In the rearview, she could see Britta slide lower into her seat.

"Harry must be changed soon." As if on cue, he began to fuss. Britta shushed and cooed, tickling him under the chin, and eventually, he settled. Clearly, he was relieved to have his beloved nanny back.

The storm let up suddenly. Kali stepped on the gas as the traffic began to move, eager to get home to Belmont Shore, get out of the car and end this weird and unsettling conversation with Britta.

~~~

Kali parked in the garage, praying that the fragile wooden structure wouldn't be flattened or swept away by the rising wind. The rain was suddenly pouring down again. The ocean was choppy, with the biggest waves Kali had ever seen. She ushered Britta and Harry safely inside, then ran back outside, latching the garage door and struggling to secure the gate to the deck. The thunder and lightning were coming quickly now, close together. The ocean level was rising, the waves were crashing against the retaining wall. Kali wouldn't have believed the waves could even reach the wall, even though its purpose was to hold it back.

She recalled news footage of the last hurricanes in Florida and Texas, of homes smashed into splinters, looking like the pick-up-sticks she and Sofia used to play with as children. A she ran back into the house, dragging open the back door, fighting with the wind, she wondered whether a tidal wave or tsunami was possible in Long Beach. Of course, it was, she concluded, worriedly. Outside the kitchen window, the power lines were swinging crazily, whipped sideways by the wind like children's jump ropes. Suddenly, there was a tremendous crash followed by the sound of breaking glass. Britta burst into the kitchen carrying Harry, who was howling in terror. "*Mein gott! En flud*! The ocean is coming into the house!"

# Chapter 34

Kali rushed into Britta's room which was now a swamp. She saw with horror that the back window had been shattered, burst open by a torrent of water. Shards and splinters of glass littered the soaked carpet. The stench was overpowering. She pulled off her sandals, as she held her nose and gagged, she hopped through the mud, yanking electrical plugs out of the sockets as she went. The mess was even worse in the bathroom, where the toilet had indeed backed up. Kali shut the door on all of it – she would have to find someone to remove all the water. No mere towels would be of any help now.

Britta put Harry into his playpen in the living room giving him a teething biscuit and a bottle of juice. He seemed to be settling down, as the storm outside finally began to subside. The peals of thunder were fading, the lightning flashes less frequent. Kali almost cried with relief.

As soon as the rain stopped, she went out to the garage to lug in Britta's suitcase and backpack. As she put the backpack down on the kitchen floor, something fell out of a side pocket. It was the framed photo of Britta in her Lucia outfit with the candles on her head. As Kali picked it up, it fell apart in her hand. A piece of cardboard and some other photos slid out of the back and dropped onto the floor.

"*Jidda inte!*" Britta was suddenly there in the kitchen and quick as a cat, grabbed the cardboard and photos, glaring at Kali.

"Britta, really, I was only trying to  help."

"No, is okay. I can fix." She turned her back to Kali, hastily stuffing all of the pieces back into the side pocket of the backpack.

Kali didn't have time to try to interpret this bizarre reaction. She grabbed a tea-towel and dried off her feet, noting the muddy footprints she'd tracked all over the buckling kitchen tiles. She would have to wash it with disinfectant—God only knew what sort of bacteria and other crap were being carried into their house with all that sewage.

"You'll have to sleep in the living room," she said to Britta, "on the pull-out sofa, until we figure out what to do about your room. I'm sorry." Britta nodded, without expression. From the living room, Harry started fussing again from his playpen. Britta hurried out of the kitchen to tend to  him.

Morosely, Kali stared out the window at the grey sky, and the rolling ocean, wondering how much everything was going to cost to repair. Huge cartoon dollar signs that flapped away on wings was all she could see. These were no mere *Proctors* they would have to deal with to save their investment from total ruin.

Her shoulders sagged as she looked out over their little backyard swamp. As she watched in horror, the retaining wall suddenly collapsed, allowing a muddy landslide to flow out, carrying the remains of Kali's garden of weeds to join the rise and swell of industrial pollutants and human excrement that was pouring into the ocean from the sewers. Kali yanked the blinds down over the window, unable to watch any longer.

She had to call Alicia and explain her absence, let her know she would not be in for a while. She felt bad for her –it would not surprise her if Alicia had already quit. Kali could hardly blame her if she had. Or maybe Kali had been fired herself. It would be there in her e-mail she never had a chance to read: *'Kali Miller is no longer with the firm. Please join us in wishing her well in her future endeavors.'* But she couldn't call Alicia right now; she had to make emergency calls about the house and yard before the remains of both floated out into the Pacific.

On her cell, she Googled and (amazingly) found a listing under FLOOD IN L.A. It was FLOOD DAMAGE RESTORATION, to be exact, with a subheading: 'See also Water Damage Restoration'.

'Mahmood's Moisture Control' didn't sound serious enough: they weren't talking mere moisture here, they were talking deluge. Then there was 'With Discretion Home Inspectors.' What was the implication there? That the others would kiss and tell, but these guys would pull up in an unmarked truck, collars upturned on their trench-coats, so that the neighbors wouldn't find out that you had a dampness issue? The Millers didn't need a cloak-and-dagger service; the whole of Belmont Shore was probably talking about their backyard already, soon to be roped off with yellow emergency tape, like a crime  scene.

Kali continued to search until she found a listing that had the right tone: 'Home-Buddy's 24-hour Water Extraction and Deodorizing'. They sounded friendly, eager and no-nonsense; the kind of guys who wouldn't mind the stench. Kali called them, surprised when a polite and friendly man (in LA?) answered, right away, and told her what she wanted to hear. They were busy, because of the sudden storm, of course, but he would send someone over to do damage control and give her an estimate within the hour. They already had a guy over in Long Beach.

Feeling more optimistic about the house, Kali turned her attention to the backyard. There were no Google listings under LANDSLIDES, although there was one for LAND CLEARING AND LEVELING. 'See Excavating Contractors – Residential'. There was also 'Excavating Contractors,' and 'bobcat and backhoe excavating'. They also did demolition, but Kali didn't need that. Demolition, they had already, in spades. Her cellphone buzzed. Alicia.

Kali answered. "I'm so sorry, Alicia, but I'm literally swamped right now," she said, before her assistant had a chance to say anything.

"Well, you're making me very nervous," Alicia complained. "I don't even have anything left to file here! I can't afford to be redundant. I need this job, Kali! I'm not going to float again!"

"We've had serious nanny problems, and now I've got a floating house and a disappearing backyard and Matt's not home to help. What am I supposed to do?"

"The world goes on, Kali. Don't you care about your practice? How long do you think you can put clients off before they get pissed off and demand to speak to someone else? The sharks are circling around here. So, don't kid yourself, Amiga, that everyone's all understanding and supportive of  you."

"Of course, Alicia, I understand. But Harry has to come first. If you'd seen some of the nut cases we've had looking after him lately..."

"Kali, you haven't put in any time for almost a month. We're supposed to be billing this week. What am I supposed to bill? You haven't done anything!"

"I don't know what you can bill. Bill Mike Potochnik. Just bill. That's the attitude around here, isn't it? Nothing else matters."

"I've been trying to hold down the fort here, putting your clients off with all kinds of excuses, but you stopped responding to anything. How long do you think we can go on like this?"

"I don't know, Alicia. You'll have to do the best you can. Just give me a day or so to get things straightened out. I'm sorry about all of this, you're doing great and you're saving my ass. No one's going to fire you."

"Well, I hope you're planning to come in on Friday. Exec wants you for some big meeting."

"About what?" Kali felt a surge of panic.

"No idea—it's in your e-mail. I just need to tell them you'll be there."

Kali swallowed. "Yeah, I'll be there." To face the firing squad, she thought.

# Chapter 35

Kali leaned against the kitchen counter, not sure what to do next. In the living room, Harry and Britta were watching *Reading Rainbow*. Britta's backpack was still on the floor in a corner of the kitchen. Now was the time to look, Kali thought, if she was ever going to. She went over to it, reached into the side pocket and pulled out the glass, cardboard and photos that Britta had so quickly shoved back into it. Her hands shaking, she turned over the photos of Britta: Britta holding up a dead trout, a fishing rod at her side; Britta in a red ski-suit and helmet; Britta in a tiny string bikini.

Then there was a picture Kali wasn't ready for but had somehow suspected she would one day find: Matt and Britta sitting together on a bench! Kali was suddenly on a rollercoaster, as the floor dropped away from under her, then rolled back up, sweeping her high on the crest of a sickening wave. They appeared to be in a European cobblestone square, with red brick shuttered buildings and planter boxes of flowers in the background. Britta was wearing a simple blue dress, hiked up at one side to show off her long, sun-browned legs and she was holding a loose bunch of flowers tied with white ribbons, that cascaded across her skirt. On her arm was the little gold bracelet of stars, and on her finger, a gold ring! Matt had a slightly dazed smile on his lips, and one hand rested on Britta's thigh. He was also wearing a ring! Kali turned the picture over. '*Brollopsdag – Angelholm*' was written on the back in a cramped European-style scrawl.

*Brollopsdag, brollopsdag...* '*Dag*' was day, she knew that much. '*En san underbar dag.*' Wasn't that what Britta often said? It's a beautiful day. Well, there would be no beautiful day for her today, that was for sure. The jig was up, oh yes it was! Breathless, Kali stuffed everything back into the backpack except for the photo of Matt and Britta which she shoved into the pocket of her jeans.

"Kali?" Britta had turned off the TV. "I will make dinner now? *Fiskpinne?*"

"What?" Kali yelled.

"Fish sticks. I should make them now?"

"Sure, whatever." Kali grabbed her briefcase and carried it past Britta and Harry, into her bedroom. She shut the door, snapped open her briefcase, took out *Swedish in Minutes!* and flipped through to the dictionary at the back, looking for '*brollopsdag.*' She stared, not believing her eyes, which were filling now with tears: '*brollopsdag [bro-lops-dag] n. wedding day'.* Kali sank down onto the bed. They were married! Matt and Britta were married! Kali was married to a bigamist, and her husband's *wife* was now Harry's nanny!

Did Matt squeeze in sex with her, in the mornings after rounds, darting home between his call schedule, his O.R.'s, seminars and Britta's slapdash housework duties? It didn't seem possible... he couldn't even get time off for a haircut, or so he told Kali. She pictured Harry dropping off to sleep for his afternoon nap—then Britta paging Matt, using some secret code they'd agreed upon to signal that the coast was clear, the baby asleep, the old *satkäring* back in her office, pushing papers around and trying to look busy. Would Matt then spring into action, yank off his surgical mask, hustle out of the operating room, and leaving his patient intubated, while he dashed home for a quickie with his son's nanny, who also happened to be his *wife*? Maybe they wouldn't even wait for Harry to fall asleep—maybe they let him watch!

Through the bedroom window, Kali could see the Home-Buddy truck pulling up to the house. Then, incredibly, Matt's Jeep turned onto Pine Beach Road! She took a deep breath, wiped her eyes and charged into the living room. She lifted Harry out of his playpen and hugged him to her, ignoring Britta's surprised look. It was time to start kicking butt at 67 Pine Beach Road!

# Chapter 36

"Kali! Come back!" Matt yelled, as he leapt out of the Jeep and Kali, on the flooded front walk, struggled to release the safety brake on Harry's stroller. She hadn't bought a new Perego, and was now obliged to maneuver its much cheaper, heavier replacement that she'd found in a Goodwill store. Not only was it almost impossible to open up, fold down and get going, but it had a twisted, sadistic mind of its own once it was moving. Each wheel rolled along independently of the others, wobbling in all directions. It was a nightmare to steer and control, especially now, in the deep pools of water on the sidewalk.

Britta stood in the front window, watching them, anxiously twisting a lock of blonde hair between her fingers. In fact, everyone on Pine Beach Road was probably watching, but Kali didn't give a shit. Not anymore. "Go back to your *wife*," she shouted at Matt "She's waiting for you! Bigamist!"

"I'm not a bigamist!"

"You got a better word for a guy who's married to two women?" She yanked and heaved and pushed the uncooperative stroller. Harry, however, seemed to be enjoying the ride, and all the drama.

"I'm not married to two women!"

"Oh? Then you're divorced! That's a relief. I feel so much better knowing that you hired your *ex-wife* to look after my baby!" Kali charged on with no idea where she was going.

"*Our* baby," Matt said, blocking her path.

"Get out of my way!" She pushed passed him, the stroller wobbled wildly on the wet sidewalk.

"Where do you think you're going?"

"Away from you, is all I care about!"

"I never married Britta!" Matt protested, close on her heels.

"Okay, great! Way better!" Kali was still working to get the stroller moving in a straight line. "She just *thinks* you married her, is that it? You went through some phony marriage—some *brollops*—to make her believe you married her? That's so much better! What a relief!" The brake on the stroller jammed suddenly. She gave it a savage kick which, surprisingly, released it, allowing her to quickly wheel Harry up Pine Beach Road, towards 2nd Street. She would have preferred an escape to the beach, to clear her head and think about what to do next, but since they no longer had a backyard, they had no access to the beach or boardwalk either. And the beach would be covered in deep slimy sludge by now anyway.

The man from Home-Buddy was back in number 67, squelching around in Britta's room and complaining that someone (Kali) had dumped Drano into both the sink and toilet, causing all sorts of problems in the century-old plumbing. The excavators were due to arrive at any moment, but Kali no longer cared about any of it. All she wanted was to take Harry and run away, turn her back on the whole soggy and sordid mess, and leave it for Matt and his *real wife* to deal with.

"I never married Britta and I never pretended to marry her! Slow down, Kali. Come on—hear me out!"

"Then why does it say *wedding day* on the back of that picture of you two?" She dug into her pocket and pulled out the photo. "You and her! On a bench, all kissy-face! Wearing wedding rings!"

Matt took the photo. His face fell; he looked suddenly broken. "I can explain. It's not how it looks."

"It never is, is it?"

"Kali, I never married Britta."

"She's holding a fucking bridal bouquet!" Kali snatched back the photo. It was evidence that she would need for the divorce, and Matt's criminal trial. "You expect me to believe you weren't married? How stupid do you think I am? You thought I'd never find that picture, but I did, right behind that innocent Lucia photo. *Brollopsdag!* It's right on the back! *Angelholm!* Hello? Does that ring a bell? Or maybe you were you too drunk to realize you were getting married. Is that your alibi, *Doctor*?"

"Can we stop for a minute and talk?" Matt pleaded. "You don't even know where you're going."

"Away from you is all I care about."

"At least slow down a bit, so you'll understand what I 'm saying. That's not Britta, in that picture." He was raking his hands through his hair, clearly very upset. "That isn't her in any of those pictures she has. If you weren't working so hard to find a reason to break up our marriage and get rid of her, you'd realize it couldn't be Britta. The girl in that picture is twenty-four. When I was in Sweden, Britta was only fifteen. Do the math, Kali."

"Do the math? You're trying to gaslight me now. Do the math! The *math* adds up to bigamy and you and I both know it! But none of it even matters anymore." Kali walked faster, pushing Harry in his stroller. "Go away, Matthew, I can't even look at you."

"Hold on." Matt grabbed her arm. "Kali listen to me. It's her sister. Okay? In those photos. Her older sister. They look a lot alike. Looked, I should say."

"You married Britta's sister?"

"It's complicated, Kali."

"I'll bet! I'll just bet it is. I bet the whole sordid story is a doozy, a dilly!"

"Let me help you with that stroller. Harry's all lop-sided—look at the poor little guy."

"We don't need your help. You're a bigamist, and bigamy's a crime. And I'm going to report you and end your brilliant career before it even starts. And me and Harry won't even visit you in prison, not ever! That big Harvard speech is never going to happen—not with you and Britta there in the front row."

"What?" Matt looked frightened now. "Are you insane? What are you talking about?"

"Nothing. Never mind." She didn't need him to try and have her committed, Kali thought; that wouldn't help poor little Harry. She walked on faster.

"Come on, Kali. Harry's getting whiplash! Look at the way his head's hanging over the side."

"He loves it, are you kidding? He loves a rough ride. He's used to it. A rough ride is what he's been getting since the day he was born, thanks to you—packing me off to work so you could canoodle with your *wife*, back in our house! The house that I'm paying the mortgage on!"

Exasperated, Matt jumped in front of the stroller and grabbed the front bar, stopping her in her tracks. "Please. At least let me take Harry out of this thing—carry him."

"Don't you touch him! You married some Swedish underpants model, then hired her clone—your own sister-in-law—to look after our baby! And what happened to this wife of yours? Or should I be expecting another house guest from Sweden to pop in one day, so the three of you can have a great big cluster-fuck?" Kali could feel the big artery popping out in her temple. Her vision was blurring. Maybe she was going to 'stroke out' as Matt would say, right there in the middle of the sidewalk. Would he even try to resuscitate her? He would probably just grab Harry and make a run for it, leaving her sputtering on the ground as the life ebbed out of her, and run back to his real wife.

She took a deep breath. She couldn't let that happen; she owed it to Harry to protect him from this monster in surgical scrubs who just happened to be his biological father. That was the *only* thing Kali was sure of anymore. She had to hold it together, for Harry's sake. She struggled on, pushing the stroller, trying to ignore Matt.

"Okay, forget it, then." He stopped chasing after her. "You don't want to try and understand. So, go ahead and break up our little family. But you don't even know why you're doing it."

The word 'family' hit Kali hard. That's what she was about to do, wasn't it? Break up their little family? But it was *him*, it was Matt who had done it, not her! She walked on for a few yards, then turned to look back at him standing dejectedly on the sidewalk, his hands in his pockets, scrubs flapping around his legs, his dark hair whipped around by the wind. She slowed down but kept walking, glancing back at him over her shoulder. After all, she *was* married to the guy. She stopped walking. "I'm not making any promises about anything." she said, "but I owe it to Harry to at least hear what you've got to say."

"Finally!" Matt looked relieved. "Can we go inside somewhere and talk?"

"Not home, not with your wife, or whoever she is, probably going through our stuff right now—which I don't even care about."

"A restaurant, then?"

"Okay. Jack in The Box. But it's not going to change anything."

"Can I push Harry?"

"Yeah, that'll happen," Kali snorted.  Matt continued to walk along close beside her, his hands still in the pockets of his scrubs, his expression grim, as they made their way towards 2nd Street.

# Chapter 37

"Can I get you anything?" Matt asked, as soon as they were inside.

"I'm not here for the food." Kali wheeled Harry over to a table and busied herself with unloading him: pulling off his hat, fluffing up his bit of blond hair, adjusting his blanket. She took a couple of red plastic straws out of a dispenser and gave them to Harry to investigate and experiment with. When she looked up again, Matt was standing at the counter, placing his order. "How can you eat at a time like this?" she demanded when he returned to the table with a tray of fries, chicken fingers, and pie.

"I'm starving. We had a case that started at seven this morning and didn't finish 'til four-thirty."

"But your family is falling apart, Matthew. Right here, right now. I will probably kick you out after I hear whatever gruesome confession you need to get off your chest."

"I don't think you will, Kali. At least, I hope not. It's not how it looks, it's not what you think." He dug into his fries. "Though I'm not excusing myself."

Kali stared at him in disgust. Men were incredible in their ability to just get on with things—essential, basic things, like sex, food and sleep—and usually in that order. It was women who became the bulimics, the anorexics, who lay awake at night, crying, scheming or plotting revenge, or playing the *'I should have said'* game for hours after a big fight. She supposed it was nature's way. Somebody had to get back out there and hunt for food, bring it home and slay the wolf at the door. "Let's just hear this story of yours," she sighed. "Get it over with and spare me the disgusting details."

Matt tore open a ketchup pouch with his teeth, then smeared ketchup over his fries. "You probably aren't going to like me any better after you hear it. Except that it will show you how much I've changed. Matured." He stuffed some fries into his mouth. "Why don't I give Harry a fry? See what he does with it?"

"He's doing fine with those straws. And babies don't need greasy, fried food. Come on, talk. Time's running out here." Her heart was thumping unpleasantly. What if he wasn't even a real doctor? she worried.

"Okay." More ketchup, more fries. "As I'm sure I've told you, I had a bit of a drinking problem when I lived over in Sweden. No, more than that. I basically got shit-faced every night. And I was always getting into fights, getting laid."

"Your disgraceful glory days. I believe I've heard all about your male bravado, many times."

"But you've got to understand how much peer pressure there was. I know I have to take full responsibility for my actions, and I do. But you have to put all of what I'm about to tell you into proper context. Okay?" He raised an eyebrow, waiting for Kali's grudging nod before continuing. He smeared sauce over the chicken fingers. "Sure you don't want some of these?"

"You're wasting my time. I've got packing to do—yours."

"Anyway," Matt continued, his mouth full, "there were a couple of times that I know I went too far, crossed the line. I remember waking up one morning in a ditch in Germany, covered with mud, the autobahn whizzing over me. But the day I got married..."

Kali's heart sank. Married! "So, it's true! Oh, Matthew."

"It's a long and complicated story, but you have a right to hear it. I should have told you all of this way back. I didn't want to get married in Sweden. I don't even remember doing it. I didn't want to stay there and work my whole life for a little apartment and maybe a cottage somewhere, paying ninety percent income tax. I told Petra—Britta's sister—that I didn't want to get married. I told her I couldn't stay over there. But she had no interest in moving to the States."

"Petra? Is that the girl in the picture?" Kali swallowed. "You married her?" Matt nodded, concentrating on his food. Oh, God, Kali thought. "So, I was right. You're a bigamist."

"No, I'm not. You need to hear the rest. Let me finish. Please."

"So, this Petra got you drunk and took advantage of you? Slapped a marriage license on you when you weren't looking?"

"Sounds stupid, but that's basically it. They make this homebrew over there—it's kind of like a rotgut vodka called *hembrant.*" He shook his head and sighed. His appetite, however, soldiered on as he hunkered down over his food. "Well, she got pregnant, Petra. I don't even think it was mine, but you aren't going to believe that, because I know that's what all guys say."

Kali swallowed, a lump in her throat. Matt not only had another wife, but a child? "Where are they now? Your wife and child?" She held her breath, dreading the answer.

Matt stopped eating. "Well, the story gets worse at this point."

"How could it possibly get worse?" Kali stared at him, her heart sinking, stomach churning.

"Petra was big in that free-Skane movement, like in those pamphlets you found. I have no idea why Britta is still dragging them around. Those, plus the flag, a few photos and some letters is all she has left of her sister, I guess. They fought a lot, but they were pretty close at the end of the day. Britta being the baby sister and all that."

"Go on," Kali said. She knew all about sisterhood.

"Anyway, Petra always wanted to go over to Denmark. She was a wild girl, even after we got married, even being pregnant. It was a rough time. I wanted to come back to the States, she wanted to stay over there. One night, she got really pissed at me and got on a party boat. She got loaded and fell, or jumped, overboard on the way back to Helsingborg." He sighed. "Petra drowned that night. That's about all there is to tell. They couldn't resuscitate her and couldn't save the baby." He leaned his head back, pressing his lips together, eyes closed, waiting for Kali's judgment. There was a smear of ketchup on his chin.

Kali stared at him. Matt, the widower. Father of a dead baby. Was she actually thinking about forgiving him for the big lie on which their marriage was based, and for what he had done to this poor girl, Petra? "Well," she sighed, "before I take Harry and walk out of your life forever, perhaps you could explain exactly what you thought you were doing by bringing Britta here to be Harry's nanny."

"I didn't bring her over. After all that I just told you about, do you think I ever wanted to see her again or anyone from her family? They all hated me, and I was so ashamed. And rightly so, for all of it."

"Oh, sure you were."

"Come on, Kali. This girl *died*. And a baby too."

Kali pressed her lips together, looked away and swallowed. "I'm sorry, it's really horrible and so tragic."

"Britta got here on her own. I hadn't even heard from her for over five years. I hadn't heard from anyone in her family. But she knew I went into medicine and she somehow found out I was in L.A., maybe from Gosta or some other mutual friends or Facebook, whatever. She found out what hospital I was at, and started sending me letters, asking if I would help her get her green card or a work visa. I didn't want to see her—she was the last person I wanted to see again, really. A voice from the past, like a ghost. And of course, she looks almost exactly like Petra did at her age."

"So, why didn't you tell her no?"

"I was afraid if I didn't help her she would tell you the whole story."

"She threatened you? With blackmail?"

"No, but I was afraid. I never wanted you to know all of this, not any of it. I was afraid you would never marry me, if I told you before, and that you would leave me, if I told you after."

"So, you hired your sister-in-law to be Harry's nanny?"

"*Ex*-sister-in-law."

Kali was at a loss how to process all of this. Harry was kicking fitfully in the high chair, bored now, tired of playing with plastic straws.

"And for all Britta's faults, and you need to believe this," Matt said, "I knew she'd be good with Harry. If I seriously thought she was a psycho or something, I wouldn't have let her anywhere near him. And she has been good with him, we have to give her that. She only wanted to stay for a year anyway. She has plans for getting a real job or going back to school. Britta's ambitious. Plus, I knew she was from a good family. Her parents are awesome. I thought I was helping them too. After the way I wrecked their family, it eased my guilt a bit about Petra. Kind of like giving back, something at least."

189

Kali sighed, staring out the window. It was true: Britta was great with Harry, and he adored Britta.

"I figured she'd be out of our hair soon enough," Matt continued, "and you'd never need to know about what happened in Sweden. And we'd have a good nanny for Harry, for a while, for his first year anyway."

"Men can be so stupid." Kali wanted to be furious but was feeling her anger ebbing away as she looked at her husband's sad, tired face.

"I have zero attraction to her, and I never did. I admit I kind of liked having her around at first. It was good to talk about old times, catch up on everyone I knew back in Sweden. But I was getting nervous that she might say something to you, about my past. Then she had that big fight with your mother and left on her own."

"But you told me to go and get her back!"

"I was worried she'd be mad enough to call you and tell you the whole story, out of spite. I didn't want to risk it. Look at the stakes. I could have lost you. Lost Harry. Still could, I guess." He looked lovingly at their son happily babbling in his stroller. "But then time went on. We tried those other nannies and I didn't hear from Britta. I thought maybe she went back to Sweden."

"So, the agency fee that you said you paid for Britta? Another lie?"

"I still have the money, or had, I guess. I spent it on that necklace I gave you for Christmas. I'm sorry I lied to you, but I justified it in my head, because I bought you something nice with it."

"What's a *satkäring*?"

"What?"

"You heard me."

Matt looked away.

"Well?'

"A bitch," he sighed. "Maybe a bit worse."

"No wonder it wasn't in my phrase book."

"Look, all you can really fault me for is my past, that I didn't tell you I was married before. It's a big deal, no question. But other than that, I'm clean. Lots of people have things in their past they don't want anyone to know about. I never wanted to marry Petra, but I *did* want to marry you. Big time."

"Is that supposed to make a difference?" Kali asked.

"I'm a desperate man, grasping at straws, just like little Harry here. What else can I say? I love you, Kali. I love Harry. I love our life together, and I love our future. Which, hopefully, we still have?"

Kali looked helplessly into his dark, troubled eyes. Was this the way to end a marriage? In the hot, close atmosphere of Jack in the Box, the air thick with the smell of grease? Was there any good place to end a marriage? To end a family?

"Look, I don't want you to leave, or throw me out. But I guess, seeing all this from your point of view... I could understand it."

"It's pretty hard to want to have you around."

"Although, I am a great fun dad. You've got to admit that."

"When you show up."

"I've almost finished this residency, Kali. Don't bail now. Things will get better when I get a job or start my own practice. You can quit work, stay home with Harry. We can have another baby. Come on, Kali, everybody makes mistakes. But I'm not a lost cause. I've learned a lot since then. I've learned how important my family is to me. And I hardly even drink anymore, right?"

Kali busied herself by struggling with a squirming Harry, straightening out the blankets in his stroller. She zipped up Harry's jacket, and tugged his hat down into place. "Are you going to eat your pie?"

"You can have it."

"I'm on a diet."

He looked at her, his eyes questioning. "So maybe we should get a box, and take it home with us?"

Kali looked at him, in silence, for a few moments. "Maybe we should," she finally said.

~~~

"You can go ahead and fire Britta, if you want," Matt said later, as they wheeled Harry down the street. "You'd be totally within your rights, and I wouldn't blame you."

As they turned together down Pine Beach Road, the sun peeked out from behind the clouds and Kali felt her spirits start to lift. They were still together— they were still a family! The only thing that had been seriously damaged was their house, and Kali didn't even really care. It was just a thing: bricks and mortar. Houses could be bought and sold; houses could be replaced. People, a family, couldn't. The day was turning around, and as the sun shone brighter, Kali could see it becoming an *underbar dag*. "I don't want to fire Britta," she said, "even though she called me a bitch and other names, which I probably deserved. She's alone in this country, her sister is dead and she's a great nanny for Harry. Not having a job isn't going to help her. I can't blame her for trying to make her life better, for having ambition, for taking advantage of any situation she could. She's not a criminal, she just asked you for help. That's what a lot of women—a lot of people—would do. That's how it is. That's life." As they neared number 67, she turned to look into Matt's eyes, "Hey, just one more question."

"Uh huh? What's that?" He looked apprehensive.

"That day you came to get me and Harry from the hospital, there were two champagne flutes in the dishwasher. Who were you drinking champagne with?"

Matt frowned. "Not sure what you're talking about."

"Don't you lie to me," Kali said. "Please, Matt. No more lies or half-truths."

"I'm not going to lie. I'm honestly trying to remember. Oh yeah, it was your sister!"

"Sofia? You were drinking champagne with Sofia?"

"She came by to congratulate us about Harry. For some reason, she thought you were already home with him. I only had a tiny bit of the champagne, since I was coming to get you guys. She had a couple glasses. Then she took the rest of the bottle home with her, cheapskate that she is."

"Weird she never mentioned this," Kali said. Had Sofia set up the whole scene to upset her, to fuel the flames of Kali's paranoia, for her own sick enjoyment? To make her think Matt and Britta had been happily swilling champagne at 67 Pine Beach Road while Kali was in the hospital, struggling to pull up those tiny Capri pants and make herself half-way presentable for when Matt arrived? She was never going to ask, she decided, because she didn't care about the answer, and she was done being Crazy Paranoia Kali, for good. Life was too short. "Well, that's family, I guess," Kali sighed. "And I'm in a pretty forgiving mood, when it comes to family."

# Chapter 38

"Your meeting starts in five. They're waiting for you." Alicia was standing in the doorway of Kali's office, polished and professional-looking, as usual.

"Right." Kali sighed. "Ugh."

"Look on the bright side," Alicia said. "It's the end of the day, end of the week."

"End of my career, too. So, where's this meeting?"

"Main boardroom."

"Really? That's weird." The main boardroom could seat twenty-four people; if the walls were moved back, forty. Kali expected Mike Potochnik, Rick Durham, a couple of boys from Exec. But there was no way they needed the main boardroom. Unless the whole State Bar Discipline Committee had been invited. Maybe Exec was hoping to intimidate Potochnik by the scale of the firm and the grandeur of the boardroom. If that's what they had in mind, they were dreaming. Scale and grandeur would piss him off even more; he would see the cost of it on every invoice he'd ever received from the firm, as if highlighted in big red numbers and dollar signs. "Listen, Alicia," Kali said, "if this ends the way I think it's going to, I'm going to help you find another job. You can even come with me, if you want. I mean, I'll take care of you. I can't pay what you get here, with all the benefits and so on, but..."

"No problemo, amiga. I have another offer."

"Really? Wow. Well you're good, and I guess I can't blame you for looking." She blinked at Alicia, suddenly very sad. "We've been through a lot, you and I."

"Alex wants me to work for him. I wasn't looking, don't think that. It was a standing offer from him, in case you didn't come back from mat leave."

"Oh, Alex, wow…" Kali nodded, "that's great. You're sure to get a big raise, since he's a name partner and all. Congratulations."

"Only catch is, I have to walk his damned dog."

"Ah yes, that famous dog we keep hearing so much about."

"Jada was also bugging me to work for her, FYI."

"You're kidding!"

"Nope. For the past year."

"That scheming bitch. Well, why am I surprised? You're the best. I guess can't blame her for trying."

"I don't think they're going to fire you, Kali, unless you're late, so go. We'll talk later." As usual, she was the more professional of the two: all business, while Kali teetered on the verge of crying. "Go," Alicia waved her off. "*Vamos!*"

As Kali headed along the corridor towards the boardroom, Jada was suddenly behind her, catching up with long strides. "I heard about the problems with your house. I'm so sorry! What a disaster! Is the City paying for any of the repairs?"

"Unfortunately, not." Kali decided not to mention Alicia. It wouldn't help anyone for Jada to know Alicia had ratted on her. Better to just play nice. Kali was on her way out anyway, so what did she care? "The retaining wall collapsed because it wasn't built properly. Matt wants to sue the guy who sold us the house, but he's moved several times, probably skipped the country. The City of Long Beach might actually sue us, for having an illegal retaining wall."

"Oh, that sucks so bad!"

Kali stopped in front of the main boardroom door and turned to Jada. "Well, this is where I get off."

"You're in the big meeting?" Jada was obviously surprised.

"In it? I'm the star attraction."

"Really? What did you do to deserve that?"

"You don't want to know."

"That's where you're wrong. I'm dying to know! Talk to me when you get out."

As she stood outside the oak-paneled doors of the boardroom, Kali thought she could hear music. She pushed open the door, and the music swelled. She was not prepared for the carnival atmosphere in the  room.

On the long granite table was a smorgasbord of cold foods: herring, stuffed eggs, caviar, sauerkraut, pickled beets, ham, and Ukrainian vodka. A huge map of Eastern Europe was projected on one wall. All the partners of Biltmore, Durham & Spears were there, even old Mr. Biltmore, looking dazed and—unnervingly, Helen Sharpe, too. The only outsider was Mike Potochnik. He had a Band-Aid on his forehead and a bruise on his cheek. Was this what it took to sweeten client relations that had soured? Kali wondered. Was Potochnik such a huge threat that he had to be seduced by all of the partners with caviar and vodka? Had Kali screwed up that badly?

"Kali!" Rick bounded over to greet her. "*Christos rodyvsa!*" He took her hand in both of his and pumped it.

"Pardon?"

"He's a little confused with the greetings, my friend, Roman," Potochnik said, standing at the buffet. "His Ukrainian is a bit rusty."

"Roman?" Kali smiled, so that Mike wouldn't think she was criticizing him.

Rick was still gripping her hand. "Yes, Roman Durko. I changed my name before law school. I'm ashamed to admit it now."

"Have some of the pickled herring," Potochnik said, "it's not half bad, for Santa Monica."

Kali looked at him suspiciously. "Sorry, I'm a little confused right now by what's going on here."

"Mykhail landed a deal to open a chicken franchise in the Ukraine," Rick said. "And Alex brokered it."

"Chicken Kiev!" Mike announced, proudly. "Great name, for a change."

"It's too descriptive," Kali said, launching into her trademark consultation mode. "Over here at least. I don't know about the Ukrainian trademark office."

"Kali, we're going to need you to do the master franchise agreement and get everything rolling," Rick said. "You can handle the minor details later."

Kali was stunned. So, Alex had stepped in to take over, fix things, make everything right, and now Kali was in line to grind out the paperwork? A year ago, she would have been thrilled to get the work. "Congrats, Mike," she said, "I mean, Mykhail. I'm really happy for you."

"You must be shocked, Kalinka Wolaniuk. You tried to buy me off with a janitorial job! Now here I am, a major client, one of the big shots."

"I suggested we might be able to use your talent and expertise in IT. I didn't say anything about janitorial, and I certainly didn't try to buy you off."

"It really wasn't your place to be offering anyone a job," Helen said, looking peeved. "You should have talked to me first."

"Anyway," Rick said, "all of that's in the past, forgiven and hopefully, forgotten. Mike's going to function as a bridge between our cultures—east and west. Since he was born over there, he'll be doing all the hiring, the property scouting, get everything computerized, and we will get his franchise rolling. It's a big win-win."

Kali studied first Rick and then Mike. "So, sorry? Hiring for what? And what does all this have to do with me?"

"Well, if you read your e-mail occasionally," Rick said, still smiling, "you'd know that the Executive Committee would like you to go over there with Mike. Work with him on his new business and set up a satellite office for our firm. We're seeing great potential in Eastern Europe right now."

"You want to ship me to Siberia?"

"Nobody mentioned Siberia," Mike laughed, "yet!"

The others joined in with loud courtesy laughter.

"It would be a fantastic opportunity for you, Kali," Rick said, "and the firm would compensate you very well."

"But I can't go over there! I have a new baby. And my husband's still a resident."

"Yes," said Mike, "there is the husband to consider. He's a very persuasive man, your Dr. Miller." He smiled thinly. "Like KGB."

"How do you know my husband?" Kali asked, with a tinge of apprehension, looking again at the Band-Aid and bruise on Mike's face. No connection, hopefully, but she had a sinking feeling.

"Let's just say, we've had words."

"When? When did you have words?"

"Not important, for purposes of this discussion."

"I know it's a big step, Kali," Rick said, "with a lot of complex arrangements to be made. Just agree you'll at least think about it. The firm will pay for your apartment – a very upscale one – give you a huge entertainment allowance, top security, a good school for your son. Whatever you need."

"Well," she said, "I've thought about it, and I'm sorry the answer is no."

After a moment, Rick added. "We would even consider buying out your present home."

Buying their house? Taking 67 Pine Beach Road off their hands? They were pulling out all the stops now! "That's such a great offer, Rick, but I still have to say no." A murmur of disappointment swept through the room.

"Kali, this is a big decision. Go home, talk to Matt. See what he has to say. He could even play hockey again over there. He'd love it!"

"Hockey?" Are you serious? There isn't even a league anymore in Eastern Europe, not to mention that he's a surgeon now." Rick had to be really pathetically desperate to try that one. Matt giving up medicine to play for some junior league in Belarus or someplace?

"I think you are being impulsive, Kali. Not really thinking this through."

Impulsive, was she? Still the irrational, hormonally-charged new mom who needed to talk to her husband before making any decisions at all, even about her own work. Kali bit her lip, holding in the response she so badly wanted to give.

"A year in Europe would be a fantastic experience," Alex added. "All expenses paid. Matt can take a year off—this gig wouldn't be forever, just to get things set up. You could use your maiden name, too. It would be a big benefit. What is it again? Wally-something?"

"Wolaniuk," Kali said, irritably. "But I'm pretty happy being Kali Miller, to be honest. And I'm not ashamed to admit it." She looked pointedly at Mike.

"Well, you don't have to decide now. Just think about it and talk to Matt first." Alex said.

"But I have decided. And it has nothing to do with the proposal, which I truly appreciate. It was my intention to tell all of you today, what I'm about to say." The murmur in the room was now a disgruntled muttering, with many frowns being exchanged. I've decided to take a leave of absence. To resign, actually, since I have no idea how long my leave is going to be, and I know the firm wouldn't be willing to keep my Aeron chair warm for me. I'm also sure someone else would enjoy having my office, with its fabulous view."

"That was a business decision," Rick reddened. "Didn't Helen explain?"

"Rick, of course I did!" Helen protested. "I even apologized on behalf of the firm."

"Well, we should have consulted you about the change, Kali" Rick said. "My bad. Not Helen's fault."

"Nor my decision," Helen added. "Not entirely."

"Kali," Alex jumped in, "don't be so quick to resign. What does your husband say? How will you guys manage without your income?"

Kali couldn't believe it. What business was it of his what Matt thought, or how they were going to manage financially?

"Besides, all you had to do was ask," Rick argued, "about us holding your spot here. We, the firm, recognize that women have the right to stay home. Take a few years off, raise the children, and not have to give up their careers. We're happy to work with you on any arrangement that works for you. Leave of absence, part-time, work from home, whatever you need. Women lawyers are highly valued by this firm." The others nodded and murmured in agreement.

"So, why isn't there a single female partner in Biltmore, Durham and Spears?" Kali asked.

"What's that?" Mr. Biltmore still had enough synapses left to recognize his own name, apparently.

"You are well on your way, Kali," Rick said, "as I'm sure you know."

"No, I don't. And I didn't. I came in here today expecting to be fired."

"Well, that's ridiculous," Rick chuckled. "Way out there, Kali."

"Ridiculous!" Mr. Biltmore echoed, as he tried, unsuccessfully, to get some caviar to stay on a cracker. No one paid any attention to him.

"You are definitely on the partnership track," Rick said, "and so is Jada."

"It's a pretty long track since she's supposedly been on it for two years. You'll be lucky if she sticks around." Jada was a big biller, a hard worker, and a real credit to the firm, but never properly rewarded, in Kali's opinion. "And what about Gillian?"

Throats were cleared, ties straightened, lint flicked off sleeves. "Gillian, ah—well, she's a special case," Rick said.

"Head case? Nut case? What?" Kali ignored the warning look from Helen.

"Who's this Gillian person?" Mike asked, as he loaded sauerkraut and pickled beets onto a paper plate. "She sounds intriguing."

"Kali," Rick began, "this is not the forum for airing the firm's dirty laundry."

"Dirty laundry? that how you see Gillian?"

"Not at all, Kali," Helen interjected. "We, the firm, appreciate Gillian's unconventionality. And her work is both necessary, and first rate."

"She's in a class of her own," Pete said. "*Sui generis*. You went to law school, Kali. I'm sure you know what that means." The partners all nodded, though they looked uncomfortable.

"Well, I've decided to stay home and be a good mother to Harry. Maybe I'll work for myself and start my own little firm. This, all of this – the fighting over profit share, office space, support staff and assistants..." Kali purposely avoided looking at Alex at that moment, "and all the stressing-out over billing and receivables, while my son grows up without his mom... Well, it's just not worth it. The law will still be there, if and when I ever decide to come  back."

"I think you'll regret this, Kali." Rick was clearly both surprised and disappointed. Was Kali imagining it, or had his fox head buttons and penny loafer pennies lost some of their luster?

"I'm positive I won't regret it." Kali extended a hand for a professional goodbye handshake with everyone in the room. "Thanks for the offer. It's been a gas but I'm going to have to pass, as my mother would say."

~~~

"So, when did you have this mysterious little chat with Mike Potochnik?" Kali asked Matt later that night as they cuddled on the sofa with Harry. The plastic film covering the blown-out back windows rustled, as it was gently sucked in and out by the wind.

"Oh, you know about that?" Matt looked uneasy.

"I just heard today."

"Last week, I think it was." Matt yawned. "I got his number from Alicia, called him up and asked him out for a beer."

"You had a beer with Mike Potochnik?"

"Yeah, and I reasoned with the guy. Convinced him to drop his complaint and give up on the idea of suing you or complaining to the State Bar." He paused. "After I offered to punch his lights out."

"Oh, Matt, no! You threatened my client?"

"It was a man-to-man talk. He understands. He wasn't pissed off. My days as a goon on a hockey squad still come in handy." He grinned. "I've still got my chops."

"You didn't... hurt him? He had a Band-Aid, and a bruise on his face. Did you do that? Tell me you didn't!"

"I may have roughed him up a little. But he took it like a man. I have to respect the guy. He didn't go down easy." Matt cracked his knuckles, one by one.

"Oh my God, you assaulted my client! I could've handled him! I'm a professional, Matthew."

"You were losing it, I could tell. You were on the edge, all drugged out, paranoid and nutty. He'd gotten to you; gotten under your skin. I did what I had to do to protect my wife and son. Pretty basic. The guy needed to learn not to send flowers with nasty messages and go around stalking people in his old Mustang. It was outside our house a lot. Since Harry was born, but I didn't want to freak you out by passing that bit of intel along."

"He told me he couldn't afford a car anymore, because of me and how I screwed up his deal."

"He lied. I knew he was up to no good, when you told me about that lunch you two had." His eyelids were drooping. In the kitchen, Britta was rattling around, getting the fish sticks into the microwave. She had agreed to stay on to help Kali with Harry, just for room and board, while she studied to become a nurse practitioner: a twenty-month, online course. Her parents were grateful to Matt and Kali, the past at least partially forgiven. Even more grateful was Gosta Lindgren and his wife.

Matt began to snore loudly with Harry asleep on his chest, drooling and snoring as well. Sleeping husband, sleeping baby. Overcome with love and happiness, Kali smiled, content to be the one left standing, the only one in the family still awake, the one in total control. It was good to be Queen, if just for one day.

~ *The End*~